DISAPPEARED

Also by Bonnar Spring

Toward the Light

DISAPPEARED

A NOVEL

BONNAR SPRING

OCEANVIEW ⌾ PUBLISHING

SARASOTA, FLORIDA

ISBN 978-1-60809-560-5

Published in the United States of America by Oceanview Publishing

Sarasota, Florida

www.oceanviewpub.com

10 9 8 7 6 5 4 3 2

PRINTED IN THE UNITED STATES OF AMERICA

For all the sisters who have found me when I was lost

DISAPPEARED

CHAPTER ONE

Friday, January 14, 2005

F ay's not back yet. It's late, and I'm hungry.

The maroon and orange plaid bedspread on her side of our hotel room—not to be confused with the one with dark green swirls on my bed—is rumpled, so she must've taken a nap before heading over to the *Centre Artisanal.*

On our day trip to Ait Benhaddou, Fay stopped at every single display of the geometric-designed Taznakht carpets from the villages around Ouarzazate—running her hands along the wool, doing that squinty-eyed appraisal that meant she was measuring for the floor in her den. Fay can pretend all she wants that she's just looking, but we had to share a bedroom until our older brother went off to college. She borrowed my clothes without asking. She hid her Halloween candy and, later, her push-up bras behind a gap in the baseboard in our closet. Fay can't fool me—I *know* she's going to end up bringing at least one rug home, even if she has to pay for an extra bag.

Deciding on a quick shower while I wait, I cross the hotel room and toss the postcards I've just bought onto the little table with a view of the Atlas Mountains. The bathroom, almost as big as the bedroom itself, is illuminated by light filtering in from the setting sun. The walls are covered with Moroccan *zellije* tile—tiny pieces of blue and red and yellow and white. Triangles, hexagons, diamonds, squares. The mosaic flickers, creating a now-you-see-it, now-you-don't pattern, like a kaleidoscope, only with a mesmerizing illusion of depth. It gives the impression that the walls are undulating, the room breathing along with me.

After my shower, I pull on clean pants and a warmer sweater. I finger-comb the damp curls making an unruly ruffled fringe around my face and add my signature carmine lipstick in anticipation of dinner in one of the fancy restaurants in this very upscale Moroccan tourist town.

No Fay.

So I'll get started on postcards.

A light breeze drifting in through the hotel-room window flutters the cards. Steve and the kids get an upbeat version of my first two days in Africa—leaving out the fiasco with the police on our drive from Marrakech to Ouarzazate. I send a view of the dizzying heights of the Tizi-n-Tichka pass to our brother Greg, and an artsy card to my bosses, the trio of orthopedists whose office I run.

Night falls quickly in Morocco. Pen-on-paper becomes indistinct; daylight has faded to sepia tones. The rugged contours of the mountains—lavender and rose when I began writing—appear dark purple.

After a few more minutes with no whirlwind Fay appearance, I decide to head over to the *Centre Artisanal*. We've already heard plenty of stories about the languid pace of rug-buying—mint tea and haggling, hundreds of stunning choices to unroll before your eyes and a thousand more in the back room. The way Fay was fondling those rugs this morning, I can easily imagine her getting lost in a rug merchant's salon. But if instead she's stuck trying to be polite, I'll rescue her.

I grab my jacket and close the window. Seeing my postcards on the table reminds me to ask the desk clerk where to buy stamps when I give him a message for Fay letting her know where I've gone—in case we miss one another in this unfamiliar town. But when I pass the front desk, no one is manning it.

The artisan shops are a quarter-mile away, down the main street and across from the local medina. I walk toward the main gate with increasing bewilderment: it's shut tight. The streets are empty, displays removed, lights off. A brisk wind blows down a side passageway, rustling dead leaves and clanking the metal frames of closed awnings. I spot a dim light at a distance and move toward it. It's a miniature open-air store—shelves built along an outside wall with a selection of newspapers, bottled water, cigarettes, candy, condensed milk, shampoo. When I come near, an old woman sitting beside the shelves on a folding metal chair struggles to her feet. She's swaddled in layers of black fabric and further wrapped in a blanket, so I see only her face, rosy and wrinkled like a dried apple.

As best I can understand from our limited language overlap, most stores close early on Fridays. Everyone goes home to have dinner with their families after evening prayers. I buy a bottle of water. As the shopkeeper counts out my change, a cold dread prickles, a chill that has nothing to do with the wind or falling temperatures. Fay left our room while I was out buying postcards, sometime between three thirty and five. It's now seven thirty-five and fully dark, stores closed, the whole town apparently shut down.

Fay must've found the market closing and decided to wander around town instead. She's always been a walker, taking off for hours at the drop of a hat—to organize a term paper, memorize material for a test, get over a messy breakup—returning home exhausted but clearheaded, ready to take the next steps.

That comment of hers . . . When I told her I was going postcard-hunting, Fay mentioned she might walk over to the handicraft market to *clear her head.*

She wasn't completely done being annoyed with me.

I'd apologized last night, but only for my bitchy tirade at dinner, not for my ongoing fright at the damage Fay's la-la-land approach to the police stop could have caused. I didn't start out bitchy, but when I kept going over how the thing with the police didn't make sense, Fay suggested it was a shakedown.

She had to know how ridiculous that sounded, but Fay trotted out a meandering tale about cops preying on tourists in rental cars to make a quick buck. "We were in the wrong place at the wrong time, Julie," she finished. "Why not?"

"*Why not?*" My jaw dropped. I could feel blood rushing to my head. "It's because they were way too interested in *us*." I scowled and, holding my index finger across my top lip in a parody of the mustachioed policeman who had scared me so, I cycled through my litany of objections. If they wanted money, I reminded her, they would have been more direct. I flapped my arms wildly enough to knock over my water glass. "I mean, seriously, Fay—how can you be so blind?"

Well, I *did* apologize later. Anyhow, that was far from the first time we'd argued. My temper—Fay often says—comes out of nowhere and accelerates to sixty before she can fasten her seat belt. And, just as often, *I've* told *her* not to worry when we argue. Instead, she should worry if we stop because that means there's nothing left for us to care about or fight for.

Last night, although Fay turned off her bedside lamp with a quiet, "G'night, Julie," I never got her patented scrunching half-hug of forgiveness—or even her more usual amused eye-rolling *whatever*. Yesterday, though, had been one serious humdinger of a bad day.

She just needs solitude to finish sorting things out.

Since I don't know what path she's taken, I retreat to wait for Fay at the hotel. A garish yellow light spills from the ornate but not highly effective fixture on the ceiling. I sit in bed with all the pillows in the room at my back. Eight o'clock. Nine. Ten.

Every minute or so I think: *Now—the next footsteps I hear will be hers.*

Fay ... but there my imagination fails. She—what? Got lost and no one could give her directions? Decided she'd rather have dinner alone instead of coming back for me?

I don't believe that. I won't believe that.

And it wasn't *my* fault.

I mean, I *was* driving when the policemen stopped us, and I *was* going a little over the speed limit. But then ... that whole part about Fay insisting we pretend we couldn't speak or understand French and how they'd yanked us out of the car and ransacked our suitcases, the whole car ... and, oh God, it had escalated from there.

CHAPTER TWO

Saturday, January 15, 2005

My feet slap the cold tile floor. Nausea bubbles deep inside, and I hurry to the bathroom. When the queasiness subsides, I return to the bedroom and sit at the little table by the window where, twelve hours earlier, I was writing mundane wish-you-were-heres.

Fay is *not* here. She didn't sneak into the room overnight without my noticing, though I hardly slept deeply enough for that to be plausible. I lean across the table to open the curtain, letting in weak early-morning sunlight. It brightens the room only minimally more than the dim bulb I'd kept on all night.

A late return because Fay wanted alone-time to walk off her moodiness is the only benign explanation. The *only* one. But she would never stay away the entire night. Something—or someone—prevented her return.

I'll call the hospitals first, I decide, but if she hasn't been in an accident, I have to get help. After the bizarre incident on the road to Ouarzazate, I'm really reluctant to involve the police. And Mom will freak out if I call to say Fay is missing. Sorting things out logically is way outside her skill set. Besides, she doesn't know anything about Morocco. Maybe Fay's husband—no matter what, Gil needs to know what's going on. *He* can help me figure out the next move.

Because no US cell phone carriers include Morocco in their coverage, Fay and I planned to buy Moroccan SIM cards with minutes and data to use in our phones. We stayed in Marrakech such a short time, though, and spent our only afternoon doing touristy stuff at the Jmaa-al-Fna, so I haven't bought one yet.

Getting my phone working is my first task. Then I'll have to figure out how to find Gil's number. He and Fay ditched their landline when they bought their new house. I've never needed to phone him; I can always reach Fay on her cell phone or at work. Oh—work. I'll get the number for Gil's law office and call him there. Later. It's still the middle of the night on the other side of the Atlantic.

Shit. When dawn breaks in North America, it'll be *Saturday* morning. Maybe someone will be working at Gil's office, maybe there's an emergency line. Oh, geez.

I shake my head without thinking, but also without a return of the queasiness. I throw on yesterday's clothes. If I can't reach Gil, I really ought to call Steve. *That* is a call I dread.

My husband made it pretty clear he thought we were nuts—two women traveling alone in Morocco barely three years after 9/11 changed the world. This vacation *is* a fairly significant uptick in "adventure" than, say, when Fay and I went camping in the Grand Canyon or took the diving expedition in the cays off Belize. Starting in our early twenties, we've taken a dozen trips together, each one more fun that the last.

I hadn't realized, though, how much I counted on our getaways until Fay's marriage to Gil two years ago. They moved to New York almost immediately when Gil transferred to his firm's main office. Goodbye to our weekly lunches; farewell to antiquing jaunts. Fay, who'd studied computer science and worked in tech for years, landed a supervisory position at a company doing research into distance learning. Between her new husband and her new job and all the diversions of a new city, she was so busy she seldom called. Last year, for the first time since Molly, my younger daughter, was a colicky newborn, we didn't take a trip together.

A couple of months ago, however, Fay phoned me, full of excitement, to suggest vacationing in Morocco. With the horror of 9/11 fresh in my mind, I hesitated. But Fay cited reassuring statistics about safety—fewer terror attacks in the entire country of Morocco than in New York City—and for days afterward, she deluged me with brochure-filled emails. Fay understands better than anyone how twitchy I get when I'm stuck too long on the never-ending hamster wheel of my life. And she knows I'm a sucker for exploring off the beaten track. I would've gladly met her at a truck stop in the middle of nowhere for hamburgers and a milkshake just for the chance to catch up and hear more about her life in the Big Apple, more about her husband, whom I hardly know at all. Not that I blame him for uprooting Fay.

Morocco: sand dunes, camels, kasbahs and oases, hiking in the Atlas Mountains. Oh yeah, she hooked me.

But after I agreed, Steve started up. Armed with Fay's statistics, I deflected his misgivings about the post-9/11 political climate, explained how we planned to stay clear of obvious targets. Then Steve pivoted to warnings about parasites and waterborne diseases, an area where my microbiologist husband has a distinct advantage. I quoted the World Health Organization on water quality, but even my promises to steer clear of raw vegetables and drink only bottled water didn't sway him.

While I understand Steve's concern, I don't share his pessimistic conviction that danger lurks in every twisting passageway or leafy green salad. We often have variations on this discussion—and it's not an argument because Steve *almost* gets my craving for "away" time. He'll wrap me in his arms when I curl up next to him and sniffle about how I spent the entire parent-teacher meeting watching Molly's kindergarten teacher's earrings sway and her eyes blink in rhythm, how I'd driven home on autopilot and couldn't even remember stopping at the store for a week's worth of groceries.

Steve is full of suggestions, but his idea of "getting away" is our annual family vacation to his brother's place at the lake. Don't get me wrong—I love it there, but I love it the same way I love our home, our family, the familiarity and peace of knowing where I belong.

But when my life gets mechanical, when I daydream instead of appreciating what I have, I need *away* away. I need an interruption from my internal map, the one that lets me drive well-worn paths without noticing the roads or scoot through the grocery store without wasted effort. What works best is a foray into unfamiliar territory where my mental map doesn't work, where I need to use all my senses to get through the day.

Look where it got me this time. Alone in Morocco. My sister is missing, and I'm afraid to go to the police.

I can hear Steve, incredulous: "You were stopped by police and searched"—no, I have to leave out the part about the search and my angina attack—"and then Fay went out for a walk and didn't come back." Ending, no doubt, with, "Call the embassy about Fay and come home immediately."

Calling the embassy is a great idea, though. They'll know what I should do, and I can get started without any emotionally charged conversations. Ashamed of my nighttime paralysis, I resolve to put the whole matter into more capable hands.

Hamza, the talkative morning clerk, is a stout man with perfect half-moon dark circles under his eyes. He's on duty when I come downstairs. Yesterday when Fay mentioned our plan to visit Ait Benhaddou, he showered us with enthusiastic suggestions and overly detailed directions. It took us a while to get out the door.

"*Bonjour, madame.* How are you? You sleep well? Everything quiet?"

Hamza only works mornings, but he'll remember Fay and perhaps he knows something. "Have you seen my sister?" My hand automatically stretches six inches over my head—this tall—and then pats my short, dark curls. "The blonde."

"No, but there *is* a message in your box." He pivots and plucks a folded sheet of paper from a cubbyhole behind him. He places it in my outstretched hand. My name. Fay's handwriting. *Fay*. My hand trembling, I flip it open and read:

> *Dear Julie,*
> *I have to take care of an urgent errand for my husband.*
> *I promised Gil not to tell you in advance. It was for your*
> *protection—at least it was supposed to be. I'm so sorry for the*
> *deception, and I'm beyond horrified about that awful experience*
> *with the police yesterday. I don't know what I would've done if*
> *they hadn't handed over your medication in time.*
> *Please, please forgive me. And Don't Tell Mom.*
> *I'll be back day after tomorrow. Meanwhile use the car, see*
> *the sights. I bet anything you'll enjoy exploring on your own*
> *too much to miss me! And we'll have more fun when I get back,*
> *don't worry.*

She signed it with the illegible flourish that stood for her name.

My fingers drop the note like a hot potato. Fay is doing an errand? An *errand*? For her *husband*? I slap the note, pinning it to the counter like I'm squashing a bug. She's *safe*?

Hamza's looking at me, his forehead wrinkled with concern. "Your sister, she is all right?"

"Ye-e-es." With my train wreck of insecurities and fears upended by this note, I'm not altogether sure. "When did you get this?"

A quick scrunch of his face as he considers. "It must've been here when I arrived at six this morning," he says, "but I only noticed it a few minutes ago when I placed a room key back on its hook in the box directly above."

The lobby's an oblong space with an arched double-door to the street at one end and a curving staircase to the rooms at the other. The high reception desk on the right side and the wall behind it are plastered with colorful sightseeing posters and suggestions for tours. Another arching doorway on the left leads to an airy breakfast room with floor-to-ceiling windows opening onto a flower garden. There are a few overstuffed chairs near the door. Four royal-blue couches with an abundance of embroidered pillows, arranged in a square around a massive wooden coffee table, occupy the middle of the room. The little TV on the table is always on. The floor is tiled, like every floor I've seen so far in Morocco.

I close my eyes to visualize how it looked late yesterday.

I walked through the lobby three times: when I returned from my postcard expedition, when I went out to find Fay, and when I came back. The first time, the afternoon man was there. He wasn't chatty like Hamza—in fact, the day we arrived, he scarcely tore himself away from a soccer game on the lobby TV long enough to show us a second-floor room and complete our registration. The desk was unoccupied the last two times. I didn't pay any attention to the little white cubbyholes, each crowned with a small decorative arch, that were lost in the sea of gaudy travel posters. The damn note was there waiting for me all along. If only the clerk had been doing his job, I would've been spared the agony of my night's worry.

"Family is everything to me," Hamza says with a sympathetic glance, "but sometimes it gets complicated."

There's a minefield of emotion lurking behind his words. When Fay and I chatted with him before we left for Ait Benhaddou yesterday, he told us his sister's husband owned the hotel. I get the feeling that, if Hamza weren't the epitome of a Very Proper manager, he would've favored me with a wicked eye-roll.

"You can say that again." I sigh. Breakfast next—not canvassing hospitals. I have to rethink this.

A skinny boy with too-short sleeves on his white jacket greets me at the door to the breakfast room. He escorts me to the same table-for-two where Fay and I sat yesterday, then pours coffee into my cup from a silver carafe. Each table is covered by a cloth of a different jewel-tone, each has a red rose—the national flower of Morocco—in a cut-glass vase. About half the tables are occupied, and a buzz of conversation in French, Spanish, Arabic, and other unidentifiable languages fills the room.

I unfold Fay's note again and carefully smooth it on top of the pale lavender tablecloth. I'm having trouble shaking off the dread that immobilized me as the nighttime hours passed without Fay's reappearance. Once I concluded our argument couldn't be the deal breaker keeping her away, my mind returned like a Ping-Pong ball to the policemen who searched us.

But the jerky combination of print and cursive is unmistakably Fay's handwriting. Nothing in the note suggests Fay wrote it under duress and was trying to put me on guard. There are none of the subtle warning touches anyone who's read a thriller knows about—my name is spelled correctly; there are no uncharacteristic smiley faces. She even added that gratuitous, personal *Don't Tell Mom*, and her signature is the same as I've seen a thousand times on a thousand other notes.

She wrote it yesterday afternoon before leaving the hotel because she referred to the police incident as "yesterday," and she planned to return "day after tomorrow." In other words, tomorrow—Sunday.

I can't find any way to assail that logic.

Fay *didn't* need more time to cool down. She *didn't* leave to shop for a rug and get mugged or kidnapped. Or worse. She wrote me a note and waltzed off into the sunset. She wrote a damn note—instead of *telling* me her plans—and disappeared.

I can't believe my sister would do that. But she did.

The young waiter brings me homemade yogurt, fresh fruit, and a plate of square Moroccan crepes, slightly puffy and fresh off the griddle. He refills my coffee cup without my asking. I lift my cup and take a sip. Then set it down, muttering under my breath, *What the fuck, what the fuck am I supposed to do now?*

I feel like a rubber band that's been fully extended and then released, spinning out of control.

CHAPTER THREE

Around me, a dozen other travelers with maps spread on the table are eating breakfast and chatting about their day's plans, much as Fay and I did yesterday. I'd read aloud snippets from our guidebook about Ait Benhaddou, a UNESCO World Heritage site that has also served as the location for dozens of recent movies, from *Jewel of the Nile* to *Gladiator*. We did a coin flip to see who took the first shift driving—a tradition since our parents made us share the car when Fay turned sixteen and got her license the year I was a high-school senior.

I stab a section of cantaloupe. Then another and another, eating the whole bowlful before I put down my fork.

And all that time—climbing the slope to the granary that crowned the hill, posing for silly selfies, wandering through twisting passageways and into restored *kasbahs,* ogling the rugs—Fay never said a word, not one single word, about leaving in the afternoon. Sure, if the desk clerk had been around to give me her note, I would've been spared my emotional roller coaster last night. But he wasn't, and my escalating panic as the hours passed is still too vivid, too raw to dismiss.

I pick up my knife and spread wildflower honey over the square crepes, here called *msemen.* I slice through the crepes as though I could excise those stubborn aftereffects of the night's whipsawing misery: Fay's shopping. She's taking a walk. She's embarrassed. She's still upset with me. She's worried. She's hurt. She's dead. She's running an errand for her fucking husband. Which she neglected to mention.

Fay lured me off on vacation under false pretenses.

I've wolfed down both pancakes without noticing. I push the plate away and swirl my spoon around in the bowl of creamy yogurt.

That's what her enthusiastic lobbying for a Moroccan vacation was about.

Fay reaching out to *me* about this vacation came as such a relief. Last year when I lobbed a few trip ideas at her, she made excuses, stayed vague. I was reluctant to keep pushing her by making more suggestions if her disinterest meant she'd moved on as well as moved away. I thought our traveling days were over.

Anyhow, Fay's moving away wasn't the only reason we seemed to be drifting apart. There was me—married with three kids and a boring office job, my days filled-to-overflowing with repetitive essentials. And Fay—in a hot and heavy new relationship, a childless executive in a tech firm. I've been alternately envious of the excitement of her life and guilty about all the ups and downs she's experienced. I hoped this trip would be the fresh start we both deserved.

When I agreed Morocco seemed the perfect sort of exotic to scratch my itch for a new perspective—and after I tuned out Steve's protests—*then* Fay proposed heading for the Atlas Mountains first. Although a lot of travelers hang out in Marrakech before venturing into the countryside, she made the very sensible case that, with shopping on our minds, we'd be better off buying in Marrakech's amazing *souqs* at the end of our trip so we didn't have to carry extra bundles around for two weeks.

Gil's a hotshot lawyer with a big New York City firm. Obviously, his mission requires our presence in *this* area *this* week. But if it's *his* business, I don't understand why *he* didn't come himself. Maybe he was just too busy—or too full of himself. *Nah.* True, my impression of Gil is that he tends toward the high-handed and egotistical, but this trip was meticulously planned over several months. He set it in motion; he sent us off. He didn't come because . . . because he'd be too noticeable. Because Fay and I were more likely to escape detection. That feels right, once the thought surfaces—two middle-aged women, tourists with cameras in hand, shopping and sightseeing.

After I drain a third and final cup of coffee, I pick up Fay's note and walk back through the elegant arched doorway into the lobby.

Hamza leans across the high scarred counter and waves me over. An acrid whiff of cigarette smoke wafts off his starched white dress shirt. "*Madame* Welch, I am desolated to have to ask of you a very large favor." He turns his limpid eyes on me.

"What's wrong?" *What now?*

"I am very sorry for the inconvenience, but the room allocated to you and your sister when you first arrived was given by mistake. It's the room with two large beds, correct?"

"Yes, the one in the back on the second floor overlooking the garden."

"You see, *madame*, that's our largest room, and Ibrahim was in error in placing you in it instead of in a room with two smaller beds."

"I told him we wanted a quiet room, with no street noise."

"Ah, I understand. The problem is that the room you have occupied for the past two nights is reserved beginning tomorrow for a family of four visiting from Germany."

But how will Fay find me again if I have to leave the hotel?

"Please." Hamza holds up his hand as if he's reading my mind about Fay. "Please, *madame*, do not distress yourself. We have several very nice doubles in the newer wing of the hotel. You may take your pick of any of them for you and your sister. There's one on the third floor from which you can see the *palmeraie*."

Compared to the other problems jostling for space in my mind, a room change in the same hotel is a manageable proposition. We arrange for one of the maids to come up and show me the empty doubles. I'll pack, and after breakfast tomorrow, someone will carry all my belongings to the new room.

* * *

Packing will only take a minute or two. I haven't taken much out, nor has Fay. When I go into the kaleidoscope-tiled bathroom to give it the once-over, I don't see Fay's toothbrush or her zippered case of toiletries. That finally gets me thinking, instead of doing my emotional pinball routine. I hurry back into the bedroom. We flew with only carry-on luggage to avoid the possibility of being temporarily stranded without clean clothes. Fay's suitcase still sits in the corner where she left it, but when I fling open the door of the imposing mahogany wardrobe, the red cotton tote she used as her personal item has disappeared.

Fay left, and she took overnight stuff in her bag. That realization makes me feel unexpectedly better. She really did walk away under her own steam. *And, if not Hamza, someone else at the hotel might've seen her leave.* I'll keep asking.

A soft knock announces the presence of a girl in a pink-striped pantsuit, the obligatory head-covering tied under her chin, babushka-style. She jingles four keys in her hand—the promised maid—and motions me to follow. We go back to the main staircase, thread our way through a maze of twisting hallways with low ceilings, then take a different staircase up one level to the other side of the hotel.

The first room she shows me has generic pale blue walls and crisp matching floral bedspreads. In this newer wing, I could be at the DC Marriott except for the woven rugs scattered on the blue-tiled floor and the view through the window of an ocean of dusty date palms stretching off to the right until they fade into faraway hills.

"Cette chambre est bien," I tell the girl, but my attempts to ask her about Fay are met with a burst of giggles behind a hand pressed to her mouth. She calls out to another girl who's coming down the corridor with her arms full of sheets.

The second maid has somewhat more French, but not enough to understand my questions about Fay, and speaking with hand gestures is clearly inadequate for asking about my sister's departure. When the girls linger, shyly casting looks at my red lips, chunky turquoise necklace, and sling-back sandals, I point to myself and say *Julie Welch*—experiencing an unwelcome flashback to the ordeal with the police trying to question me—and then in turn point to each girl.

"Tadefi," says the giggler.

"Sihan." Her friend is a sturdy, moonfaced girl.

Haltingly, I learn that Sihan is sixteen and Tadefi fourteen—my daughter Erin's age. Both went to school for only three years. I try, without success, to imagine my cell phone–chattering, soccer-playing Erin in their place—school a distant memory, working a fifty-hour week. I suppose it's culturally insensitive to assume that Sihan would prefer studying algebra to sweeping and making beds, that Tadefi would embrace shopping malls and dating.

Sihan is a cousin of Hamza and has worked at the hotel since she was twelve. Tadefi, newly arrived from the mountains, is living with relatives in a neighborhood in the *palmeraie*. The two do most of the cleaning in the hotel, although a third maid, Amina, is busy upstairs.

I'll try the remaining maid later. These women roam the hotel, in and out of rooms, up and down the stairs. They're the natural people to ask about Fay.

*   *   *

Since I no longer need to call Gil—an Extremely Good Thing because I feel like ripping him to shreds for insisting that his wife, *my sister*, lie to me—I decide to get out and enjoy myself. While it's easier to be pissed off at him than my sister, there's nonetheless a certain *you betcha I'll have fun* directed at Fay in taking her advice. She went along with Gil's intrigue, after all. We definitely need to have A Talk when she returns.

First, a visit to the Saturday morning market, then maybe a drive along the *palmeraie*—the palm grove on either side of the Draa River.

The labyrinthine passages of the old town are packed. Vendors, squeezed in like sardines, spread cloths on the ground to display their wares. Squares of burlap sacking strung between poles act as sun shades. Merchants hunker behind their offerings. The entire town seems to be out chatting and marketing. The sound of a man announcing specials with a loudspeaker fills the air. Women wait their turn in front of a stall filled with cackling white chickens. Boys pick through the selection of used jeans and sneakers laid out neatly on the ground. Throughout stand patient blanket-covered donkeys lashed to simple wooden two-wheeled carts.

I keep stopping and starting as one thing after another catches my eye. The vegetables are amazing: glossy purple eggplant, red onions by the truckload, oranges with dark green leaves still attached, potatoes, squashes—yellow, bulbous, green, mottled, oval, striped, round, and some spectacularly odd ones—gallons of green beans, waxy parsnips, ruby red tomatoes, crimson beets, hot peppers, carrots, limes, and—everywhere—bundles of mint.

Each time I ask vendors the local name for a vegetable or how to cook it, they're curious about me, too: Where are you from? Where is your husband? How many children do you have? Is this your first trip to Morocco? Are you enjoying yourself?

I show several women my favorite photograph of the kids, the three of them beaming at the camera from our old porch swing the day Alex lost his first tooth. Although the snapshot is five years old, I keep it in my wallet as a reminder of the uneasy balance between constancy and change: Alex's tooth milestone, new baby Molly, Erin taking her first experimental steps toward womanhood. I took the photo that day knowing they'd grow older, grow away from Steve and me. I was wondering what sort of adults they'd become. I saw them simultaneously as the precious children they were *and* as the promise for an unknowable future they brought with them.

I don't mention to the market women that the impish girl with the long braid is now almost as tall as I am, that the freckled boy with the wide snaggle-tooth grin is a serious skateboarder, or that the bald baby squeezed between them is into costume jewelry and twirly dresses. Many women proudly whisk their own special photographs from interior pockets in their voluminous kaftans. Although my French is fluent—Fay and I grew up speaking it with our paternal grandparents who lived in Montreal . . . plus I took it all the way through school for easy As—I'm afraid it might seem too pushy to ask what's special about *their* snapshots.

On the far side of the market are clothing stalls. A display of *babouches* like a wall decorated by a pointillist painter catches my eye. The soft, pointed Moroccan slippers come in a dizzying variety of colors—and there's a bright magenta pair on the bottom row. I pick them up and measure them against my palm. My younger daughter Molly's size and a perfect match for her favorite princess dress. *No, there will be other markets*, I think, but the man quotes me a price so low that I know I have to get them. I'll tell Molly it was the first thing I bought on my trip. For a third child that means a lot.

A couple of times, once wheeling sharply to avoid a collision with a hand truck carrying cases of Coca-Cola stacked six feet high and once when I reverse course to retrieve Molly's slippers I set down when the lady selling almond pastries gave me a mini-cooking lesson, I glimpse the same young man—a slender pale-skinned man wearing a faded gray-and-brown striped djellaba with the peaked hood covering most of his face. Both times, he paused mid-step and shifted his gaze to look at store windows, when all his body language indicated he was still focused on the street. Given everyone's curiosity about a lone foreign woman in their midst, I discounted his attention the first and the second time. But when I stop at the hotel entrance and hold the door open so a workman can remove a tall stepladder, the same man is twenty feet away, staring resolutely into a display of vitamins in the window of the pharmacy across the street.

He *is* the same man. Unless I'm getting paranoid. A bit I once read in a John le Carré novel flutters into my mind. *If you suspect someone of tailing you, notice the shoes. They're the hardest thing to change.* I look at his feet, concentrating as best I can without appearing to stare. Brown sandals buckled on top, socks that would be white except for the accumulated dust, big toe peeking out on the right side. He's probably nothing but a bored and curious local youth. Still, it won't hurt to keep my eyes and ears open.

I turn and walk into the hotel.

CHAPTER FOUR

brahim, the afternoon man, is at the hotel desk when I return from my afternoon drive through the *palmeraie*. Ibrahim affects an exaggerated up-tilt of his chin combined with incessant swiveling of his head. It's possible he's mimicking a snooty maitre d', but the look is more like that of a vain actor on a quest for the best camera angle.

"*Bonsoir, madame.*" Eyes focused on the chandelier that graces the center of the ceiling, he drops my room key onto the counter—now he resembles a seal balancing a ball on its nose. "Hamza asked me to find out which new room suits you best."

"Three-seventeen will be fine." While I pick up the key, Ibrahim underlines my name in the register and draws a snaking line across several columns and marks an *x* in the new space.

I haven't asked what he saw the day Fay left. "Ibrahim, do you remember my sister, the tall woman with the blond hair?"

His eyes brighten. "*Bien sûr, madame.*" Ibrahim, like many men, admired Fay's generous curves.

"She's . . . gone away for a couple of days, and I missed seeing her go. I wonder if you noticed when she left the hotel."

"*Malheursement,*" says Ibrahim, "I don't believe so, but how would I remember"—accompanied with an impeccable Gallic shrug—"one time out of many?"

"She would have been carrying a small red bag."

Ibrahim shakes his head. *"Désolé, madame."*

Upstairs, I kick off my shoes and flop onto the olive-and-lime-green coverlet of my bed, already nostalgic at the thought of leaving this offbeat room with its mismatched furniture for the tasteful, "modern" new room.

I am *beat*. Thankfully, no suspicious strangers were lurking outside the hotel a few hours earlier when I left for my afternoon excursion. The market had folded for the day and street sweepers were busy plying their brooms. Otherwise, the streets were deserted. I filled the car with gas and took the bumpy path that followed the river.

The green line of the *palmeraie* extends south from town, curving out of sight. Around each bend another vista—a ruined kasbah set in a glade of ancient date palms, a glimpse of the rushing river, a group of women washing clothes at the river's edge, the laundered items spread over prickly bushes to dry.

Plus, I had my very first camel-sighting. Alex, my ten-year-old budding naturalist, specifically requested camel pictures. Of my three children, Alex is the one most like me, the kid who worries about climate change and asks questions for which there are no easy answers—most recently, "Mom, how do I really know if I'm awake or dreaming?" That one stumped me. It's something I wonder about, too.

I spotted the camels on a rare straightaway. Wind-blown sand whipped across the road, making it hard to see what was moving toward me. Animal, not vehicle, I guessed, because of the herky-jerky motion. When I drew nearer, I saw long legs and humped backs. My mouth opened wide, then a smile split my face in two. I'd never even seen a camel in a zoo before. "Oh my God," I said out loud.

I stopped the car and hunched as far as I could over the steering wheel to watch them approach. When they were opposite me, I cranked down the window all the way, got out my camera, and clicked and clicked while the line of a dozen camels sauntered up the middle of the road.

I sat there until the camels disappeared into the thicket of palms. Then I let my head loll, took a deep breath, felt the tightness between my shoulder blades dissipate.

This is what I came here for. This—the unexpected, the unfamiliar, the fleeting lagniappe, the surprise that refocuses my attention on the present.

It set me up for the rest of the afternoon, finding peace while losing myself in the beauty of the lush green valley, marveling at its contrast with the ochre hillsides and stark purple-blue mountains rising in the distance. The nearer peaks were dramatically lit, each crevice picked out, each fold highlighted by the play of light and shadow, while those in the distance faded to silver, topped with the occasional patch of white that could be a cloud, but was probably snow.

My sense of wonder kept me driving much farther than I intended. By the time I got back to the hotel, I wanted a shower, a nap, and a glass of wine—preferably in that order.

Looking across the hotel room at the garish plaid comforter on Fay's un-slept-in bed irritates me. I went out to forget about her deception and my lingering hurt of not being trusted. Well, that *and* also to prove that *you betcha* I could have fun on my own.

Fay and I never did much together when we were young. In fact, for a couple of years, a line of silver duct tape divided our room in half—which, of course, our mother blamed *me* for—and, of course, she was correct. Fay's side overflowed with stuff, stuff that ended up on my side so often I'd throw it back—hard—like I was trying out for the shot-put. There were her stuffed animals and her art supplies and her jewelry box and don't get me started on her sewing machine and all the fabric and other crap that involved.

Fay's thing has always been fashion and clothing design. After she whined for one, Mom bought her a kid-size sewing machine the Christmas she was, I think, eight. Right from the start, though, she was seriously good. Fay could look at something in a store window and go home and make the damn thing. And it wasn't just creating. If she borrowed my shirt, I'd get it back with the frayed cuff re-stitched. Because I was striving for a grungy early-teen look, I didn't appreciate her efforts.

My side was neater, but pretty basic, just the essentials. I didn't spend much time in our room. Fay was always just so . . . so fuzzy-pink-sweater cute, so chipper, so focused and talented. I hung out with our older brother, Greg when he would let me, and we both ignored Fay, a goody-two-shoes brat who spouted tell-Mom-on-you at the slightest snub.

Not as smart as Greg; not as pretty as Fay. I grew up knowing that in the same bedrock instinctual way I knew the sun rose in the east. The only positive thing I had going for me was my mother's oft-repeated sentiment, "Julie, you're more trouble than your brother and sister combined." So trouble became my go-to, the teenage me having long ago figured out that negative attention was the best way to get noticed.

It was also a remarkably easy way because I'd inherited from my dad what he called his "wonky ticker," a congenital heart rhythm condition that causes fast, chaotic heartbeats. It's controlled 99.9% of the time by a tiny once-a-day pill—but triggered by stress or strain—which meant that any time I overexerted, my parents fussed.

Another girl might've lapped up the warnings and cuddles and solicitude, but Another Girl didn't have to compete with Fay as a little sister. I did, and she had me beat hands-down in the Good Girl category. So I developed a vast repertoire of ways to push my limits. My mother's protesting "It's just not safe for you, dear" was my cue to go full speed ahead. Kind of like this trip.

When I flunked out of college in the middle of my sophomore year, my parents made me come home to live. Since Greg had just started the first year of his pediatric residency at Northwestern Memorial in Chicago, I inherited his big room on the third floor. Free from enforced togetherness—each of us with our own closet and our own music—Fay began to seek me out. Maybe it was history repeating itself, this time with *me* being the older sibling, but we started having real conversations. I discovered we had more in common than I thought. Fay's mama's-girl routine, for example, was an act, every bit as much as my rule-bending acting out. We just had different ways of getting our parents' attention.

One thing I'd always wondered was why the heck Fay, with her fashion sense, would sometimes sneak my clothes. It was for the days she had homeroom, Fay told me, because the coolest boy in her class sat right behind her . . . and my black leggings and tunics and dangly earrings made her look older, sexier. Now, *that* was an unexpected revelation. I looked at my little sister with renewed interest—from her sparkly purple toenails to her boobs to the single gold stud in her nostril.

Fay started hanging out with my friends. Although she dated far too many of the boys, my girlfriends tolerated her. She was our designated driver, the shopping companion who always knew which outfit would look best. In a group, she did a good Kid Sister act—agreeable, funny, and self-deprecating.

Also, quick-thinking.

An incident on our first trip together cemented our sisterhood. It happened a few months after I had to move back home. I didn't really flunk out, but my dad made totally unrealistic demands on improving my GPA. A guy I met at a party when he was home in Virginia for Christmas extended an inebriated invitation to "come visit sometime." He went to Tulane and gave me tingly feelings in all the right places, so I got the Great Idea to surprise him for Mardi Gras.

There were a few problems—like I didn't have enough money to fly. Also, the car was now Fay's, and she was a high school senior who needed it for school. When Fay got wind of my idea, instead of telling me to forget about it, she made up a bogus story for our parents about a senior class field trip to visit a couple of Ivy League colleges and blurted it out with exactly the right mix of excitement and trepidation. Then she added that since Julie (she didn't *say* "poor Julie" but her expression did) wasn't in college, she'd asked the history teacher who was chaperoning if her sister could come, too. He said it was okay, she told them, as long as Julie paid her own way. If I'd made that pitch, they'd never have believed me, but suck-up Fay nailed it. I even got spending money.

Fay and I drove the thousand miles to New Orleans—sixteen hours straight. It was clear the second we got out of the car the guy I was surprising had no idea who I was. Still, he took us along to some party in the French Quarter—where he promptly disappeared, leaving Fay and me not knowing where we were, boxed in by a sea of plastered Mardi Gras revelers brawling between us and the exit, watching police surround the building.

Fay saved the day by pulling the fire alarm. The commotion distracted the police and created a disorganized logjam, giving us time to ease away from the crowd and out a side door without being arrested.

The next year, we spent spring break on the beach in Cabo. Much more fun. Our trips became a yearly ritual we both enjoyed—time together, a change of routine and scenery, and, in the early years, occasional what-happens-in-Vegas escapades.

But that was then, and this . . . this *now* is a real pain in the ass.

Casting about for a distraction, I decide this might be a good time to find Amina, the remaining maid. I climb to the fourth floor. More rooms, but no maid. A narrow stairwell at the end of the hall leads up and there, on the roof, I find her. The roof is the laundry room. Lines strung high between the parapets crisscross much of the space. Huge

steel tubs, steaming hot water, long hooks for stirring—it's an oper-
ation out of the nineteenth century. To one side, a long table is piled
high with folded stacks of clean sun-dried linens. Behind the table, a
corrugated metal shed houses the hotel's unused stock of sheets and
towels and pillowcases.

Amina is round and solid, an older woman with a fleshy nose and
tired eyes under uncompromising black eyebrows, dressed in unrelieved
black. Her skirts are hitched up, and while we talk, she bustles, beefy
biceps flexing as she stirs the tubs.

Her answer is like Ibrahim's. She remembers the tall woman with
yellow hair, but can't say whether or not she saw her the previous afternoon. She never saw her carrying a red bag.

Fay didn't just disappear into thin air; *someone* must've seen her
go. Before I leave, I ask Amina to find out if the other two maids saw
anything.

CHAPTER FIVE

Saturday night in Ouarzazate. Jam-packed, noisy streets crammed with strolling families. Neon signs flashing, music blaring. The smell of roasting meat and other tantalizing aromas—ginger and coriander and something like cumin but with a sharper bite—waft out of the cafés. Although I don't generally enjoy eating alone, my high from this afternoon's excursion lingers. No hanging around in my hotel room with a take-out sandwich waiting for Fay. I'm going out to have a good meal.

I look over menus posted at the entrances, conscious of the paradox that the most crowded restaurants, those mobbed with people eating and laughing and waiters running around on dancing feet, are probably the best places to eat, while the quiet spots with only a scattering of customers—places where I might feel more comfortable dining solo—are the local losers.

I walk farther down the street.

Maybe this is a lousy idea. I can ask Ibrahim to order something for me and eat it in the room. *Chicken*, I squawk at myself. *Come on, give it a try.* I could look beyond the main street, perhaps, for a quiet and upscale restaurant. I'd pay a little more for a peaceful refuge. Turning the corner, a movement behind me catches my attention. Or rather, the cessation of movement. A man in a djellaba, perhaps the same one who followed me this morning. I don't know if I'm a fool, a scaredy-cat convinced I'm being stalked. Or if I'll be the fool if I don't pay attention.

I pretend to examine dusty trinkets in the barred display of a closed jewelry store, afraid to turn away from the crowds and the streetlights. Through the reflection in the shop window, the man appears to be lounging against a wall on the opposite side of the street.

Don't panic, think. To find out if it's the man from the market this morning, I can walk back the way I came. And if I keep my eyes down demurely, I'll see his feet.

When I turn to retrace my steps to the main street, he stays suspended in inaction. It looks like he's biding his time until he figures out which way I'm going. Lowering my head modestly, I stroll toward a restaurant near him. Same toe sticking out of the same dirty sock. It *is* him. A quick, casual glance at his face reveals only a thin young man with dark wavy hair and a hint of a mustache, indistinguishable from many other Moroccan men.

L'audace, toujours l'audace—it comes to mind in a split second, although I can't remember which French revolutionary used that phrase to urge bold action.

I walk up to Djellaba Man. A jolt of adrenaline lifts me, and I swish past him to examine the menu scrawled on a chalkboard by the door. Specials include lamb with prunes and almonds, stuffed eggplants, and *pastillas*—pigeon pastries—which I'm dying to try.

The dining room looks inviting. I'll have plenty of company—or witnesses, should he follow me in. I'm still standing at the entrance when a tall white-haired man dashes from the kitchen. With a generous smile, he says, "*Soyez bienvenue, madame.* Please come in. We have one small empty table, but if *madame* does not wish to dine alone, may I invite you to join my family who is on the far side—over by the wall, you see? —my mother and father, along with my wife and three of my children and five grandchildren. We are having a party tonight to celebrate the return from France of my son, Ali—there, at the end of the table."

I start to demur, but the proprietor has already tucked my hand into the crook of his arm to walk me into the restaurant. I feel a brief flutter of anxiety, but my audacity at sauntering across the street into the teeth of danger buoys me. I smile and nod, savoring my triumph. "That sounds wonderful. Thank you."

Another chair materializes, and I squash into a place next to a statuesque brunette who greets me in English. "I'm Fatima. Please, be welcome at our table." My seat offers a clear view of the door, and I keep a close watch on it all evening. Meanwhile, Fatima makes introductions, cuts her grandson's chicken into smaller pieces, and wipes another's chin while she peppers me with the steady stream of husband/children/are-you-enjoying-our-country questions I've come to expect. But Fatima is also curious about politics, and she doesn't shy away from tough questions about US foreign policy toward Arab nations. And her English is good enough that, for hours, we switch languages back and forth the way the way we do at home when my French-speaking grandparents visit.

The man who greeted me is her husband, Hassan, the owner and head chef. He keeps popping back and forth from the kitchen carrying one platter after another. I never manage to order anything.

We sample everything the specials board advertised and much else besides: Chicken with honey and fried almonds, the perfect combination of crispy and tender. Chunks of eggplant cooked in olive oil with garlic, tomatoes, peppers, and onions. Melt-in-your-mouth carrots with a cilantro and spicy pepper sauce that makes my eyes water. And the ultimate comfort food, *kefta*—meatballs—baked with tomatoes and topped with a fried egg.

Couscous is the only thing not on the menu. When I ask about it, Fatima tells me that couscous is always served on Fridays in Morocco.

"We don't usually make it on Saturday." She throws her hands into the air and laughs. "Anyhow, it's not the same in restaurants, even a traditional one like ours. You really ought to have couscous family-style." The room's noisy and the table so crowded that our shoulders are almost touching, but Fatima scoots even closer so she's speaking directly into my ear. "Next week, on Friday, no matter where you are, find a nice Moroccan woman and say to her, 'please, Lalla,'—Lalla is how we call an older woman to honor her years—you say, 'I've never eaten authentic couscous. Do you have room at your table for me to join you?'" Despite her lighthearted words, Fatima taps my hand to underscore her sincerity. "When she says yes, bring her a beautiful bouquet of flowers to show your appreciation. And then you will eat true Moroccan couscous!"

In between mouthfuls, Fatima tells me that two of their children work in the restaurant, but that Ali, her youngest son, followed his brother Mehdi to France where he makes good money working construction. Fatima puts down her fork and bites her lower lip. "Mehdi's been in France eight years. He married a French woman, and they have two children. They don't return, even for the biggest holidays, like Eid al-Adha. I despair of Ali adopting his brother's Western habits, "but"— Fatima squares her shoulders—"but for now, he still comes home."

Eid al-Adha, the "Festival of Sacrifice," as Fatima translates it, is the time every year when Muslim families come from all over the world to be together. Ali arrived that morning, a few days early, to beat the flood of young Moroccans in France who would soon be clogging the buses and planes. "Perhaps this year, we can talk him into remaining in Ouarzazate." Fatima smiles ruefully over at me, one mother to another, acknowledging her protective parental wishes. "With his European clothes and money in his pocket, he's in a good position to settle down with a nice local girl and, who knows, maybe come to work in the restaurant."

Fatima's description of the once-yearly journey home to have a feast with family makes me think of Thanksgiving, my favorite holiday. In fact, it's been feeling a bit like Thanksgiving ever since Fatima and I began talking.

Steve and I give the holiday an international twist. The university lab where he works employs scientists from all over the world, many of them young single men and women. So they won't be alone at a time when families get together, Steve likes to invite several for Thanksgiving dinner. We add all the extra leaves to the dining-room table. With us and the kids and our extended families and the scientists, it's a big crowd.

Our guests often bring something special from their cuisine to add to the traditional turkey and stuffing meal. Sampling *moussaka*, potstickers, *pão de queijo*, and more—it's like a mini-getaway for me. And we probably have the only five-year-old in town who's hooked on tzatziki.

Plus, it leavens the awkwardness between Steve's parents and my mother.

The *best* part for me is the opportunity to mingle with people from other cultures—asking Fatima-like questions, having conversations about schools, families, jobs, the hopes and dreams of people all over the world. With the harrowing start to this trip, it's taken me until today to unwind into vacation mode—first, with this afternoon's drive awakening my senses and now sharing a meal with my new friends. I hope that tonight's welcome invitation to share Hassan and Fatima's feast has added to their enjoyment as our guests always add to mine.

Later, when the crowd dwindles, Hassan finally sits down with us. Ali is on his mind, too, but *his* take is different. "Young people have a new way of negotiating between the old and the new," Hassan says. "I have one foot in both worlds, but look at my father over there. He grew up in a village in the hills, the youngest son in a family of farmers. He came to town as a boy because there were more stones on the farm than there were leaves on the plants. And then came the struggle for independence."

Hassan sips coffee while he talks about the challenges of his father's life during the war years. Then, "Me, I was born in 1956, the year of independence. I grew up here. I went to school—to the *lycée*, even. I met Fatima, whose family took a chance on me when I had little to offer but hard work. From that, we created this restaurant." He smiles broadly.

"And here is my son." Hassan waves his hand to the far side of the table, where Ali is regaling his nieces and nephews with stories. Ali, perhaps misunderstanding the gesture, waves back enthusiastically. "My son with his blue jeans and his music, his Internet and his cell phone. He loves his grandfather but does not understand his old-fashioned ways. Ali is a good boy. He lives in a new century, and he'll find his own way."

Hassan continues in that vein for a while, but I'm distracted by something he said: *his son with his blue jeans*. I look around. None of the young men wear djellabas. They're all in Western dress, with heads and arms bare, chains around their necks. Even most middle-aged guys like Hassan have on slacks and neat button-down shirts. Only those of his father's generation wear the body-cloaking robes.

I ask him, when I get the chance, about my observation.

"In town, it's mainly true," Hassan says, "but in the country, in small towns, some boys and young men still follow the old style of dress."

So, my stalker is either an authentic and curious country bumpkin or a deliberate fraud. Ali and one of his brothers walk me back to the hotel.

CHAPTER SIX

Sunday, January 16, 2005

In the morning, after a lovely breakfast I never thought I'd be hungry enough to eat, Hamza reminds me in his flowery way that now would be a good time to move to the new room. I promise him to pack our belongings right away, and he promises me a young man to carry our bags. When I get to my room, Amina, the senior maid, is standing in front of the door.

"Oh, *madame*, I have news for you."

She lifts her voice and speaks in a language I don't understand. Tadefi's face pops into view over the upstairs railing, and she runs down to join us. Amina resumes speaking French to me. "When I asked about your sister, Tadefi said she thinks she saw her when she left. She saw a red bag. It was big like . . ." Amina says something else, and Tadefi's hands move out to show the dimensions. More translating back and forth. "But your sister, she was not carrying this bag."

My forehead furrows, but before I can make sense of it, Amina says, "It was the man who carried the bag."

Fay left with a man? My stomach lurches. "Man?" I say when I can speak calmly.

More translating. "It was a Moroccan man. Tadefi says he looked rough—I will ask what she means by that."

Another torrent of words.

"She says his clothes were not clean. And his hair was too long."

Tadefi chimes in with more chatter.

Amina translates. "She thinks your friend was unhappy to be going with this man."

I tug at the collar of my sweater. All of a sudden, the hallway feels furnace-hot. "Why?" I swallow hard. "What happened?"

Another round of consultation in what I assume is Tamazight, the Berber language. "This child doesn't know. It's only an idea of hers." Amina drops her voice, as if to keep Tadefi from hearing—although the point of this translation service is that Tadefi doesn't understand much French. "She's young and fanciful. I think she's afraid of men."

I'm not so sure. Still, I have a million questions, and with Amina's help, I learn that Tadefi saw Fay with the man when Tadefi got off work Friday afternoon and was waiting for Sihan, the other teenage maid, to come down to walk her home—about four o'clock. She thought neither Fay nor the man saw her because she was sitting alone in the breakfast room with the lights off. They initially went over to the desk, where they stopped for a minute—*my note*. Then they turned and walked out. Fay was in front and the man, holding her red tote, walked behind her.

Tadefi doesn't think he was pushing her or touching her at all. I ask about that, of course, because I'm horrified that Fay really *was* forced to leave and I wasn't clever enough to unravel her clues. When I exhaust all my specific questions, I ask, "Is there anything else you can think of?"

Tadefi surprises me by speaking at length to Amina, who relays, "She thinks she's seen the man before, but she's not sure. She'll try to remember."

* * *

The picture in my mind after talking to Tadefi and Amina is disturbing. Once I got her note and recovered from my night of panic, I was sure Fay was okay. I figured she was being secretive—like when she hid things she didn't want me to know about—in order to do something confidential, but was generally okay. I have no doubt she wrote the note, but she left the hotel with a rough-looking man and, if Tadefi is to be believed, she was scared.

I try to shoehorn that into an "okay" scenario: I should've guessed Fay would require help to accomplish this *very important errand*, this mission that was going to take two days. She'd likely need transportation, and she left me our rental car, so a man in general—a driver or a guide—isn't a huge problem. Maybe Amina is right, and I could dismiss Tadefi's impression as that of a young country girl in the big city. Maybe. But if I were in Fay's size nines at the point of doing whatever it was my husband couldn't do himself *and* I decided it was a bad idea—yeah, I'd be scared, too. I work through the idea with increasing certainty I'm on the right track. If *my* feet were becoming progressively colder—if, say, I was stopped and searched by unfriendly policemen—I might become distracted and testy with my sister as I brooded about what was to come.

Memories of the traffic stop surface, specifically the way Fay refused to admit we spoke French or understood what they said—as though she didn't want to be asked any questions. *Those men* can't possibly be the people/thing/event she's helping, so perhaps they were trying to stop her.

After the police let us go, I was so shaken that, had I been driving, I would've reversed and dashed back to the airport. I kept repeating, as if repetition would somehow bring clarity, that I didn't understand why they asked all those questions about where we were going, why they pawed though all our stuff. "Why?" I asked. "Why us?"

Fay had taken over driving when we got back in the car. Her hands tightened on the steering wheel. "I can't imagine how they could . . . why they would go after us."

"How they could *what*?" I snapped at her telltale flub. "What were you going to say?"

"Oh." Fay licked her lips. "I guess . . . how they could let us go without giving us a ticket."

Even then I should've suspected it had to be more than that.

I've assumed this errand she's running for Gil has to do with his business as an attorney. I only hope it isn't, in fact, a task too dangerous to entrust to his wife. To his wife and to me. Wherever she is, I'm *here*, vulnerable, in plain sight. Since seeing the man in the striped djellaba again last night, I'm positive I'm being watched. But I don't know *why*. The surveillance could be to protect me. Or to determine my involvement.

Oh dear God, I think with a gasp, maybe the watcher lost track of Fay when she left and is monitoring me in hopes of locating her. I pinch my lips tight to keep from whimpering, and freeze in place, wishing I could disappear. But I can't leave my sister; I have to stay. I have to wait for Fay.

My shaky breathing calms. *Right.* I exhale with a whoosh. I'm staying here. Whoever *they* are, I can't help them in any way. I don't know anything. I'll take it easy today. Thank goodness it's already Sunday, and Fay will be back soon to explain.

We haven't done much unpacking, so it only takes a minute to clear my toiletries from the bathroom and pick up a few things from the bedside table. Hamza's promised young man appears. He sticks Fay's suitcase under one arm and mine under the other. Leaving me to bring up the rear, he marches off to my new quarters.

The man unlocks the door and opens it with a flourish. He deposits our suitcases inside the door and hands me the key before walking off. The room is a utilitarian rectangle with two single beds along the right side, a window at the far end, bathroom and closet opening off the left side. The bathroom—I'd forgotten to look when the maid brought me here to inspect the room—is boring dove gray paint with a tiny ceramic shower stall. I already miss my gorgeous undulating kaleidoscope tile.

Oh, well. The room is cramped and nondescript, but we plan to spend only one more night in Ouarzazate, so it'll be fine. I claim the bed by the window and wheel my suitcase around to the far side to get it out of the way. Then I push Fay's suitcase over by the bathroom wall.

I'm troubled by these new questions concerning Fay's whereabouts, never mind the *why*-abouts, and equally troubled by how I've become involved. When I shove her bag against the wall, I wonder if Fay left behind any hints about her clandestine journey. Snooping isn't something I think a sister should do, but then neither is disappearing.

So I unzip and peek. And find nothing out of the ordinary. We traveled light, one small suitcase apiece. Fay's is not quite filled with the basics—bra and panties, socks, slacks, shirts, a sweatshirt, her quilted jacket, a pair of nice shoes, camera, two paperbacks. Her passport is in a side pocket, along with her return airplane ticket.

I shake out her clothes. I riffle through the books; no slips of paper fall out. I look at the photos on her camera; the last pictures are from Ait Benhaddou on Friday morning. I flip back through the remaining pictures, like my life flashing in reverse sequence before my eyes. Like the credits at the end of *Thelma and Louise*. No menacing stranger lurks in the background; no evidence Fay is documenting anything besides the beautiful scenery.

I pick up her suitcase and shake it: empty. I put everything back in as neatly as I can. An uneasiness niggles at the back of my skull. I stare into the bag in front of me as if I could pry out its secret, kneeling on a faded blue and yellow prayer rug on the cold tile floor until, at last, my knees and back rebel. I'll have to wait for Fay to explain.

I don't know exactly when to expect her, probably not this early in the morning. Since Hassan and Fatima waved away my wallet, I never managed to pay for last night's meal. One thing I need to do is return to the restaurant and, if they still won't take my money, thank them again for a wonderful evening.

I grab the backpack I use on vacation instead of a purse—much better for hands-free convenience and for the ability to stuff more *stuff* into it—and head down the twisting staircase once more. Hamza's sweeping the lobby floor. He has his shirtsleeves rolled to his elbows and secured there with rubber bands. The main door is open, letting in bright sunshine and a warm breeze laced with diesel fumes.

Hamza leans companionably on the broom. *"Bonjour, madame,"* he begins, and my excursion is delayed while Hamza checks on my satisfaction with the new room, my opinion of the hotel's breakfast offerings, what sights I've seen . . . I assure him I'm having a wonderful stay in Ouarzazate and the weather is perfect and I'm looking forward to seeing more of Morocco. I fudge a bit on our itinerary because Fay's absence may have screwed up our plans—or what I *thought* our plans were. Only then do I escape down the street, much quieter in the early morning than it was in the bustle of Saturday night.

Fatima is slumped at a table near the restaurant's front door, elbow on the table, chin resting on her open palm. A stack of papers lies before her on the table.

"Julie." She straightens and a wide grin lights her face. "Wonderful. Just in time for me to take a break. Come, sit. Would you like some tea?"

"No, thank you. I just finished breakfast," I say, reluctant to accept more food from them. "What do you need a break from?"

"I'm the bookkeeper for the restaurant, but this week has gotten totally out of control. I'm so far behind." She makes an exaggerated grimace and runs her fingers through her thick curly hair. "My father trained as a bookkeeper, too, and he could do this in half the time. Normally, I bring the paperwork to him when I get overwhelmed, but Hassan had to use our car today."

Better than offering money. "How about if I take you?"

"Oh, but my father lives in the Valley of the Roses. It's an hour's drive."

Bingo. The Valley of the Roses, the closest gorge, is one of the places I most want to see. "I'm dying to go there," I tell Fatima, "but didn't know if I'd have time. Please let me take you, and you can point out all the sights."

CHAPTER SEVEN

The compact and picturesque urban center of Ouarzazate ends abruptly just beyond the *Centre Artisanal*. An instant later, I'm driving through caramel-colored hills that resemble the high desert of the American West, a semi-arid expanse of rolling hills covered with scrub vegetation. The hills become sharper, steeper, browner. Driving east under high, thin clouds takes us past a huge lake. "That's the dammed-up River Draa," Fatima says. The lake's zigzagging contours are defined by the sharp ridges of mountains the water has engulfed. Only a few dying palms still keep their heads above water.

Fatima tells me she studied environmental sciences at the university and explains how the dam, built in the '70s to control the flow of water to the fields and bring clean drinking water to local villages, has been a boon to the Draa Valley. But thirty years after the dam changed the water supply, soil erosion and excess salinity, exacerbated by the ongoing drought, have destroyed many villages downstream. "Man-made intervention," she scoffs and crosses her arms with a scowl.

"What was so out of control about your week?" I ask Fatima in the lull in conversation.

"It was Ali's plane. He emailed that he was arriving Friday afternoon at two on Royal Air Maroc. His brother Samir and I went to the airport, but he never got off the plane."

"Oh, no." I steal a look at Fatima, remembering Alex's awful first day of first grade when he got off the school bus at the wrong stop and was lost for hours. "I would have gone crazy with worry." I *did* go crazy.

"Oh, *yes*." Fatima slowly nods. "And he didn't answer his phone and we didn't know what happened or if he was okay or how he was getting home."

I'm old enough to remember a time I think of as BC—before cell phones—when a missed connection or a flat tire on the highway or a child who didn't come home on time meant anxiety—like Fatima's and mine—or danger or endless complications and confusion. We've gotten spoiled so quickly by instant communication. If Fay had gone off like this in the States, I would've picked up my phone and demanded to know where she was and what the hell she was doing.

But *we* were the foreigners-lacking-SIM-cards here, surely— "Couldn't the people at the airline desk tell you what flight he was arriving on?"

Fatima's been looking out the car window at the rocky watercourse that parallels the highway. Now she turns to me, shaking her head, lips thinned in exasperation. "They didn't know."

"What?" That's their *job*, all those agents tapping on keyboards. "How could they *not know*?"

Fatima explains, with words tumbling out faster and faster as she relives her frustration. Apparently, in Morocco, passenger manifests exist only on local computers until the fight is boarded and the door closes. Because the pinging of constant traffic can overtax the computer system, they hold all the data and just upload it once. According to Fatima, a supervisor in Ouarzazate had no trouble finding out that Ali boarded his flight originating in France—Marseille to Casablanca. Since he didn't arrive in Ouarzazate, then he must've been stuck in Casablanca. "But more than that, we couldn't find out," she adds tartly. "You'd think by 2005, Morocco would have joined the twenty-first century."

Another glimpse at how technology is changing our lives. When a sudden snowstorm blew across the Rockies the day I was flying home from college for Christmas—this was the late '80s—my only option was a flurry of long-distance-collect calls from airport pay phones to my parents as one flight after another was canceled.

"So when Ali wasn't on the flight to Ouarzazate, there was no way to find out how he'd been rebooked until . . . until he was already in the air, I guess?"

"Right." Fatima spreads her fingers wide and reaches her hands up to touch the roof of the tiny car. She raises her face to the sky, beseeching heaven. "Samir and I waited around the airport all day, but Ali's name never came up on the passenger list for any of the flights from Casablanca. When he wasn't on the last plane, we finally went home."

"Such an awful experience. What happened to Ali?" *Okay to ask because, obviously, he arrived safely.*

Fatima throws back her head and laughs. "Ali showed up on our doorstep early yesterday morning. His father was furious, but Ali showed him the messages he'd sent—they call them text messages. Apparently, he uses them in France all the time, but the idiot didn't realize that our phones aren't set up to receive them."

The knot in my stomach relaxes at the happy ending, and I'm laughing with sympathy. *Yet another technology changing how we communicate.* "My daughter Erin has started doing that, too, but I don't use them either."

"Ali's flight was overbooked. They called for volunteers to give up their seats in return for a travel voucher, but everyone was in a hurry to get home. When they upped the offer high enough to pay for another whole trip home, Ali took it." Fatima claps her hands. "He'll use it to return in the summer."

"That's wonderful."

*   *   *

The Valley of the Roses begins in the commercial town of El Kelaa M'Gouna. Once away from the urban sprawl of endless cinderblock suburbs, the road follows the Mgoun River as it meanders along the bottom of a wide valley. Oncoming traffic plays chicken on the not-quite-two-lane road. Whoever turns their wheel in avoidance first—that would be me—jolts into a rut on the nonexistent shoulders. But the farther I drive, the fewer cars we encounter.

The road climbs away from the riverbed revealing a vista of opulent greenery, brown-black rock, striking red cliffs. Modest mud-brick dwellings made from the soil rise up artlessly—open, rambling, and unpretentious—not hidden behind tall fortifications. These are farms, where the eponymous roses grow.

Higher on the mountain, occasional rocky outcroppings, often the site of a romantically picturesque kasbah, interrupt thickets of yellow winter leaves.

Fatima directs me off the main road at the entrance to a small hotel. The air is cool, the sun warm, the view—river, trees, farms, cliffs, sky—incomparable.

"I grew up near here, but this place is my father's new hobby," she says. "Since my mother died, he's tried one distraction after the other."

While Fatima conducts her business, I sit under a brand-new awning of lashed bamboo poles, which, one day, will be heavy with vines and provide shade. The djellaba-clad man was not skulking around the hotel this morning. Even if he had accomplices, no car paralleled our journey up the mountain, and I'm the lone customer in this brand-new establishment.

I sit in silence, save for occasional birdsong and the distant whine of a chain saw. It would be fanciful to imagine the scent of roses in the air on this January afternoon—still, a redolent perfume permeates the air, a mix of sweet-smelling flowers, savory wood smoke, and baking bread, all lifted by the breeze and mellowed by the sun.

It's peaceful here on the hilltop. My mind wends along that circuitous path it often follows when life pauses and the wonder of "how I got here" rises to the surface. From Fay's disappearance and my fear, to her note that turned everything on its head, to the success of yesterday's drive and then dinner with Fatima and her family.

I run my fingers along the rough-hewn table. I reach out to pull a single pale-yellow flower toward me. It smells like honey, and I memorize its contours. I close my eyes to better hear the birds and the rustling of other life.

You never know what you'll find, I think with a smile, when you go searching.

So here I am. Not exactly where I'd planned to be. But sometimes the best excursions turn out that way.

A few years back, Fay tried a shortcut to get from my house to an antique store she'd heard about in a small town in the Blue Ridge Mountains. The road turned into a dirt track, narrowed to the point that bushes were scraping the side-view mirrors. We came, finally, to an opening wide enough to turn around. Fay had only to raise her eyebrows and give me her secret smile of intrigue.

I smiled back my agreement. *Let's see where this road goes.*

It went to a field of wildflowers overlooking a pond nestled in a hollow. We lunched on Fay's stash of emergency granola bars from the glove box and returned home, not with an antique lamp, but with armloads of magnificent flowers.

Turns out neither of us needed a lamp. What we needed was the serendipity of getting lost and discovering where the road led.

I'll bring Fay here—show her my discovery.

CHAPTER EIGHT

atima returns with her sheaf of papers, and I stand, assuming we'll leave, but she waves me back into my seat. Behind her, the housekeeper carries a platter containing an elaborate *salade composée*—an artistically arranged pinwheel of cold green beans, chunks of tuna, marinated baby potatoes, olives, sliced tomato, eggs, beets, and avocado. So much for not accepting any more of their delicious food.

"Didn't you say last night that your mother was taking care of your children while you're on vacation?" Fatima asks after she serves a generous helping of vegetables onto our plates.

I laugh. "My mother-in-law." Because the French word *belle-mère* can mean "stepmother" as well as "mother-in-law", I clarify, "my husband's mother."

"Ah, mine is a veritable dragon." Fatima makes a face as though the potato chunk she's just eaten were a bitter lemon.

"I don't know what we'd do without Donna," I say. "The kids adore her, and she's so good with them. Where she lives, winters are cold and snowy, so it's become a tradition for her to visit us for a month every winter. We all do stuff together for a couple of weeks, and then she shoos me out the door and tells me to go have fun and let her spoil her grandchildren."

Her son, too, I think. But Donna's "spoiling" is all about hugs and kisses and extra ice cream. Ghost stories and pillow forts that don't get taken down for days on end. And a little gift for me, often as I'm heading out the door. "For you," Donna will say, pressing a small package into my hand—a scarf, a journal. This time it was the slim nylon neck pouch where I'm safeguarding my passport and an emergency stash of funds.

"So that's when you go on vacation with your sister?"

I'd told Fatima at dinner about some of the trips Fay and I have taken.

"You're so lucky."

"I am." I smile—and deflect the conversation to Fatima's family.

The less said the better about why the *belle-mère* babysits and not the *mère*.

Yeah, the house will be a disaster when I get home, but that's a small price to pay for family harmony. My mother long ago labeled Donna "inattentive." To my mother, the micromanager, *not paying attention* is a serious charge. But I can't bear the thought of her constantly critiquing Erin's school outfits of skinny jeans and crop-tops, correcting Alex's homework, or nagging Molly, whose thumb slides into her mouth when she's tired or worried—*so you won't need braces like your mother did, dear.*

I'll take a messy house and happy children any day. Even if Molly *does* need braces.

* * *

A wide-ranging conversation with Fatima over lunch is a welcome distraction. During the drive back to Ouarzazate, however, I start wondering what I'm going to say to Fay when she returns. Her complicated deception in orchestrating this vacation is *way* out of my experience with her, but not totally out of character. Fay has a private side—her solitary walks to mull things over—and she certainly managed to keep the troubles in her first marriage from me until the week she filed divorce papers. She met Gil a couple of years later when they were both playing in an over-thirty soccer league, and they married love-at-first-sight quickly.

If Gil needed a discreet emissary, for example, I could see her volunteering to help. Perhaps she carried important papers or is meeting someone. I hope that's all. The mysterious watcher in town worries me, but I can't believe Gil would ask Fay to do something illegal or dangerous.

*   *   *

The note I left for her is still in the box. Fay is not back. *Not back.* In my fantasy, I return from the Valley of the Roses, confident and cheerful— *oh, Fay, I took an amazing drive today with my friend Fatima. I'll have to show you . . . nice to see you again, and what the hell was so secret and important you couldn't tell me?*—not like the nervous wreck I'm going to be if she keeps me waiting much longer.

I try to figure out when I can realistically expect to see Fay. I assume her destination lay in a remote place. If not, she could easily have invented up a compelling reason why we simply *had to* visit some town or other that had a wonderful . . . fill-in-the-blank. Fay could have slipped away for a few hours, no challenge at all compared to the present circumstances. Admitting I can only guesstimate, I do the math. Leaving at four on Friday meant only a few hours of travel before dark. My tentative conclusion—a few hours' drive on Friday afternoon would result in a few hours' return today. In other words, she could easily be back by now.

My feet move me up the stairs and through the halls while my thoughts swirl. I automatically take the path to our old room. Luckily,

I hear people inside speaking German and, realizing the new occupants have arrived, reverse course.

I walk into our new room and toss my sweater onto the bed. It misses, falling limply to the floor. *It fell limply.* Something else was limp, something that shouldn't have been—what was it? I nibble a fingernail, tap my toes. It was here, here in our new room, that I saw something . . . Fay's suitcase is on the floor. That's it—the answer to what vexed me so when I looked through her things: something had happened to Fay's puffy quilted jacket.

I unzip her suitcase. Lying neatly folded under the black pants and sweater she wore to Ait Benhaddou is Fay's beautiful striped jacket. Neatly folded—and nearly flat. When I admired it, she told me she'd sewn it herself, which segued into my teasing Fay about the mess her sewing created in our room when we were kids. Really, though, I was glad that, as busy as she was, she still maintained her interest in couture.

On the plane, she rolled it into a fat pillow. At dinner the first night in Marrakech, its metallic gold and silver threads winked in the shimmering light as she snuggled in it against the cool breeze at the rooftop restaurant—and by the side of the road, its billowy warmth enveloped me when Fay placed it around my shoulders after my angina attack.

I spread the jacket out on my bed. It looks and feels different now. Only a thin layer of batting inflates it.

Since Fay made the jacket, she could have concealed something inside, something rather bulky. Not just an important document. It would have been bigger, pliable, or perhaps in small pieces. What was it? Fay knew damn good and well what those policemen wanted, and she fixed it so we couldn't answer their questions. She safeguarded something concealed in her jacket, and now she's taken it with her.

I pace up and down the length of the room.

Back by the side of the road, Fay threw our belongings helter-skelter into the handiest suitcase. That night at the hotel in Ouarzazate, when

I returned to the bedroom from my shower, Fay was sorting our clothes into piles on the beds.

Fay's jacket lay on the top of her pile, *and* Fay had her little sewing kit out. I'd thought nothing of it at the time; Fay is famous for keeping needle and thread close at hand to ward off the horror of a loose button or a pulled seam.

Consumed by my hurt feeling and not troubling to be tidy, I go through Fay's suitcase once more, thoroughly, methodically, to see if I missed anything.

There *is* something. I almost overlook it, and it's easy to imagine anyone failing to notice it. A piece of yellow legal paper, folded several times, is wedged in the inside pocket of Fay's Villanova Wildcats sweatshirt. The outside of the paper has numbers scribbled in pencil, all three or four digits, so probably not phone numbers. They could be amounts of money. Maybe mileage or distances. Or even the combination for a lock. But when I open the paper, I hit pay dirt: short lines of writing in Arabic. A list of words, I think, rather than sentences. What Fay is doing with it, though, I can't fathom. She doesn't know any Arabic.

Since I can't read it either, it isn't much of a clue. I tuck the paper back into her sweatshirt pocket for safekeeping.

CHAPTER NINE

At six, I dash out to the café around the corner where we ate the first night in Ouarzazate, leaving Ibrahim instructions to have Fay meet me there. Although it's chilly, I take a table on the patio so Fay can easily spot me. It's a pedestrian street, full of men and women hurrying home from work, most in Western clothes and carrying briefcases. But for the scent of mint permeating the air and the *chaabi* music floating through the air from the record store next door—and the decorative scarves more or less covering the women's hair—I could be in any large American city. I wolf down my lentil soup and run back along the obvious, shortest path. Ibrahim shakes his head. No Fay.

The evening wears on. Calm deserts me. My pleasure with solo successes—shopping, excursions, dinner—ebbs. The worry I kept at bay returns, crashing over me like a tidal wave. I jump at every door slamming. I freeze at every footfall in the hall. I pace restlessly. I open the window. The *palmeraie* stretches in a green ribbon off to the right, but looking left brings an oblique view of the street. Most shops have closed, lights shining only on wares displayed in the front windows. Traffic is light, bringing with it relief from the scent of diesel that hangs over urban Morocco. I stare at every car that passes, hoping against hope to see one stop at the curb and Fay descend with a cheery good-bye wave.

Pressure builds, my chest tightens, and my breathing becomes erratic. I curl up in bed, pretending I'm safe at home watching Saturday morning cartoons with the kids huddled around me, but I can't sit still. A hot shower doesn't help; neither does scrolling through the day's scenic snapshots on my camera in an attempt to recapture carefree memories from my visit to the Valley of the Roses.

I stand at the window again. I close my eyes, count to ten, look down at the street, don't see Fay, close my eyes, count to ten, look out. Fay never appears. My anxiety loop spirals higher. A cold lump gathers in the center of my chest, and fingers of icy adrenaline-fueled disaster radiate outward—the beginnings of an arrhythmia attack.

I sit, try to calm down. I'd swallowed my daily atenolol, the drug that regulates my uneven heartbeat, after lunch with Fatima, so this episode can't possibly be as severe as the day the police frightened me so badly.

The only tricky part of my medication is taking it at the same time every day. To adjust to the time change from Virginia to Morocco— five hours ahead—it's easiest to switch the timing to lunch instead of my at-home breakfast routine. So that awful morning when the police stop turned menacing, I didn't have enough left in my system to stem the flood of adrenaline. My heart had raced out of control, and I came close to fainting.

Tonight's surge of anxiety does prompt me to take an additional small piece of atenolol in an effort to quiet the questions making my heart beat frantically in my chest as though a trapped bird is struggling to escape: Why is Fay delayed? Where is she? Should I sleep? *Could* I sleep? And—what in heaven's name will I do if she doesn't come back?

Monday, January 17, 2005
In the end, like Friday, I do sleep, although I spend a restless night, marred by dreams of war, snowstorms, and loud blasts. I awake, alone,

to find I forgot to close the window—which would account for the imagery of cold and the sharp noises in my dreams.

Although it's barely light, sleep has fled for the night. Downstairs, the overnight man, whom I've only seen once before, sits slumped in an overstuffed chair near the front of the lobby. Hamza, still in his overcoat with a Lakers watch cap covering his curly hair, crouches next to him. The men are speaking quietly but fall silent when I approach.

"Are there any messages for me?"

The night man shakes his head. Hamza doesn't even bother to turn around with his habitual *bonjour, madame.*

Perhaps we all need to wake up a little more. I stumble into the breakfast room and sip coffee while I take stock: Julie Welch. Monday morning. Alone in Morocco. I have to get help today.

I'll call the embassy first. Surely someone there can tell me what to do. It would be a relief to dump the entire problem in their lap and let the United States government earn their tax dollars, but at best, I figure advice, perhaps a local contact. Despite my misgivings, if they insist I report Fay's disappearance to the local police, I will.

Although several stores around the hotel sell phone cards, when I rush out after breakfast, they're all closed. According to signs dangling in the doorways, the earliest I can expect to find one open is nine a.m.

*　　*　　*

Like déjà vu all over again, as the Yogi Berra quote goes, my return to the hotel brings the tableau of Amina and Tadefi waiting by my door. In this newer part of the building, the halls are wide enough to drive a car—although a car couldn't cope with the funky twists and turns the corridor takes. The women have been sitting on a low bench scattered with rose petals from a remarkably luxuriant bush that's thriving in a green pottery urn the size of a mini-fridge.

The women rise when they see me, and I hurry down the hall. *They must have more news.*

The information comes out smoother than the day before, Tadefi having relayed her narrative to Amina in advance.

"Tadefi remembered that the man who left the hotel with your sister was an acquaintance of her cousin Driss, so she went to her cousin's house to ask about him." Amina tells me that Driss wasn't home, but his mother knew who Tadefi meant. Here, Amina's normally severe features morph into snickering. "Once Tadefi satisfied her aunt that she wasn't *interested* in the man, she learned his name was Mohammed. He'd been staying with their neighbors and had taken Driss to some clubs that angered his mother. Fortunately, Mohammed returned to his village a few days earlier." With a brisk slap-slap, time to wash her hands of the situation, Amina concludes, "That was Friday afternoon."

I keep silent, thinking over what to make of this new information. When Tadefi resumes speaking, Amina translates, "She says her parents live in the same area as Mohammed's family. Should you wish to follow your sister, she can draw a map of the roads you must travel."

Without giving it a huge amount of thought, I agree that might be useful. I pull my spiral travel notebook and a pen from my backpack, then open the notebook to a clean page. Tadefi sits on the bench again, lays the notebook down, and begins sketching. She keeps up a stream of conversation, which Amina dutifully recounts, explaining that I should take the N9 south about one hour to Agdz, and then another hour or so to Zagora, where I'll turn onto the N12.

Tadefi draws an arrow pointing left, looks up to make sure I'm following her, then speaks again. Amina translates. "From there, roads don't have numbers. There's a signposted turning for Ait Tazigout several kilometers down the road on the right." Tadefi sketches a line curling off to the south and, despite her limited education, neatly letters the name in crisp Arabic script. Amina continues to relay Tadefi's comments that this was the beginning of the black desert, a barren area where I'd likely see only rocky hills and perhaps boys herding goats. But when I get to an old house with no roof on the left side of the road and a tree in a hollow protected from the wind, I should take the path between them. "Go down the track until you come to a cluster of houses around a well. This is Taghabene." Tadefi inscribes another name. "There you will find the family of the friend of Tadefi's cousin Driss."

Head reeling from an excess of hard-to-digest information, I focus on the words Tadefi lettered on her map. "I can't read Arabic," I tell Amina. "Would you say those town names again so I can write them phonetically in a way that I can read them?"

When I concentrate on writing the phonetic equivalents beneath Tadefi's careful lettering, the ornate curlicues begin to look familiar. Amina is shuffling her feet, anxious to get back to work, but I have an idea and need to know one more thing.

"Excuse me a minute." I turn and jab the key into the lock on my door, dash into the room, and remove the folded yellow paper from Fay's sweatshirt. I bring it out and compare it to Tadefi's map. There!— the name of the mysterious Mohammed's village. It matches the top item on Fay's list. Her destination. I'm positive.

Tadefi continues reading from Fay's paper. She tugs at Amina's arm, gibbering a mile a minute. Amina, lost in her role as translator, continues to relay Tadefi's words. "Those people, they were bad people, traitors, enemies of the king. Now dead."

Before Amina finishes speaking, pint-sized Tadefi has somehow managed to drag her halfway down the hall.

CHAPTER TEN

The closest place that sells phone cards is a small electronics store on a street parallel to the hotel, near the café where I'd eaten dinner. I'm pacing outside when it opens. A frustrating half hour later, their tech-support guy finally gets my US phone to play ball with the Moroccan network—something about "resetting the APN" that goes totally over my head.

They look up the US Embassy number for me, and I go outside to phone—though not too far in case of further technical difficulties.

My call to the embassy yields the information that services for citizens of the United States visiting Morocco are handled at the US *Consulate*. The woman who answers the embassy phone provides the consulate's phone number. "But," she says, "I think the office is closed because of some upcoming holiday, not sure what the deal is."

"Eid al-Adha," I tell her. That tiny bit of insider knowledge from my visits with Fatima lifts my spirits briefly. "It's like Moroccan Thanksgiving."

I dial the consulate anyhow. The person who picks up the phone is a fast-talking Midwesterner named Sam Monatti. He says his name so quickly—Samonatti—that I have to ask him to repeat it several times before I understand. The consulate is *not* having normal business hours that day, but Sam's the on-call duty officer. I've reached him at his apartment and interrupted an unspecified task he seems impatient to resume. While he doesn't actually "help" me, he does permit me to take up perhaps five minutes of his extremely valuable time.

He breaks in before I finish. "So you're telling me that you came to Morocco with your sister, a Mrs. Fay Ohana, age thirty-six. She left you a note stating she was attending to business for her husband. You expected her back last night, but she didn't show up. There's no evidence of foul play. Sunday afternoon. Monday morning. No big deal. You're not in the US here," he says. "Do you have any idea how bad the roads are? Ever hear any jokes about third-world time? They're all true."

Although I plead with him to reconsider, he tells me there's nothing he can do unless Fay is injured or there's evidence she's the victim of a crime.

And the second I mention she left accompanied by a *man*, a *Moroccan* man, Sam's minimal helpfulness vanishes. "Call the local *gendarmerie* if you like," he says. "You can give them that note and the left-behind slip of paper with Arabic writing." Sam's acerbic rendering of "left-behind slip of paper" makes it clear he isn't impressed with my fears.

I imagine his shrug as he disconnects.

Traitors, enemies of the king. I was already afraid to involve the police, and Tadefi's words have magnified my reluctance tenfold. It's Monday, so Gil is my next move. I look up his office number online, but it's scarcely ten a.m. in North Africa. I don't know how to come up with his cell phone number, so I'll have to wait another three or four hours until it's reasonable to reach a human at his office. This is all Gil's idea, I think, let him take responsibility. Dumping all my resentment on him still feels better than blaming Fay for my frustration.

I clomp back to the hotel from the cute urban park where I made my calls. A white car with angled green-and-red stripes is parked in front of the hotel.

Police.

Adrenaline kicks in as I relive the moments by the side of the road when the two policemen yanked Fay and me from the car and tore through our belongings. *Calm down*, I command. *There's no reason this has anything to do with Fay.*

Still, my stomach roils; my mouth goes dry. I thrust out a hand to steady myself, managing only to scrape my fingers on rough stucco where my hand lands.

A uniformed man reading a newspaper inside the idling vehicle pays no attention to me as I steal past him and walk into the hotel. Hamza slouches on one of the blue sofas in the lobby taking jerky puffs from a cigarette. Ash scatters in little gray snowdrifts over his normally impeccable white shirt. *Something* is wrong. I move toward him. "Is there a problem? The police?" I gesture vaguely.

His mouth opens and closes a few times; no sounds come out. Hamza is ashen. The hand holding his cigarette trembles. "Oh, *madame*, it is a tragedy such as never before happened at this establishment. *Madame*, it could have been you!"

A sharp pain, like a sucker punch thrown by an invisible man, tightens my gut. I flop onto the couch opposite Hamza. My hands quiver like his. "What could have been me, Hamza? What happened?"

His mouth opens again, and this time words tumble out in a rush. "In the middle of the night, men with masks came in the back door and surprised Moulham, the night clerk. They hit him and tied him up and threatened to cut his throat if he made any noise."

"How awful." So that's why they looked so shaken up when I first came downstairs this morning. "No one heard the men attacking your clerk?"

Hamza shakes his head. The men were quiet, he tells me, threatening Moulham with whispers, then locking him in the supply closet and going upstairs.

I squeeze an embroidered throw pillow to my chest. "The poor man must've been terrified."

With trembling fingers, Hamza lights another cigarette from the stub of the one he's finishing. "Yes. Moulham said when they were leaving, the men sounded so angry that he feared they would kill him." Hamza inhales several steadying puffs in a row before he takes up the story again. "One man said something like, 'God help us when they hear about our mistake. Your idiocy has ruined us.'"

My fingers pick ineffectually at loose threads on the brocade pillow.

"But," Hamza continues, "the men went out into the night, and all became quiet once more. When the kitchen staff arrived at dawn, Moulham kicked the door loudly enough for them to hear. The cook freed him and phoned me."

"Thank goodness." I'm hugging the pillow to my chest. "I'm so glad he's all right."

Hamza clasps his palms in front of his bowed head. "At first, we couldn't find any damage to the hotel or any theft, but later a guest came down to complain about loud banging coming from a nearby room. We found four people tied up and gagged, two of them badly injured. It was your former room, *madame*."

Ice water surges through my veins. *Our old room*. Not where I slept last night, but the room registered to me and Fay. Lackadaisical Ibrahim merely drew an arrow from our names to a different spot on the chart. The newcomers were undoubtedly jotted down in a handy margin. The German family—"Are they going to be all right?"

Hamza blinks rapidly to ward off tears while he tells me that the children weren't injured, but the father had cuts on his hands and arms. They bandaged him at the hotel so he could stay with his children, but the mother was taken to the hospital with knife wounds. "There was so much blood," he says.

My hand rises involuntarily to my mouth. I suck my skinned knuckle, taste my blood. *Blood*. I shudder.

"So much blood," Hamza repeats. "It is unheard of, this sort of violence." He shakes his head once more.

"Do you—" I have to be careful about what I ask. "Do you know why they were attacked? Was it a burglary?" I can't ask the question most on my mind: Did they want *Fay*?

"They speak little French. I believe the man said the intruders shined a light—I suppose they had a flashlight—and woke up his wife by shaking her." Hamza demonstrates this, much as the German man probably had to him. "One man asked her for something, asked again when she did not speak. It's curious, but he said they spoke to her in English."

My dreams of war, noises in the night. Danger has arrived. I have to get away.

"They cut her when she didn't answer them. One slashed her again as they were leaving." Hamza gestures a backhand swing. "These people were already tied up. The woman could not protect herself." He looks up solemnly at me. "The Prophet says, '*Kindness is a mark of faith, and whoever is not kind has no faith.*' These were not men of faith. I am ashamed."

The tears Hamza has been trying to keep at bay run a slalom course down his stubbly cheek, and he brushes them away roughly with his palm. Not knowing or caring if it's proper, I pat his hand as I stand to go. "I'm sorry."

CHAPTER ELEVEN

I run up the three flights of stairs to my room. I have to pack, have to get away. The men who knifed the German woman and terrorized her family, the men who asked questions in English—they wanted me. I *know* they did. They want me to tell them . . . something. But I don't know anything.

Perhaps I do, though. Since talking to Amina and Tadefi, I have a good idea where Fay went. And I have an inkling of the mess she must be involved in. Dead enemies of the king—holy shit, what a disaster.

Last night's attack has also removed all doubt that hostile forces are stalking me. My watchers have ceased merely observing. Perhaps they also expected Fay's Sunday reappearance and her continuing absence has provoked them. Provoked them to attack and terrorize a woman, a woman who could have been me.

Okay, then.

The consulate won't help me. I can't reach Gil yet. I'm afraid to go to the police.

That leaves me. I have a car, and I know where Fay's gone.

If I drive away this morning, I can reach Mohammed's village before dark. Find Fay. Perhaps I mean *Find her before someone else does*.

I race along the third-floor hall, imagining unseen attackers pursuing me. An abrupt car horn sounding on the street brings tears of terror to my eyes. The caress of a billowing window curtain on the back of my neck drives my stomach up into my throat. Imaginary assailants' footsteps pound in the hallway while, with wobbling hands, I stuff everything into our suitcases. I run downstairs and have our bags brought down while I check out, exchanging a quick goodbye with Hamza. Although we only reserved a room through last night, Hamza knows I'm supposed to be waiting for my sister who, I told him, is off exploring on her own for a few days.

Family is complicated, he'd commiserated, after my initial shocked reaction to Fay's note. Perhaps he's chalking up my abrupt departure to more of that complication. If so, he'd be one-thousand-percent right.

I load the car and drive away without a second's pause. *South on the N9, south on the N9*, like a drumbeat in my brain. *Drive south, get away from here.* I long for telepathy. *Fay, I'm coming. I'm coming.* I want Steve sitting beside me—heck, I want Steve *driving.* I want him to reach over and squeeze my hand, as he did when we were rushing Erin to the hospital after her boogie-board accident last summer. Steve doesn't need words to talk to me; his hand in mine says it all.

For a while, the road out of town runs straight and true over gently rolling hills. I keep one eye on the rearview mirror, but I have the narrow strip of black asphalt to myself except for the occasional rocketing *grand taxi* flying past me. The most common intercity transport, the tan Mercedes *grand taxi* sedans shoehorn in seven to nine passengers and their luggage, dropping off and picking up passengers as space becomes available. The quicker the better, the more fares the better. Driven by madmen.

The taxis leave me eating their dust.

My stomach settles. I'm doing it.

I'm still scared, still wishing I'd wake from this nightmare. But that isn't going to happen. No one else can help me find my sister, and I can't do *nothing.* I'm going to keep driving south toward the black desert.

Here, the desert isn't black, but pink, and dotted with tufted straw-colored scrub brush. In gullies and shallow depressions, tangled greenery indicates where water occasionally collects. Purple mountains rise to the south, one range superimposed over another, until the farthest, barely visible, takes on the gray-blue of the sky.

No one appears from behind and paces me. Once I'm positive no one is following me, I fish Tadefi's map out of my backpack and spread it on the passenger seat. I'll need it later, after I turn off the numbered highways.

*　*　*

Agdz comes into view just before noon. It's a sleepy little pink and tan town situated in the shadow of an improbably twisted mountain eroded into spiky peaks and spires and candy-cane stripes. It reminds me of the lopsided castles my kids make at the beach by drizzling wet sand from their fingers.

They won't be at the beach on a chilly January morning. It's Monday anyhow, a school day. With the five-hour time difference, the kids will just be getting up, and I bet Donna's made them pancakes for breakfast half the mornings I've been gone.

It's soothing to imagine what they're doing. Not everyone understands, but I actually enjoy missing them—in an "absence makes the heart grow fonder" way. Donna loves them, loves to make special meals and go to their soccer games and—once upon a time when they were young—she could be cajoled into reading endless bedtime stories. These days only Molly can't read, but she likes to *tell* stories, and so Granny will sit by her bed until Molly's voice slows and her eyes close. Then she sings a lullaby, dims the lights, and tiptoes out the door.

And when I get home, I see them with fresh eyes—see how Molly's flyaway hair is turning darker like mine, how much Erin has grown. All the little things that get lost in the shuffle of day-to-day-to-day.

It's the same with Steve. Two weeks without sex makes for a sizzling reunion. And it's not just that, although *that* is awesome. Two weeks without sharing a glance across the dinner table—*look at the wonderful family we've made*—when one of the kids says or does something especially cute. Two weeks without his off-key singing in the shower, without the stubble on his chin tickling me as we curl up to sleep like spoons.

The best part about getting away from it all is returning home, open to life pulsing around me. This trip, I just have to retrieve Fay—then, I think, I'd like to go straight home into his arms.

South of Agdz, the road parallels the oasis created by the Draa River, a serpentine strip of lush date palms, with their coruscated bark and a bushy topknot of tumbling branches. Mountains that were a dusty blur on the horizon from the hotel in Ouarzazate take shape—craggy buttes crowned by crenelated towers, embellished with deep fissures, witness to eons of accretion and additional eons of erosion. Beyond lies the Sahara.

It's almost one thirty when I arrive in Zagora, the last town on my route. I have the car filled with gas, then grab a quick lunch of grilled kefta kabobs and French fries. Hearing Fay's amused voice in my head as I devour my food: *You eat like a bird, Julie.* Hearing my standard reply: *Yeah, yeah. I know. Twice my body weight every day.* Seeing Fay roll her eyes at my full plate and settle for tea and a salad.

While I could have passed for a boy until I left for college, Fay's been all curves since she hit puberty. She and Mom were always on my case for me to let my hair grow longer, but they didn't understand how annoying the wispy hairs floating around my face were. Or how much I didn't want to spend time primping. My sole concession to femininity is my slash of red lipstick. Three seconds tops, and I'm good to go.

When I go to the cashier to pay, the ubiquitous portrait of King Mohammed the Sixth stares down at me. With frustration born of twenty-twenty hindsight, I realize that, from almost the first minute we were in Morocco—on our taxi ride from the airport into Marrakech—Fay was griping about the king. A wide modern boulevard lined with elegant palm trees had led us from the airport into the unknown.

"Your first trip to Morocco?" the driver turned around to ask.

Because Fay was absently drawing circles with her fingers where her breath fogged the window, I replied, "Yes, we just arrived."

"You American ladies, yes?" Without waiting for a reply, he continued, "American people very welcome in my country. Poor country, but rich in soul of people. Beautiful culture. Modern king, many schools. I am Abdulazziz. I take you to hotel through olive grove, okay? Same price, no problem. Is very beautiful. Street here is Avenue Mohammed Six. Mohammed Six is name of king. Modern king." By then, he was three-quarters turned in his seat, watching me instead of the road.

"King Mohammed in Marrakech now. Here his favorite palace." He resumed looking forward to my intense relief.

"Hey, did you hear that, Fay?" When she didn't reply, I jiggled her arm. "The cab driver said the king was in Marrakech."

Without looking away from the window, Fay muttered something under her breath that sounded like "bastard." At the time, I thought I misunderstood.

The cab ride itself was a delightful introduction to Morocco. Abdulazziz played tour guide. "Is beautiful hotel here. *Le Meridien*. Next is Café Excelsior. Good place for tea—womans come in, not only mans. This very famous Hotel Mamounia."

Traffic built up after we turned onto another wide boulevard. This one was a sea of red flags with centered five-pointed green stars. Ahead, the city walls appeared just like in the pictures—dusky ochre red, tan, rose, pocked with square holes. We squealed through an acute-angle turn and jounced to a stop behind a line of stationary donkeys loaded with sacks of onions.

"Okay, ladies. Thank you very much. I give you card." Abdulazziz revolved around in his seat to hand it to me. Then he curved his thumb and baby finger and held his hand to his ear to mimic speaking on a phone. "You call me, I show you old city."

I was staring at the massive wall where we stopped. It had a tiny keyhole entrance. A series of intricate designs decorated the perimeter of the opening, and a lovely arabesque surrounded the whole works. "Arab-*esque*," I said out loud.

I've been so excited about exploring Marrakech at the end of our vacation. Now, who knows if I'll get the chance.

The second I finish my kabobs and eat every last bit of potato, I dash across the circular plaza to return to the car. A dozen fruit trees, oranges and lemons, line the perimeter like points on a compass; the ubiquitous fountain decorates the center. The plaza is empty in the heat of the day, although a few dogs lie panting in the shade.

Just as I reach the car, I notice the neon-red flashing sign on a nearby building: *téléboutique*. The little electronics store in Ouarzazate was a *téléboutique*, too—a place that makes phone calls for the dying breed who have neither a landline nor a cell phone. Several older men, however, came in to make calls while the staff was trying to configure my phone.

Don't forget to call Gil. The electronics-store salesman cautioned me that reception is often fluky in rural areas—scary to think I almost drove off into god-knows-what remote place without remembering to call him.

I wrench the key to the off position and pull out my cell phone. Punching in Gil's office number, however, results in a beeping like a fast busy signal. The *téléboutique* can be my fallback, but first I put the car in gear and drive around looking for a cell tower. I find one on the far side of town in a commercial area. I cross my fingers and call again.

The first time, I get the fast busy signal, but I get out of the car and take a concrete path that goes up the hill. Charcoal smoke wafts from doorways. Sharp pinging sounds are accompanied by physical thuds so strong I can feel the thumping in my stomach. I peek into an open door. Workmen, each one armed with hammer and tongs or a small hatchet, are making fountains. The percussion of a dozen miniature hammers tapping fills the air. Two to a stall the size of my walk-in closet, the men hunker down on their haunches, piecing together intricate designs from tiny pieces of tile. *Zellje* under construction.

At the top of the hill, I try the phone again. It works.

I thread my way through the law office voicemail to Gil's personal assistant, but there I dead-end: Mr. Ohana isn't in. He isn't available. He can't be reached at a different number.

"His wife is missing?" A sharp intake of breath and a tremulous exhale. "I'm really very sorry," she continues, her executive persona dented but intact. "Mr. Ohana is on his way to a conference in Denver. His flight has already left—I checked on Flight Tracker just now. There's no way to contact him for almost four hours. If you explain to me what happened, I'll make sure he gets your message the second he lands."

Walking farther, I've found a spot away from the hammers of the fountain factory, quieter and with better reception on a high point of land overlooking a massive olive press being loaded with fat black olives dumped from huge barrels. Two donkeys lashed to poles are idly swishing their tails while they wait to tread the well-worn circle that will tighten the screws and produce virgin olive oil.

I tell Gil's secretary everything I know, making particular mention of the police stop and the knifing of the woman in our former room, stressing the fact that Fay is overdue and her note said she was running an errand for her husband. "I'm on my way to the village where Fay went on Friday with that man I told you about," I say. "Since Gil asked her to do this, surely, he knows what's involved and can take steps to defuse the situation, do whatever he thinks needs to be done. I'm working blindfolded here."

"How can Mr. Ohana contact you?"

I leave my number, but considering my difficulties in getting a signal, I add, "If Gil can't reach me, I'll call back tonight." Then I suggest that, if he wants to act quickly, he could contact Sam Monatti at the American Consulate in Casablanca. "Gil might have to light a fire underneath him to get him moving, but I'll bet he's better equipped to do that than I am."

She gives me Gil's cell phone number. "I'll alert Mr. Ohana, but please call as soon as you find his wife."

The secretary finishes on a hiccup, and we both know she's not saying— "or if you don't find her."

I walk down to the car again and start it with relief. Not all I hoped for, but it was easier not to have confronted Gil directly. Better to get his efficient secretary to relay the story minus my emotional baggage— like, *what the hell have you gotten my sister mixed up in?*

CHAPTER TWELVE

I locate the N12 and accelerate out of town. After days of denial and dithering, the wind blowing through my hair becomes proof that I'm finally taking action.

I'm traveling east now, away from the oasis and toward the approaching mountains. The land becomes stony and barren. Grays and browns replace the pinks and greens. A few forlorn trees, stunted and shabby, hunker in depressions and against the steep cliffs. Soon after I turn onto the N12, Tadefi's description of "several kilometers" being imprecise, I begin looking for the sign pointing to Ait Tazigout. I keep her map on the seat beside me so I can easily compare words, not trusting my memory with such an unfamiliar script.

After ages of slowing down at every potholed turnoff, I spot a dirt track worn with twin ruts for tires and a sign almost identical to Tadefi's lettering. With relief at finally spotting it, I assume the girl made a mistake.

I drive for miles on a narrow track, up and down lumpy black hills. I see no one. No cars. No houses, standing or otherwise. No trees. No boys or goats. Only a monochrome landscape—shiny basalt rocks and dull slate ones strewn like marbles on russet hills, under a leaden sky. I wonder why this road exists, who travels it.

I come to a fork in the road. No sign.

It has gradually been dawning on me that I'm barking up the proverbial wrong tree. I reverse. A bumpy hour later, back at the main road, I quiver with indecision. Left—back toward Zagora? Where I looked carefully, but failed to see the turn? Or right—onward? I've already driven twenty miles from Zagora, farther than I expected, but I have plenty of gas. What the hell—it could be just around the corner. *Onward.* I put the car into gear.

What I find, not around that corner, but around a sweeping bend in the road a few miles distant, is a man standing beside the road. He was trudging along but turns when my car approaches and pumps his arm, fingers outstretched—the local gesture for asking for a lift. Because he's walking through this empty ocean of waving hills and blowing sand, he must be from somewhere around here. I'll ask him about Taghabene.

I stop the car. The hitchhiker is a boy, a skinny teenager with a backpack, wearing French designer jeans and a fleece-lined jean jacket with the collar turned up against the breeze. He beams at me when I pull level with him. I lean over to roll down the passenger-side window.

"*Parlez-vous français?*" I'll give him a lift—he's a *kid*, for crissakes, not an ax murderer—but he isn't going to be much help finding that village if we can't communicate.

"*Mais oui, madame. Je suis au lycée technique à Ouarzazate.*"

A high school kid. I yank the door handle up. "Come on in," I say in French. "Where are you going?"

"My village is five kilometers distant from here. I had a ride as far as"—he says a totally meaningless place name—"but we left town so late I was afraid I would still be walking after dark. Thank you for your kindness," he adds, holding out a neatly manicured hand.

We shake. His name is Izri, and he's on his way home for the celebration of Eid al-Adha.

"I'm Julie, and I'm trying to locate this village." Instead of pronouncing (badly) the name, I hold out the paper and point.

"Oh, Julie, you're going the wrong way."

Shit. "Where is it then?"

Izri does a one-eighty in the passenger seat and points back to the west.

"Oh, no!" I *did* miss it somehow. I sag in the seat, rubbing my hands over my cheeks.

"What is it in Taghabene that you wish to see? There is nothing. Only a few houses. Lots of scorpions. No café." Izri's brow furrows. "No place for you to sleep."

"My sister went there."

"Your sister, she is presently in Taghabene?"

I suspect he wonders what in heaven's name she's doing there. "Well . . ." I stall, unsure what the honest answer is. "I *think* so. She went there a few days ago."

"But you are not sure?"

"No, I haven't talked to her since she left."

His eyebrows draw together. His mouth purses the way my grandmother's did when, late in her life, she no longer understood conversations going on around her. I read confusion on his face, plus a healthy concern for my well-being. At least, I hope that's what it is.

The macabre humor of it finally gets to me; I laugh, out of control. Poor Izri watches, perhaps unsure whether to join in with my incomprehensible amusement or to jump out of the car and run away from this crazy woman.

He doesn't bail, though, and when I finally calm down, Izri says with finality, "Julie, you cannot go to Taghabene now. The sun is at the top of the mountains already. It will be dark within the hour, and Taghabene is too far. And the road is impossible to see at night." He shrugs with his entire body. "And, should you avoid crashing into a ditch or falling over the side of the mountain, what will you do when you arrive? And what if your sister has left?" He stacks up his *and*s inexorably. "You must come to my village."

I guessed his train of thought was chugging in that direction. If he's being sincere—if! —his logic is inescapable. If he just wants to get home before dark . . .

But Izri anticipates me. "If you wish, I will explain exactly where to find the turn, and you can go back. I have a better idea, though." He explains that his grandfather runs a *gîte d'étape*, a guest house, and that his grandmother's a wonderful cook. "In the morning," he concludes, "with a full day of sun, you can continue your journey."

The light is already fading. Izri's right; finding Fay will have to wait for morning.

I hedge. "How about this—I'll take you home. If there's a room available, I'll stay the night." All the while thinking *and if it's too weird, I'll develop an urgent need to drive back to Zagora*. I saw hotels there and feel reasonably confident I can navigate this skinny, but lightly traveled, road in the dark.

"*D'accord*." Only then does Izri snap on his seat belt.

I put the car into gear and roll back onto the asphalt. I sense he's being honest. God help me if he's the pied piper of the black desert.

CHAPTER THIRTEEN

F ive kilometers turns into eight or nine. We encounter only a couple of overloaded swaying trucks, both heading in the opposite direction. For Izri's sake, I'm glad he isn't still out there hiking home alone in the dusk. The sun drops lower in the sky, and the stark lunar landscape softens. A rosy diffuse light picks up sparkles in the debris field of black rock. The slanting rays throw the hills into relief, revealing contours not apparent in the glare of the midday sun and texture in the different types of rock. It's beautiful in an austere way.

"What year are you in at the *lycée*?" I ask.

"It's my last year. I want to be an engineer." His unselfconscious grin of satisfaction is replaced by a shadow of uncertainty as Izri explains that his father hoped he'd stay home to run the family farm. The grin returns. "But I've been showing my cousin how to do things. He's twelve and already takes a lot of the responsibility. I think it will work."

Izri has me turn off the main road onto a bumpy path, marginally less rubble-strewn than the one I struggled over earlier. The track skirts a riverbed—no water, only rocks. Where the road crosses the river, the bridge has fallen down. A well-worn detour takes us down to the bottom of the riverbed at a crazy angle and then zigzagging up the steep bank on the far side. We circle past a grove of trees, which Izri says are olives, and spread out before us stand several dozen mud-brick and stone houses, luminous in the last gentle light from the sun.

He directs me to the far side of the village. People and dogs stop what they're doing to watch. Izri rolls down his window and waves to one and all, a triumphal return in a private Peugeot. We reach a broad plaza. Izri points ahead to a long, low building that contains a few small businesses, now shuttered with the approaching evening, and tells me to park.

It's an empty lot. No guest house in sight.

"We must walk from here," Izri says. "There's a *gardien* for the night."

I'm used to *gardiens* by now—entrepreneurial chaps who monitor the streets and, for a price, look after your car—but I'm not so sure about leaving my car all by itself in this lonely spot.

"My grandfather's house is up this way. Let me get your bag."

"No!" That was too shrill. I soften my tone. "Don't bother. Let's make sure I'll be staying first."

I lock the car, leaving my suitcase in the trunk. Izri runs ahead, calling out in Tamazight, and I follow him up a steep narrow path toward a whitewashed stone house on the hillside.

A young woman with a baby swaddled on her back stands at the front door. Her face, long and narrow with a sharp ridge of a nose, has the elongated beauty of a Modigliani portrait. Over a long maroon skirt, she wears a heavy sweater of blue and white. She has a red-checked scarf wrapped around her neck, and a gold-and-black-print headscarf, twisted tight to leave nary a hair in sight.

"The wife of my uncle," says Izri after he greets her. The girl looks all of twenty. I hope she isn't the mother of the twelve-year-old cousin. Perhaps *this* uncle is a much younger brother.

An older man comes around the side of the house wiping his hands—the grandfather. His teeth are just about gone; his hands gnarled; his beard white; his turban was once white, too. Izri does the honors. Grandfather quotes me a price of two hundred dirhams for the night, hastening to add that the price includes dinner and breakfast. That works out to less than twenty-five dollars. My concern about the availability of a room now seems humorous. A *gîte d'étape* is more like a rural home-stay. This isn't a commercial guest house; it's their *home*.

I ask to see the room.

It runs the entire length of the left side of the rambling house and is accessed by a door that opens off the main entrance hall. An entire professional basketball team could sleep in the room. They could stand up in it, too, as long as they didn't mind bending double to use the four-foot-tall door. The room is higher than it is wide. The rafters are tree trunks thicker than my waist, and the ceiling disappears into the general dimness. A single bare bulb hangs down to human level. There are a dozen narrow beds. Also, a dozen low tables. And dozens of rugs. Layers and layers of rugs. Faded kilims in the old-fashioned geometric patterns, brand-new acrylic-pile monstrosities featuring bouquets of roses and gold medallions on incandescent blue fields. Like the exuberance of Izri's aunt's robes, a single color or design seems to be inadequate.

The place is funky beyond belief. But clean. Piles of blankets. And I have the whole place to myself. Grandfather walks me outside to a small building that contains a minimal bathroom—squat-on-top toilets, a pitcher of water, a tin mirror. No shower tonight.

I agree to the price. Grandfather shakes my hand solemnly. When Izri and I walk down to get my suitcase, he gives me a brief tour of the community. On either side of the steep path are rocky fields and pens for animals. There's an attractive tiled square surrounded by a dozen stone houses and a community well where I meet several neighborhood women. Then we're back at the deserted market plaza where I left my car. Although I now understand I can't drive any closer to the house, I ask Izri again about the wisdom of leaving the car there.

"It's safe here, Julie. The *gardien* will begin patrolling after dark," Izri says. "You can pay him in the morning. Only ten dirhams."

"But where do the other cars park?"

Izri grins. "No one who lives here actually owns a car. There's only the truck for the rug co-op and a taxi. Our village *gardien* is more like an all-purpose night watchman."

We start back up the hill with my bag, leaving Fay's locked in the trunk. The sun has already disappeared behind the mountaintops. It's just after five thirty, four hours since I called Gil's secretary. If she's reached Gil by now, perhaps there's news. With my exhale, a wave of solace rocks me gently. Gil set this into motion. He'll have a better idea what I should do.

When Izri's cousin calls out that he needs help corralling some wayward goats thwarting his attempts to return them to their pen for the night, I pull out my phone and dial, but I get the same fast busy signal that means no network. *Damn.* I hadn't realized just how remote this place would be.

When Izri returns from helping his cousin, I cross all my fingers and ask where I can get a cell signal. He tells me that, here in the thinly settled south, iron in the mountains disrupts cell phone reception, and modernization, in the form of sufficient repeater towers, is slower in arriving than in more populous regions. The closest phone is apparently a *téléboutique* in Taghbalte which, Izri says, is twenty kilometers in the opposite direction from Fay. "But sometimes"—Izri slaps his palms together with a burst of enthusiasm—"you can get a signal out on the road where you picked me up this afternoon closer to Zagora."

I blow out a long, slow huff of frustration. *Okay. It's okay. I don't have more news to relay and, no matter what Gil might tell me, I can't do anything until morning. Tomorrow will have to do.*

I beg off further touring of the neighborhood. The air temperature is sinking steadily with the sun's descent behind the mountains. My energy level is plummeting, too, last night's nightmare-filled sleep being totally inadequate for the turmoil of the day.

When we get back to the house, Izri detours into the kitchen, which we reach through a large main room. Along one wall is a massive loom made from tree limbs, an unfinished *kilim* stretched across it. From the back door of the rambling stone house, we cross to a separate low, whitewashed building.

Izri has offered to talk to his grandmother, the evening's cook, about serving an early dinner to accommodate my fatigue. His grandmother is sorting vegetables, but she bustles over to me and, touching her right hand briefly to her heart in a gesture of welcome I've seen all over Morocco, launches into a lengthy welcome in Tamazight, which Izri translates into French.

While they discuss dinner, I look around. Judging by the brighter white of the whitewash, this kitchen must've been added on recently. Though small and utilitarian, it's filled with all the modern conveniences.

Then I notice the rug on the floor—intersecting diamonds in pale blues and oranges—and I'm visited by a totally unexpected flash of memory: The first time my mother visited the run-down apartment Steve and I rented after we got married, she walked into the kitchen. "Why in heaven's name did you put a *rug* in here?" my mother said. "It'll get filthy."

I'd been so proud of how we'd fixed the place up on a tight budget—Steve was still in grad school—and the rug, a thrift-store find that covered a spot of discolored linoleum, was one of my favorite new things. It's been almost twenty years, and I still get the sinking feeling of inadequacy when I hear in my head that exasperated, disapproving voice I've been trying to drown out for ages.

* * *

I retreat to the cavernous bedroom, prop myself up with pillows, and pile blankets around me. From my nest, I consider my options.

I'll skip the Taghbalte *téléboutique,* I decide, and get on the road to Fay as early as I can. If I get a cell signal *en route,* great. If not, well, when I retrieve Fay, I'm whisking her off to Zagora. With any kind of luck, we can be together in town much faster than if I start out driving many kilometers the wrong way just to tell Gil I don't have any more information.

I'm far from calm, but—the heck with my mother's disapproval—I *have* done the best I can. My instinctive decision to get the hell out of Ouarzazate was definitely the right one. Gil now knows everything I know, and I'm stuck here until sunrise. Dinner, sleep, on my way. I'll bring Fay home.

Vague sounds of clattering and conversation in Tamazight gradually resolve into the smell of cinnamon and roasting chicken. Time passes and my eyes have begun to grow heavy when a couple of children peek in the door, whisper that dinner is ready, and flee.

I dine on low cushions with Izri, his father, uncle, and grandfather. While we eat a chicken *tagine* with carrots and eggplant, we talk about everything from curing goatskins to the willingness of Abraham—here called *Ibrahim*—to sacrifice his son Isaac which, I'm astonished to learn, is what Eid al-Adha commemorates. *That's* the great sacrifice; *that's* the significance of sharing it with your family. Every family that can afford it will kill a sheep three days hence; every person who can afford it goes home. The entire country shuts down. It's about family and friends, sacrifice and thanksgiving.

In the middle of the evening, conversation turns to the challenges Morocco faces in adapting to the 21st century with its fast-growing and youthful population—housing and education, creating jobs so the thousands of young Moroccan men who emigrate, mainly to France, can stay home. Like our garrulous taxi driver that first jet-lagged day in Marrakech, these men are proud Moroccans, and they applaud King Mohammed's pace in moving the country surely—but cautiously—into the future.

As a guest in their home as well as a guest in their country, there's no good way to ask them *so what sorts of people don't like this wonderful young enthusiastic modern king of yours?* Or perhaps *what would bother the king enough to call you an enemy?* And *what would he do about it?*

The women and children are nowhere to be seen. After dinner, when I ask to thank his grandmother personally for the delicious meal, Izri escorts me to a low curtained doorway. Not sure what to expect, I duck and enter. It's a smaller version of my own chamber—low beds against the walls, a few tables, floor covered with rugs, one flickering lamp. And at the far end, on a high pedestal, sits a large flat-screen TV. They're watching *Finding Nemo*.

CHAPTER FOURTEEN

Tuesday, January 18, 2005

Rural Morocco wakes up early. Roosters crow before daybreak. Muted voices echo in the hall, doors squeak open. Children giggle. Sheep baaa.

I snake an arm out of the heavy pile of blankets I buried myself under, squint at my watch. Almost seven.

The sooner I get up, the sooner I get to Fay. My clothes from yesterday lie where I shed them, in a pile next to the bed. I curve my hand down, find them by touch, and wiggle into everything before emerging from my cocoon. Then I run a brush through my short dark hair and apply my daily lipstick, both without looking. Ready to go.

A table with a bright blue cloth is set up beside the front door. Behind the table, sheepskins cover a low ledge on the stone house, forming a long bench. The children I heard laughing earlier are outside playing marbles. When they see me, they motion me to the table and call out to someone in the house.

A minute later, the young wife brings me a pot of tea. There being zero language overlap, I thank her with smiles and the hand-to-heart gesture, which I've seen people use to express appreciation, and she responds in kind. Izri told me last night that, like Tadefi and Sihan in Ouarzazate, she attended the local primary school for three years of math, Koran, and basic Arabic—they all speak Tamazight, the Berber language, at home. And she *is* married to the same uncle who has a twelve-year-old son, only she isn't the boy's mother. The uncle, whom I found pleasantly soft-spoken and intelligent when we chatted during dinner, has another wife and four children who live in a separate house in the village.

Tea is followed by warm bread and honey. I stuff myself—not knowing where or when I'll get lunch—while I sit in a sunbeam against a stone wall looking out over a town of squat ochre houses with the rugged, snowcapped meringue of the Atlas Mountains visible in the far distance.

I'm sipping the last of my tea when Izri and his father show up.

"We're on our way to the rug cooperative," Izri's father says. "Wouldn't you like to see it?"

The rug co-op is The Big Deal in the village, and I know he's angling to get me over there to fall in love with a rug. This is such an exquisitely out-of-the-way place that, under normal circumstances, it would be a delight to pore over their selection of locally woven rugs—and would make a great story to tell when we get back home. *Be fun, if mischievous, to find a rug for my mother in the same greens and blues as her kitchen,* I think.

Not today, though. "I need to get going." I hope I infuse the words with sufficient regret to disguise my insatiable hunger to hit the road without delay.

The last moves go quickly. I pay for the room, adding ten dirhams for the *gardien*. Izri loads my suitcase in the trunk next to Fay's and remains to wave goodbye.

I turn the key. The car gives a lame click-click. I turn it again, and again there's the quiet ticking of the starter-motor trying to do its job, but the clicks aren't accompanied by any of the grinding or whirring I associate with a failing battery.

No. *No.* My head rocks back against the headrest. *Not engine trouble.* If I can't figure out what's wrong and fix it, I'll be stranded at the edge of the black desert in a village with no cars.

I open my eyes to the familiar sight of Izri watching me with concern. I roll down the car window and stick my head out. "Do you know anything about cars?"

"No, I don't, but I'll fetch the mechanic. *He* will know what to do."

The mechanic. For heaven's sake. Not to look a gift horse in the mouth, but I have to ask, "How is it that a village with no cars has a mechanic?"

"Omar was in the army for many years. He worked on the big trucks. Now he lives here with his pension; he has goats and grows onions. When there's a problem with the truck from the cooperative, he always fixes it."

In a remarkably short time, Izri reappears, a chubby old guy in a blue coverall chugging behind. He gestures for me to release the hood and pops it open in a flash. By the time I extricate myself from the driver's seat, he's gaping at the interior with a furrowed brow.

"What's wrong?"

The mechanic shakes his head. "All the wires are missing."

"What?" I get out of the driver's seat and walk over to peer into the engine compartment. Shit yeah, it's obvious even to a total mechanical ignoramus like me. No wires. I suck on my lower lip. A chill tingle of unease creeps along my spine.

Someone vandalized my car. Since there's no access to the hood release without a key to unlock the car, they must've had to pry open the hood. Perhaps they didn't make much noise, but this is a small, quiet place and sounds carry a long way in the clear mountain air. The *gardien* should have heard it.

So much for the not-very-watchful night watchman. Whether it was a malicious prank or opportunistic theft, I suppose my rented

Peugeot—the only car in the neighborhood—made a tempting target. At least Fay's suitcase was safely locked in the truck.

"Can you fix it?"

"Oh yes, *madame*. One needs only the wires and one can do the job itself in a matter of minutes."

I almost fall over with relief; I can get away, after all. I gush *merci beaucoups* at Omar.

The mechanic looks down, rocking from heel to toe and back again. "The problem is that I don't have these wires. Someone must go into Zagora to buy them."

Oh, no. That's why he's so glum.

Omar waves his outstretched hand, the hitchhiking gesture. "It cannot be accomplished before the end of today. Perhaps tomorrow."

I can't wait for tomorrow. I have to get back on track *now*. My bright idea that I'm the only person who can catch up to Fay is looking more and more reckless in the clear chilly light of a desert dawn.

"Is it possible to telephone, to have someone bring the wires you need here?"

"No cell phone reception on this side of the mountains, remember?" Izri says. "And the nearest *téléboutique* is in Taghbalte. That's twenty kilometers east of here."

"But you do have a car here!" I shout triumphantly. "Izri, you said so last night. There's a taxi. I'll hire it."

"The taxi is now in Rabat with its owner, Sidi Abillou. He hopes to return tonight for Eid al-Adha, but his wife is having her chemotherapy and is very weak."

I sigh. "Then that leaves ... a truck?"

Izri's face brightens. "That is so, Julie. The cooperative truck. I'll go and check right now. Many days, it goes to collect rugs from the houses of the women who weave. But not every day. Wait for me!" And he's off again.

Like I'm going anywhere. I lean against the car in gloomy silence.
The old mechanic wanders around the car, inspecting it like he's in
the market for a gently used Peugeot. As news of my problem spreads,
townspeople gather, wondering aloud what happened. One man says
that the *gardien*, if he wasn't sleeping on the job, is the person to ask.
He is, of course, sleeping now, having been on duty during the night.
The men deputize themselves and go to question him.

Three things happen in very short order.

Izri returns at a gallop. The cooperative truck is going out today, so
I can't commandeer it for my own use. "But there's good news, Julie,"
Izri says. "It's picking up rugs and delivering wool and cotton yarn on
the track up to Taghabene. Although it will take longer, they can give
you a lift."

"That's wonderful!"

"They are leaving soon, ten minutes. Shall I tell them you want to
come, Julie?" His voice drifts lower. "I know you're worried about your
sister. I'd invite you to stay here with me and attend the feast as my
guest, but I understand that you need to reach her. Let me say this,
though: when you find her, *please* come back to visit. Return Thursday
for Eid al-Adha if you can." He grins. "It will be an authentic Moroccan
experience complete with the killing of a sheep. Or come back later, so
I know you are both safe."

Before I can reply, a red-faced man pushes through the knot of villagers. He was part of the group who went to confront the *gardien*.

"Rafiq is afraid to show his face," he announces to the assembled
crowd. "He says he saw a light flash in the night and, when he went to
investigate, two soldiers grabbed him."

"Soldiers?" It isn't only me; everyone murmurs the same word.

"Rafiq said they told him to leave the area if he valued his life." Bushy
eyebrows become inverted Vs as the man turns to scowl at me. "Why
would the army wish to disable your car?"

All around, muttering begins. Izri moves closer, nervously licking his lips.

At that moment, the mechanic scoots out from under the front bumper of the car. He holds a small black rectangle in his palm. "*Un mouchard*," he growls. A fly on the wall. What in English gets called a "bug." A tracking device.

CHAPTER FIFTEEN

zri and I rush down the path to the other side of the village where the cooperative truck is revving its cold diesel engine. I've grabbed my backpack from the front passenger seat but leave my unwieldy suitcase in the trunk. I can easily get by for a day or two with what I have in my backpack and in the security pouch around my neck.

I hand Izri my car keys and give him enough cash to cover the repairs. Then I scribble my name and Fay's on the back of an old grocery list. I add *Sam Monatti/US Consulate, Casablanca*.

Today's Monday—no, it's Tuesday already. I tell Izri, "If I don't return by Friday, could you please call the consulate, tell them where I went." As an afterthought, I ask, "You don't drive, do you?"

He shakes his head ruefully. "But my older brother does and also my uncle." Izri puts his hand on my shoulder. "I promise I will take care of everything."

"I know I can count on you." I smile at him. "Thank you."

"*A très bientôt,*" we say to one another. "See you real soon."

The cooperative truck is an open-bed cargo truck, the kind that might be used to haul loads of produce. The agreeable driver who was willing to give me a lift has also accommodated a dozen villagers and quite a few of their animals. We all sit in back on lumpy plastic bags of yarn destined for the homes of local women. They'll weave the yarn into colorful kilims and return the finished product to the regional rug cooperative which, in turn, negotiates a better price than the women could individually. Then they divvy up the proceeds. It's a marvelously simple and efficient system, and I make instant friends by saying so. Also, the folks on the truck weren't at the developing fracas by my car, so they aren't aware that I'm fleeing town as much as I'm getting a ride to see a friend.

The truck's belching diesel engine takes forever to warm up. Then, just as it does, we stop at another village. And when we stop, black dust swirls around like a *djinn* and catches us all in its embrace.

Although some of my fellow travelers get out at villages where the driver is conducting business, I'm amazed at the places the truck pauses to let others out. Barreling full blast down the highway—the same road I took from Zagora the previous afternoon, the same vast expanse of featureless nothingness—someone would bang on the outside of the cab, rather like yanking the cord to halt a city bus. What identified that specific stretch of desert, I never knew. The truck would rumble to a stop, the dust would eddy, and the man—or woman—with animals—or children—would descend and march off onto the black rock, striding resolutely toward an uncharted destination.

By noon, when the truck approaches Taghabene, only a few grimy souls share the truck bed with me. Most of the yarn is gone; in its place are several dozen carpets wrapped in old newspaper and tied with twine.

I missed the road to Ait Tazigout the previous day because the sign had fallen down. When the driver down-shifts to turn onto the rutted road, it's lying dust-covered on the ground. We lumber through rolling hills, past the identifying characteristics Tadefi sketched in—the derelict house, the tree in the hollow. Then—Taghabene, at last—a small group of stone houses of less-than-normal architectural interest.

The truck stops in a dusty clearing by the municipal well. Like the well in Izri's village, it's a round concrete structure with tree limbs topped with Y-shaped branches embedded on opposite sides. Suspended from the crook of the Ys is a third branch with a rope, pulley, and pail attached.

A woman drawing water waves with a flourish of both hands and then darts away, calling out. The driver comes round to the back, making sure I know this is the place. And finally, it's time for me to step down into another unknown. Feeling more alone than ever, I clamber off the truck and the remaining passengers hand down my backpack.

One man stands off to the side while the village women swarm the truck. He's tall and nicely dressed in a traditional brown djellaba, with a prominent beaked nose and reflective aviator-style sunglasses—and the air of someone in authority.

I walk over to him. *"Excusez-moi de vous déranger, m'sieur"*—the polite sorry-to-bother-you—"but I am looking for a man named Mohammed."

"There are several Mohammeds here," he replies. "Which one do you seek?"

"This Mohammed was in Ouarzazate last week. He met my sister—a tall woman with blond hair—and she came here with him."

The man's eyes remain obscured behind his Ray-Bans, and his floppy hood casts his face into shadow. After a time, he clears his throat, hawks, and spits. Not *at* me certainly, but close enough that I reflexively jump back.

"Wait here. I will see if this Mohammed can be found."

A curious way of couching it, but I stay put as he pads around the corner in his soft slippers. Also, I meant to ask where *Fay* was, not Mohammed, and I'm not sure why I didn't say it that way.

The negotiations by the truck continue. At each village, the driver has taken out a little book where he notes each woman's debits and credits—debited yarn, credited completed rugs. Today, money is also changing hands—payment for items sold.

My taciturn acquaintance materializes from behind the building, two older men in his wake. Instead of answers, they have questions: Where have I come from? Why do I seek Mohammed? Did someone send me? Did I meet Mohammed in Ouarzazate? Why did I arrive on the co-op truck?

Tiring of the one-way flow of information, after I explain I had car trouble and glossing over exactly what the trouble was, I keep talking, refusing to yield the floor. "I *know*," I say, overstating for a better bargaining position, "Mohammed brought my sister, Fay, to this village. She was supposed to return before now, so I've come to get her."

This prompts a protracted discussion in Arabic. I'm beginning to notice differences in language and in style. This isn't a Berber village like Izri's, where Tamazight is spoken. Here, the language is Arabic, and the women do not merely dress modestly and cover their hair. Instead, they wear long black robes and veils. Many have a white square of cloth pinned to the front of their veil, obscuring all but their eyes.

The conversation lengthens and, in the unfamiliar tonalities of Arabic, it sounds like an argument has erupted. They're still talking, and I'm still waiting for a chance to speak, when the truck driver comes over. His business in the village finished, he needs to get underway again. Fortunately, *he* has no qualms about interrupting the caucus.

I stand by, feeling invisible—mute, dependent, uncomprehending. These men don't *see* women. Perhaps that's why I asked about Mohammed, not Fay. The truck driver asks questions. And, thank goodness, Mr. Ray-Ban responds.

Then they fall silent, looking around at one other as if unsure who will speak first.

It's the truck driver. "The men of the village are concerned you bring trouble for Mohammed, who took a big risk in conducting your sister to an enclave a short distance into the desert," he tells me. "She is there now. Because Izri, whose family is honorable, vouched for you, I told them you have no desire to make mischief. I think you'll be all right if I leave you here."

"But she was supposed to be back—"

He holds up his hand. "All I know is what they say. You." He turns to the hawk-faced man in sunglasses. "Tell her what you said to me. If Julie finds your idea acceptable, I will leave her in your hands."

The villager brings his hands up from the depths of his brown robe, spreads his fingers wide, and opens his palms to the sky. "The blond woman wished to contact someone at a compound in the desert, a place where we occasionally traded in the past." Speaking French, he explains that Mohammed had done business there, so he agreed to escort her. But he returned saying Fay's undertaking was more complicated than anticipated, that the men there would be responsible for returning her here in a few days. "So Mohammed went back to Ouarzazate to tell her companion she'd been delayed. If I am correct, that is you, *madame*?"

"Yes," I say, puzzled. "But when was this? I stayed at the same hotel for several days after Fay left."

"I don't know when Mohammed arrived in Ouarzazate, but he left here to deliver the message yesterday morning."

"Yesterday!" I feel like screaming—maddened by the missed opportunities, fed up with a country where roads are impassable after dark, where cell phone signals don't penetrate, where one car serves an entire community. If I'd stayed put, I would've gotten news of Fay. But, remembering the carnage at the hotel, I know exactly why I didn't remain in Ouarzazate.

I rub my sweaty forehead wondering how to construct a sufficiently polite way to say *what the fuck took him so long*? I settle for "Why didn't he leave sooner? I expected *Fay* to be in Ouarzazate yesterday."

"And thus Mohammed expected to find *you*." The slightest of curves bends his thin lips. "The problem was that he only returned here, to the village, Sunday night, too late to take our narrow, twisting road down the mountain."

So Mohammed returned to Taghabene from someplace in the desert Sunday night, spent Monday on the road to Ouarzazate. We probably passed each other in transit. That makes *some* sense, but if they left on Friday ... ?

"I thought you said this place was not far from here?"

"No, not far, but it's not possible to go by car. They rode donkeys."

Taking donkeys to a trading post in the Sahara Desert. Oh, Fay, what have you gotten yourself into?

"My uncle Ahmed once made the journey with Mohammed." Mr. Ray-Ban curls his index finger, and one of his companions steps forward. "He knows the compound and offers to take you there. If you wish."

The truck driver taps his fingers on his spiral notebook waiting for my answer.

An offer to guide me. That could solve my problem, but I gave most of my cash to Izri. "I didn't come prepared to pay for the services of a guide."

Glances exchanged between the village men apparently settle the issue.

"Since you lack transportation, we would arrange to return you and your sister to Zagora, where there are banks."

I've come this far as much to flee the carnage in Ouarzazate as to reach my sister. Leaving this village on a donkey with a guide for a trading post in the Sahara Desert where Fay "has business" amounts to a major red line in the sand.

There's an odd ache in my stomach, a gnawing sensation. It's almost like some kind of insect is trapped inside my body, trying to chew its way out. No, not that exactly, it's more like *I'm* the insect—a caterpillar becoming a butterfly. I have to break out, but my cocoon is so very thick. I don't know if I'm strong enough to get free.

If I thought only of myself, I would turn tail—hop back on the truck and eat a sheep with Izri's family—but once I consider Fay, the decision is simple. The man said her business was unexpectedly complicated, and I'm worried that's code for *problem*. I checked for a cell signal several times while the truck was on the main road this morning. I got a fleeting signal once, though I'm not sure how much of my message to Gil got through before it faded. And Mom will never ever forgive me if I abandon Fay.

I found a truck when I lost the car; I found the village; I've found a guide. I can get to Fay much faster than anyone else. This time, I can be the one to pull the fire alarm to foil the cops—or whatever the equivalent distraction might be in Morocco.

As we must've said to one another a zillion times in a zillion different crises from flunked tests to towed cars to unplanned-pregnancy scares, "It's the person you can call for help at four a.m. that matters." Whether Fay is in trouble or legitimately delayed, having come this far despite attempts to discourage or prevent me, I have to go to her. This is as four a.m. as it gets.

"I accept your uncle's kind offer."

CHAPTER SIXTEEN

The truck reverses and turns down the track, trailing plumes of dust. The whine of the truck engine fades, my last contact with the outside world fading with it. The men linger where we've been standing and talk among themselves. The women retreat into houses; the streets empty. Muted shouts of children kicking a ball in a distant field are the only sounds.

The dust kicked up by the truck has coated my face with a coarse grit. I wipe it off with the sleeve of my sweater. "How long will it take to get there?"

No one in the semicircle of men surrounding me speaks.

I shrug off my backpack, remove my water bottle, and take a drink to ease the dusty tickle in my throat. "Can we make it before dark?"

Ahmed, my new guide, replies, "If we go now—"

My original intermediary, the man with the sunglasses whose name I never heard mentioned, interrupts him. "You can't leave on an empty stomach. I sent the women to prepare food."

Considering what lies ahead, eat-like-a-bird Julie agrees it's best to have a meal first. They arrange a quick—by Moroccan standards—lunch of brochettes and grilled vegetables for me. Sizzling bits of lamb, sprinkled with salt and cumin, spatter hot fat onto the coals, and the aroma lingers in the air. The man who's tending the fire hands me a tin plate, the kind I've used when camping, of meat nuggets. They're brown and crispy on the outside, perfectly pink and tender inside. Eggplant slices and small onions prepared with the same spices complete my meal.

Meanwhile, Ahmed gathers the necessary items for an overnight trip. Even if we manage to arrive at Fay's desert destination this evening, we can't return until tomorrow.

Time passes; one donkey is led over, inspected. A foreleg palpated; heads shake in doubt; conversation ensues; the donkey led away. More time passes; a boy brings another donkey; it, too, is inspected. More discussion.

Although my toes are tapping with impatience to start moving toward Fay, I sense the unhurried pace will persist no matter what my attitude. I take my daily atenolol and remain where I ate the brochettes, sitting on a stool-sized stump next to the smoldering open-air firepit.

When I get home—when *we* get home—I am going to have so much fun teasing Fay about her donkey ride and the mess she got me into. Of course, I can hear Fay replying *turnabout is fair play*. Which is a good point since I've gotten her into a few scrapes over the years.

The donkey they're examining has a sweet face. A blaze of white defines his snout—or whatever you call the nose of a donkey. I take out my camera and snap a few pictures, imagining how I'll tell Alex the story of Mom riding this animal into the desert to go see Aunt Fay.

Two boys draw near, holding a death grip onto one another's hands, but clearly curious about what I'm doing. They must be brothers—one slightly taller than the other, both skinny and crowned with identical cowlicks in their tousled dark brown hair.

I change the camera display to show them the pictures I've taken, telling them a little about my son and his interest in animals. Then the older boy asks politely if I'd take their picture, too.

"*Mais bien sûr.*"

After a few snapshots with the brothers staring stiffly into the camera, they loosen up, and I take a bunch of cute pictures of them clowning around.

I only wish I managed to keep the camera.

Finally, the second donkey is pronounced sufficiently robust to make the trip. Ahmed ties a short rope around the tops of two cloth bags filled with supplies—food, blankets, water. He slings the bags over the donkey's back, one on each side. Then he lays a thick blanket on top. "*On y va,*" he says. *Let's go.*

And so we set off: Julie the Intrepid in brown corduroys and forest-green fleece, astride a mangy donkey; Ahmed the Silent striding ahead, staff in hand, his gray djellaba flapping. The well-trodden path through the village soon becomes harder to spot. We pass irregular rectangles filled with stubble.

"Those look like abandoned fields."

"It hasn't rained in this part of the desert for sixteen years," Ahmed says. "Sand is covering everything. All but a few families have moved away. It's becoming impossible to wrest a living from the land. Ten years ago, Taghabene was a thriving, if remote, village, well known for its peppers. Now . . ." He shrugs. "Now, we do what we can."

We skirt trash-filled gullies, pass two outlying cottages, roofless and partially engulfed by embryonic sand dunes. After a sharp left at the second cottage, all signs of human habitation vanish.

Ahmed shares two striking characteristics with my Quebecois grandfather: his great comfort in the outdoors and his selective hearing. When I ask about the plants, the occasional lizard, the soaring birds, he provides the answer—camel grass, acacia, dab, lark, curlew, *moula-moula*—a sort of black-and-white sparrow—he knows them all. When I ask about our destination, however, his accent deteriorates, and he scratches his bristly beard while he pretends not to understand me.

I learn only that Ahmed hasn't been there for several years, that it's beyond the nearest range of hills, and that he doesn't know who's there anymore. "No, really," he insists, "the men I saw there would be gone by now. We were trading—remember?" He raises his head and eyebrows to look sharply at me. "With the sand covering our fields, with the drought, we do what we must in order to survive."

Smuggling, I think, with a queasy feeling in my stomach.

After leaving the village with its animals and sounds and cooking fires and worn pathways, Ahmed and I traverse featureless rubble, gritty brown sand and jagged rock in gray and tan and black, without footprints or hoof-prints to mark the passage of any other large life form.

I say—out loud and mainly for the reassurance of hearing my voice— what I'm thinking. "I've never seen land so empty!"

Ahmed, of course, thinks I'm talking to him. He wheels around and points. "Do you see that mound of rocks?"

I glance where his knobby finger indicates, a waist-high pile of rocks about fifteen or twenty feet across. "Yes."

"That was once a dwelling for the ancient people who lived on this land when the water receded."

"Water?"

"Oh, yes. This section of desert was once a large lake."

"I didn't know that."

"Here, let me show you." He looks around speculatively. All I can see is a haphazard scrabble of stone, but Ahmed leads the donkey off to the right and we stop perhaps thirty yards away—near several larger rocks with a shallow depression on one side. Ahmed hunkers down and sifts through the coarse sand with his fingers. Up come a half-dozen spiral shells. "Freshwater snails."

"That's amazing." Ahmed holds out his open hand to me, and I take one of the delicate spirals. "So beautiful. Are there other things like these shells out here?"

"Of course. See those rocks, the shiny black ones near the top of that rise?"

More black rocks. "Ye-e-es," I say, doubtful what I'm agreeing to.

"That's debris from a meteor. Look." We walk up the slope. Ahmed picks up two rocks that, on closer inspection, do appear blacker and somehow denser than the surrounding pebbles. From the pouch slung over his shoulder, Ahmed extracts a magnet. When he holds it near the black rocks in his other hand, they roll toward it.

"Wow." Goose bumps spark along my arms. When I tell people about my trips with Fay, I often say, "I never know what I'll find when I go searching." Sometimes I add, "Or who I'll find."

This time *what* is seashells buried in a desert seabed, meteorites fallen from the sky—and there must be so much else to discover in this strange land. And, along with my serendipitous desert guide, Fay is *who* I'll find.

"How could you tell?" I ask Ahmed.

"I've lived in this place all my life. The *hamada*—our word for this windswept and rocky land—is a challenging environment, but life is all around if you know where to look. To you, perhaps, this land seems barren, but it has a rich history, and many objects remain to show us how life has adjusted to changing circumstance. Life—human, animal, plant, it matters not—all life will adapt to survive. You do what you can with what you have." Ahmed displays the black rocks in his palm. "And here is one example of what we have—meteorites are much in demand by tourists, so I sell them to shops in town."

Responding to my curiosity, we wander around for a while. Ahmed picks up several long skinny rocks with sharp edges. "Arrowheads." He detours to a line of larger boulders and shows me a patchwork of indistinct lines carved on the rocks; he traces them with his finger. "Turtle, antelope, hippopotamus," he says. "Neolithic drawings."

I learn to look in sheltered spots, alongside larger stones in the lee of the prevailing wind, which brings with it a coating of fine sand. In one such place, I troll my fingers through the sand the way Ahmed showed me and bring up a curved piece of—shell? pottery?—about three inches on a side, convex, a creamy golden ivory with swirls of brown, smooth on one side and slightly pockmarked on the other. With that, Ahmed's thawing reserve melts.

He lays an arthritic hand on my shoulder. "Good eye, young woman," he says. "That's a section of ostrich egg, petrified now. It is for you, who have come such a long way for love of family. Keep it for luck."

It's becoming as customary as a handshake: Still holding the bit of shell in my right hand, I touch hand to heart briefly. "Thank you."

CHAPTER SEVENTEEN

Ahmed is making for distant hills. Although our original course was southerly, the afternoon sun hitting my right shoulder tells me our current direction is southeast. At times, Ahmed meanders sluggishly, and then he lifts his wooden staff and beats the donkey, encouraging him to trot. This animation lasts a minute or two, then our speed subsides once more.

With no visual frame of reference aside from the mountain peaks and the sun, progress is difficult to judge. The absolute emptiness of the landscape disorients me. It feels oddly as though *we* are standing still and the mountains are pirouetting to advance toward us. Even watching each clump of camel grass come nearer and then disappear in our wake does little to dispel the illusion. I'm acutely aware of the particular—the rough skin of the donkey, sweat trickling down my back, my beating heart—but also of the cosmic: I imagine how we would look from space, two smidgens of dust on a lumpy surface, our pitiful progress measured in millimeters.

Soon even that progress halts. The sun disappears; the sky flames red, then dims violet and gray. We've made it to the foothills of some higher peaks. Ahmed alternately beats and cajoles the little donkey into a five-minute climb up a steep path. It leads to a broad plain with a small stone shelter that Ahmed said was once used by shepherds.

"We'll have to stop here for the night."

Ahmed can't feel the hollowness in the pit of my stomach at the thought of spending the night alone in the wilderness. Alone with a strange man.

"You'll be more comfortable inside the shelter," he says. "I'll stay outside to keep an eye on the donkey." Ahmed pats one of the bags. "I brought plenty of blankets."

I don't see what else we can do. Although a fat crescent moon is rising over the mountains to the east, soon it will be too dark to travel.

Ahmed scavenges for firewood and adds sticks from one of the saddlebags. He grills small bits of meat, which we eat with slabs of chewy flatbread.

I take out the curve of ostrich egg and admire it in the firelight. When I get home and show it to Steve, he'll probably suggest displaying it on the shelf in the living room that houses other mementos. And he'll want to know the story behind it. "Are there stories in your culture about the ostrich?"

"Oh yes." Ahmed rolls a long stick between his hands. His mouth curves to a slow, pensive smile. "An ostrich will get up and run, even after it appears to have been killed," he says, "so in the old days, many believed them immortal. A bit of the ostrich—bone, beak, and especially the egg, which is a symbol of renewed life—was thought to endow the possessor with similar qualities of endurance."

I press the shell between my hands, my fingers steepled.

"And there are many tales," Ahmed continues. "My favorite is about the triumph of cunning over strength. Lion, like your boxing champion Muhammad Ali, considered himself the greatest of all."

With skilled narrative flourishes, Ahmed tells the story of how Lion made fun of Ostrich's toothless mouth and weak call compared to his own sharp teeth and mighty roar. But instead of getting drawn into conflict with the stronger animal, Ostrich suggested a cooperative antelope hunt. While Lion attacked and devoured Antelope, Ostrich attacked Antelope's calf. But when Lion mocked Ostrich for killing only a small animal and threatened to eat *him* as well, Ostrich ran away and hid behind a termite mound. Lion followed. Ostrich leapt out and blinded Lion by kicking sand with its feet.

With raised fists of triumph like a boxer, Ahmed finishes, "Ostrich, who had no teeth and only a weak voice, did have cunning, a plan, and a strategy. And he was the greatest."

"That was lovely. Thanks, Ahmed." It'll be a great story to tell the kids.

He hums under his breath. I think to take advantage of his good humor for more information. "How much farther is the place we're going to?"

"Two or three more hours."

"Over this mountain?"

With a shake of his head, Ahmed says, "We only came up here for the shelter I knew was here. One must go back down the steep path and continue the way we were going, with the mountains always on the right until one comes to a pass."

"A pass?"

"It's unmistakable—there's a gap in the mountains that serves as a gateway to the Sahara. It's marked by an influx of the pale golden sand so different from the obsidian variety here in the black desert. To get through the pass, it's necessary to scramble up and around large boulders. But from the top of the pass, the compound should be visible."

"Can you tell me more about what sort of place it is?"

I really don't think he'll answer me. His selective hearing has prevented him from dealing with the question every other time I've asked, but he says unexpectedly, "It's for the border."

"Border?"

"Yes, just across these mountains is the frontier with Algeria."

"But that's—" I was going to say that's *mined*, that's *dangerous*, but before the words pop out, my brain registers that control of a border is a task for the army. Or perhaps for the police.

Ahmed, however, finishes my sentence with his personal preoccupation. "Yes, the border's closed—has been for more than a decade. It's another reason this part of the desert is so empty. Nomads can no longer travel the old routes."

Concern for the lifestyle of the indigenous people of Morocco would have, at a different moment, been of significant interest, but now I have only one apprehensive question. "So we are traveling to a place where there will be soldiers?"

Ahmed shrugs. "I suppose so."

"What business could my sister possibly have there?"

And—just like that—he's back to being hard of hearing, and I'm left with my thoughts. Traveling without a map, without roads, I didn't know we were close to the border. But I *do* know there's been trouble along the Morocco-Algeria border for decades, ever since 1975 when Morocco annexed a large territory to the south known as the Western Sahara. It did so with UN approval but against the wishes of a group advocating self-rule, the Polisario freedom fighters—or terrorists, depending on your point of view.

Algeria threw its support behind the Polisario, and there followed a decade of shooting war between Morocco and Algeria, then failed cease-fires and fruitless peace talks and more shooting. Morocco guidebooks caution you to steer clear of border towns. They also warn of stepped-up military patrols, of more careful checking of papers near the border.

Geez, I promised Steve I wouldn't even eat raw vegetables—now here I am traveling to an armed and dangerous border.

It can't be helped, I think, if it's the only way to reach Fay.

I've fallen down a rabbit hole where nothing makes sense. Fay is doing *something* for her husband. But Gil is a lawyer who specializes in employment and tenant rights. In my agitation and distress over the past few days, I've overlooked the obvious question: What the hell can Fay be doing for him in *Morocco*?

And now I add to that: What does Gil want to accomplish that would have Fay contacting "enemies of the king" on the border with Algeria?

I stare at the moon, already high in the black velvet sky. Ahmed stares at the fire. He's looking into the fire the same way I sometimes do, as though by divining a message in the flames you could make sense of the past and see the future; you could read the truth. I look, as well, for answers in the rocks silvered by moonlight. Finding none, I leave Ahmed meditating on the dying coals of our fire and curl up in a blanket in the little shelter. I fall asleep feeling the planet spinning beneath me.

CHAPTER EIGHTEEN

Wednesday, January 19, 2005

I awake, disoriented. On the other side of the stones that serve as my shelter, not six inches from where I lie, a chilly wind whistles. One gust shakes loose a small stone, and it lands on the heavy blanket covering me. Light is visible between the chinks. Since the moon had already passed its zenith when I curled up in the shelter, I guess I've made it through most of the night.

Ahmed, who remained outside by the campfire, should already be stirring on this cool, windy morning. My ears strain for sounds other than the wind. One minute passes; two. There's nothing. The donkey was softly braying earlier, but now all, save the wind, is silence. I need to pee; I need food, water. A cup of coffee is a miracle I can't expect this morning, but we're on our way to Fay. I can manage.

I sit, rotate my stiff shoulders, and roll my neck. Then I hoist myself to my feet, walk to the entrance, and blink.

I'm alone.

A wave of panic squeezes air from my lungs and tears from my eyes.

The sun is low over the rocky ridge to the east. To the west lies the scrub desert we traveled the day before, ending with indistinct bluish hills in the distance. Somewhere at the edge of those hills is Taghabene, Mohammed's village. Wind, in the form of dust devils, swirls on the empty plain, but there's no sign of an old man and a donkey plodding away from me.

No, I must simply be overwrought in this unfamiliar place, jumping to conclusions. I turn back toward the hut and campfire. Perhaps Ahmed has merely gone foraging for more twigs to add to the fire for our breakfast.

I'm already shaking my head.

He wouldn't take the donkey to do that. I look around. Campfire stubbed out completely. The saddlebags gone—food and water *gone*. He left with everything. Left me alone.

I sink onto the rough gravel, my back to the stone hut, legs and feet splayed out in front. And I sit, unable to think, not moving. The wind drops; the morning warms; the sky turns blue. I follow the sun's progress by shifting shadows on the lumpy ground.

The only person who knows where I am will not return to rescue me. I'm in uncharted territory. Without a map or a guide. Today, there's only me. Me alone.

So if I don't want to die of starvation or thirst or hypothermia, alone, on the side of a stony hill somewhere in the black desert, I have to get moving.

I *could* try backtracking to Mohammed's village. The distance isn't too great to accomplish in a few hours of walking, and I know the general direction. Big problem, though: Ahmed sneaked away, leaving me in the middle of nowhere. I remember that heated discussion in Arabic back in Taghabene after the truck left, when they knew I couldn't understand them. Maybe they were trying to decide how to get rid of me. Or at least how to get me away from their village where, whatever eventually happened to me, it wouldn't be linked to them.

Which brings me back to my car. The soldiers in the night who removed the wires—they tracked me to Izri's village and tried to keep me there. In the heat of the moment, running with Izri to the co-op truck, I assumed they were preventing me from continuing my journey to Taghabene. To Fay.

But considering that the men of Taghabene left me here to die, maybe the soldiers were trying to *protect* me. The "why" of that is beyond my understanding, though, and I'm out of ideas—except this: now I'm really afraid the men of Mohammed's village lied about Fay being delayed. They betrayed me, and I think they deceived Fay as well.

If I can't stay here and I'm afraid to go back and I believe my sister is in danger, my only option is to continue to Fay on my own. Ahmed told me the route. Wait—*Ahmed told me the route.* Before he slipped away in the night.

I consider whether he was telling the truth. I'm not sure my bullshit detector is reliable in Morocco. But, as I mull over the people I've met, I decide I've been right a good percentage of the time. Izri proved a solid friend, and Hamza, at the hotel in Ouarzazate, was a go-to guy. Flaky Ibrahim of the afternoon shift, who drew arrows instead of erasing the ledger, was not to be trusted. Nor, I now believe, was Mr. Ray-Ban, who set this whole guided trip into motion.

Then there was the solicitous truck driver who took time to ensure I got off the truck at the right place. He asked the men at Taghabene questions and seemed satisfied with the answers; *he* thought Ahmed would take me to Fay.

The truck driver was wrong, says my negative angel.

But Ahmed started *to take me,* I argue.

Ahmed led you as far away from his village as he could in one afternoon. That was not an accident, retorts the pessimistic me.

Well, no, probably not, I reluctantly agree. *But the second we were away from the village, he could've done something to harm me*—my mind enforces a strict no-fly zone for the specifics of "harm"—*and been home before sundown.*

But he didn't "harm" you, did he? Instead, he taught you about the desert, told you stories, and gave you those directions to get to Fay.

I can't stay here all day arguing with myself. Whatever the reason Ahmed abandoned me here, I'll follow his directions: go back down the steep path to the plain, skirting the edge of this mountain range with its serrated peaks until I come to a pass where golden sand spills through, and go over the mountains there.

I collect my meager belongings and inventory them. Ahmed's blanket. My backpack, which I'd used for a pillow. In it is a spare T-shirt. Wallet. Camera. Pen. My useless cell phone. An almost-full bottle of water. A bag of dates. A bag of peanuts. Hairbrush. Fastened to a loop on the outside is my watch, which I removed from my wrist to thwart my impatient time-keeping during the interminable delays of the previous day. Around my neck, tucked under my green turtleneck sweater, the nylon security pouch Donna gave me holds pills, passport, some money paper-clipped to a couple of business cards I collected, fingernail clippers, and lipstick.

A week in Morocco and my possessions are reduced to this. A laugh erupts, one that has everything to do with hysteria and nothing with humor.

First, I sip a little water. I stuff the blanket into the straps of my backpack. It will cushion my load and is, for now, nice and warm on my back. If the day stays cool, I'll appreciate that. If it gets hot, I'll stuff it into the backpack.

Okay, Fay. Ready or not, here I come.

I clamber down from the plateau, the downward scrabble much harder than the trek up. Tiny bits of gravel slip under my feet, acting as skids to accelerate my descent. The way forward lies along a line of round foothills, with their loose residue of stony gravel. High above towers a chain of saw-toothed mountains, windswept down to bare rock.

And so I walk. Left, right; left, right. Moving on has released a welcome spurt of energy that gets me down the slippery slope and on my way, but it dissolves like morning fog over the ocean and then vanishes altogether. My speed is so slow compared to the immensity of the fantastic peaks that, like yesterday, all sense of progress dwindles. Only today, I'm not riding a scruffy donkey, but picking my way over a rubble-strewn field of irregular stones.

Being careful not to trip and fall occupies all my visual attention, but my mind craves stimulation, and I agonize over the accumulating, unanswerable what-ifs: why Ahmed deserted me, whether I'll recognize the spot to cross the mountains, what Fay could possibly have been trying to do on the Algerian border for her husband, what sort of trouble she's in—for trouble, I'm now convinced, it certainly is—and what Gil is doing back in the States to help.

After a couple of frustrating cycles of what-if, I shift my concentration to the environment. It's a cool morning with a light breeze. Waves of high, thin cirrus clouds, looking like fish scales, dance overhead. I'm seeing fewer animals than I did with Ahmed, mainly soaring birds riding the high thermals. The tufted grasses have also disappeared. I look for the sort of artifacts Ahmed showed me, but I guess my eye isn't as keen as his. Or perhaps this part of the desert is emptier.

No donkey or camel pictures for Alex today.

That simple thought lets loose an avalanche of ferocious intensity. My guilty pleasure at missing the children vanishes. That pleasure is predicated on their stay-cation with a doting grandmother and on my safe return in two weeks. Now, each step closer to Fay takes me farther from them.

I want to count Alex's freckles. We've been doing that at bedtime since he was a baby, although I know he's growing too old for kid stuff like that. I want to hear the exhaustive, precious recounting of his utterly ordinary day—everything from what the bus driver said to what was for lunch in the cafeteria to a blow-by-blow of the entire episode of whatever TV show he's just watched. That delight in small confidences is another thing Alex is growing too old for.

And Erin—it's Wednesday, isn't it? The day of her algebra final. It's early morning in Virginia. Donna wouldn't let her go off to school with only pancakes this morning. I hope she's made eggs for Erin to help her stay focused for that third-period test. Molly's still in her room, I think with a smile, deciding which twirly dress and tiara she'll wear to kindergarten. Steve—no doubt long gone to the lab. He's always been an early riser, and this way, he's home from work early enough to coach in the after-school athletic program.

Thoughts of family always migrate to thoughts of food. I'll make blueberry muffins for everyone when I get home. Moroccan food has been amazing, but I crave a homemade muffin slathered in butter.

After a while, I realize I'm doing the same thing Ahmed did with the donkey: prodding myself to proceed quickly and then letting my pace slacken. I wonder again if he spent yesterday afternoon conflicted about what to do with me or if he was simply planning where to abandon me.

Today, my erratic pace is a struggle between fatigue and all the unknowns ahead of me. Already, the sun is directly overhead. I must've sat in a daze at the shelter for longer than I thought. Except for the crunch of my sneakers on the gravel, the silence is absolute. Here, there is no air-conditioning to hum, no refrigerator motor to whir, no clock to tick, no murmur of voices, no thrum of distant traffic on the highway. Even the wind has dropped, so the rattle of shifting stones has ceased.

For a while, I distract myself by singing songs whose words I've long ago consigned to memory and trying to walk in rhythm. Belting out "Jeremiah Was a Bullfrog" and "I Wanna Dance with Somebody" helps for a while, but singing dries out my throat, and I know I'd better ration my water to get through the day.

After a while, I need to rest, but the afternoon sun blazes down and there's no shade. I create a makeshift tent by placing the blanket on my head and holding it out with one hand while I drink some water, finish the peanuts, and slowly chew a few dates for energy.

I pull out the bit of ostrich shell. It's my talisman now. My good luck. In congratulating me for finding it, Ahmed praised my willingness to go after Fay—*for love of family*, he said. But Steve and the children are family, too, and I'm leaving them behind, one step at a time. I can only pray I've made the right choice.

I forgot to check the time when I left the hut, but I must've already walked longer than the two or three hours Ahmed said it was to Fay. Perhaps I'm going slower than we would have with the donkey. I decide that if I don't reach the pass before dark, I'll survive the night as best I can, curled up in the blanket. Then I'll go back the way I came. The deeply grooved path up to the stone shelter should be pretty clear. Once I find it, I'll cross the plain and take my chances with the villagers.

I get back on my feet and on my way again, keeping my eyes open for the pass.

With the long vista across the plain, the skin of the earth curves noticeably; distant mountains appear, one by one, rising up from beyond the planet's arc. The ground is dark sand covered over with a layer of shining pebbles. They gleam metallic silver and black, with flashes of purple. The hillocks around me shine like armor. Flanked by iron hills, I traverse a silent, purely mineral world. I walk on, stopping twice more for sips of water and dates.

The landscape changes. Foothills flatten and, at the same time, the looming razor-edged mountains near. A pool of shimmering water appears in front of me, reflecting the luminous blues of the sky—then recedes, staying just out of focus. It has to be a mirage, of course; there can't be water out here. I trudge forward until, at last, the image resolves. It is, in fact, the opposite of a pool. It's an arc of golden sand, higher than my head, spilling over to this side of the mountains. The pass.

CHAPTER NINETEEN

I hurry forward. A river of sand runs through a rocky basin. I begin to follow this riverbed uphill, but my feet sink in the loose sand. Car-sized boulders lie jumbled in heaps, as if a giant toddler tossed a bucket of stones into his sandbox.

The path stretches farther than I can see, but the slope is gentle. At first, it's just a matter of not getting bogged down in the fresh drifts of sand. I learn to stick to the edges, where the sand is packed harder. The initial rocks I encounter are huge, but widely enough separated that it's more like negotiating a slalom course. Gradually, the rocks build up into piles, stacked helter-skelter. These, I have to climb over, jockeying for position so as always to have a foothold or a handhold to get from one to the next.

Then there's a stretch of gigantic sideways slabs, an elevated highway of stepping-stones, complete with large gaps. I jump from one rock to another, head down, concentrating on each footfall. In this way, I find myself unexpectedly face-to-face with three camels walking in a depression on the far side of the boulder I'm scrambling across. The lead camel blows out twin blasts of hot snotty breath when he sees me. His comical lips quiver, and his head swivels wildly from side to side.

Startled, I stiffen and lose my footing. In a flash, I'm in a heap on the sand, the breath knocked out of me. The camels, as spooked as I was, bolt past me and thunder away, snorting and huffing. The trio regroups a short distance away, then departs single file, dark silhouettes against the spun-gold sand in the slanting rays of the late afternoon sun. In seconds, they're gone, and I'm alone in the desert again.

My only obvious injury is a long scrape where my hand rubbed against the rock when I tried to catch myself. Blood oozes from a couple of spots, but they're minor scuffs. My arm feels bruised, so I push back the sleeve of my sweater. The abrasion continues but, protected by the layer of fleece, my skin is only rough and irritated. I landed crookedly—on my left side with my chest facing the rock, my head twisted up and to the right, and my legs squashed underneath me. When I creak to my feet to check for scratches on my legs, a sharp pain makes me gasp. My eyes slam shut, sending a cavalcade of shooting stars against the backdrop of my eyelids. My ankle can't hold my weight.

I sit down again. Taking my left foot in my hand, I slowly rotate it. My ankle hurts like hell, but it moves in every direction. Not broken, then—sprained. I can recite by heart the handout we give patients at the orthopedics office I manage: "For a sprain, RICE—rest, ice, compression, and elevation."

No time to rest; no ice; no sitting with my foot up. I have to get to Fay.

I have to get up. I have to walk. I can't. I have to. I can't, I can't, I can't . . .

My breath comes sharp and fast. Hot tears of frantic frustration blind me. A new thought intrudes and overrides my panic: *You forgot to take your midday atenolol, dummy. No wonder you're coming unglued.* I ease my backpack off. Squashing it and my blanket together, I elevate my leg for a while. Then, from under my sweater, I fish out the pouch containing my pills and swallow one without water.

Time passes, and so does my panic attack. Since the goal of my medication is to block adrenaline—the hormone that's responsible for the fight-or-flight response—taking it after feeling such anxiety makes me preternaturally calm.

My heart rate slows; my head clears. But my ankle has almost doubled in size. The distended skin is shiny-red and hot to the touch. I have to climb over a bunch of rocks in the desert, and I need something to help hold my weight. I haven't seen a tree all day, only rocks and sand.

I unzip my backpack again. Five dates remain, Ahmed's blanket, water bottle, T-shirt, cell phone, camera, wallet, hairbrush, pen. A crutch isn't possible, so I'll have to devise a splint. I lay the pen alongside my left foot. It's long enough to span from ankle to lower leg. Then I create a small tear in the neckline of my T-shirt with my fingernail clippers and rip the shirt down the side. Opened up, it winds several times around ankle and pen with enough left over to make a secure knot.

Using the face of the boulder to support me, I gingerly pull myself upright. I let go of the rock. I balance. I step forward with my right foot. So far, so good. But moving forward with the next step brings a knife-like spasm, and cold sweat breaks out on my forehead. I can't put any serious weight on my left leg.

So. Balance. Right leg forward. Hold. Bring left leg up to meet it. That keeps the worst of the pain at bay.

I work into a shuffling gait, dragging my throbbing ankle behind. My fall occurred close to the end of the elevated section I was hopping over. "Over" no longer being possible, I discover that squirming between the tall slabs gets me from one gap to another—probably how the camels entered the path—and staying inside the labyrinth of rocks gives me needed bracing when I tire.

When the tall rocks peter out once more into occasional boulders, I have to step carefully to reach the next support without stumbling. If I sit on the sand with nothing to pull myself up, I doubt I could get back on my feet. When the rocks become so widely spaced that the distance is more than I can cover without stopping, I rest standing up.

At every other boulder, I lower myself to the ground, sit in the shade, swing my arms, and circle my neck and shoulders, which are stiffening in the aftermath of my fall.

Finally, even that is too much. With both hands against the rock, I roll to my knees one last time. My neck aches at the strain of holding up my head, and my forehead droops against the rough stone. And my ankle—its throbbing rivals my pounding heart for attention.

That's it. No more stress on my foot, so I crawl forward. And crawl. And crawl.

When I reach the top of the gap, gasping with effort, I inch toward a stone slab sticking up at an angle and hoist myself onto it. The sun, which has been hidden from me as I clambered through the rocks, lies no more than a finger's width above the western peaks. Beyond the pass to the east are distant mountains, shiny black and twinkling. The valley of rocky black at my feet is split in two by the pale encroaching dunes. Empty space as far as my eyes can see.

Ahmed said the compound Fay was visiting would be visible from here.

But off to the right, south of the gap I crossed, there's only a desert of brown sand. To the left, another range of mountains joins the line I was following. A cloud comes over the sun just then, and the play of light and shadow creates confusion—absent the harsh glare from the slanting sun rays, some of the black shapes seem to be vegetation. And a tall angular silhouette might be a minaret. I don't know if I'm seeing another mirage or if those irregular forms are man-made.

The cloud passes. Glare flattens the landscape. The shapes reassemble themselves into hilltops; architecture ceases to exist.

My ankle throbs. I'm dizzy from hunger and fatigue. But it will be dark soon, and I can't afford to succumb to the agony of indecision.

If I can't see the compound from up here, I'm certainly not going to spot it from down lower. It's pretty clear, though, that only flat, empty land lies to the south. The hills to the north must be hiding Fay's destination.

Either Ahmed told me the truth or—

I shut my eyes. Shut my mind to the possibility that following his directions all day has been a mistake. That my search for Fay has been a fool's mission from the start, that the day's exertion and my injured ankle have been for nothing. That instead of walking toward Fay, I've been walking away from my husband and children. I refuse to consider that Ahmed simply chose a less strenuous way to lure me farther into the desert and ensure my death.

I let go of my support and, dragging my left foot, find I can make downhill progress walking. As I descend onto the plain, the wind whips up bits of pea-sized gravel and flings them about indiscriminately.

I finish my water when the sky is purple—no longer blue, not yet black. Passage of time measured by heartbeats. A flash of panic—stars have begun winking, so I'd better find shelter from the cold. It's all that remains of self-preservation, but the second I suck down the last drop of water, I begin to fade away.

I still limp along. I keep my mouth shut against the sand. Pasty saliva glues my lips together. I fall. The first time, I pick myself up. The second time, it takes longer. The third time, I remain motionless where I fell. The wind sprays a constant fine mist of sand. It buffets my right side, stinging slightly.

After some time, I no longer notice the discomfort. Looking sideways along my flank, I see the accretion of wind-driven sand has covered my skin. A small dune is forming outside my arm. I'm a mountain, drowning in sand.

Clouds cover the stars, and the wind picks up, bringing with it noise, something largely absent all day. The shrill whooo-hooo as currents career around hillocks, an occasional emphatic hu-uhhh that rattles pebbles and leaves a momentary silence in its wake, the steady background pitter-patter of sand crystals sounding like rain—these inanimate susurrations become murmurings, whispering voices.

At first, the words are indistinct. Gradually, they become clearer and I understand I'm home again. The alarm clock has shrilled, and I'm trying to get the children ready for the school bus in the inky blackness of early morning. I inhale chill air and wood smoke from the finicky potbellied stove in the family room. It's so blessedly normal to hear Erin and Alex squabbling at the breakfast table. Molly's lost her lunchbox, and she's crying. Steve keeps telling her to hurry. I know Molly left it on the back porch, but when I try to tell her, I find I'm mute. Their voices fade. I'll never see or hear them again.

I have another fragmentary memory from a time I register as being "later": a pale face high above me—not a face, but the moon lighting the desert.

Voices again. Not speech this time; someone singing to me. I struggle to catch the words. It's the radio. News, followed by a commercial jingle. I'm hearing a radio. I smell smoke. In the remote corner into which my consciousness retreated, I can hold two opposing thoughts simultaneously: I know I'm hallucinating and I know, so long as I continue to listen to sounds that aren't there and inhale smells that don't exist, I am alive.

CHAPTER TWENTY

Thursday, January 20, 2005

'm warm. While I consider that—buried in the sand at night, yet warm—I'm struck by the total absence of sound. The wind must've dropped. Perhaps it's morning. Perhaps I'm completely buried.

Perhaps I'm dead.

No, air tickles my nostrils as it ebbs and flows. I'm breathing. Besides, I hurt too much to be dead. Frightened of what my open eyes might see, terrified of what they might not, I compromise: I try to see through my eyelids. Surely I can tell if I made it through the night and am being warmed by the sun. But no red images form on my retina. It's still dark.

I'm lying on my side, curled in a little ball. Cautiously, I extend my right leg. Not sand. Instead, there's a scratchy blanket beneath me. Perhaps I managed to retrieve the blanket from the backpack and wrap it all the way around myself. I probe with my stretched-out foot. Touch . . . a horizontal bar. Hard and cool. Metal. I try a gentle bounce. Springy. I'm lying in a bed.

A wave of relief washes over me. Sweat courses from my skin. My muscles relax. Warmth builds swiftly, a sauna under the covers. Still not having dared to look, I sleep.

Later, I become aware of voices and a draft of air, bringing with it the scent of something sweet, like clover in the sun. A patch of light falls on my face. A bent old woman stands framed in a doorway. She smiles mutely and holds up a finger—one minute—and closes the door gently behind her. When the door reopens, a younger woman has joined her.

The girl tiptoes in. "*Bonjour.* I'm Jamila," she whispers. "I'm glad to see you're awake. You had us worried for a while. How are you feeling?"

"Umm ... okay." I run my tongue over cracked lips; I taste olive oil. "Better."

"That's good. My grandmother wonders if you would like some soup."

A rush of tears spills from my eyes, probably the last moisture left in me. I manage to nod yes.

Jamila calls out something in Tamazight and helps me sit up. I'm wobbly; my hands tremble like leaves in a windstorm. "Where am I?"

"You're at Ksar al Rima, on the road between Merzouza and M'hamid."

"On the *road*?" Ever since the cooperative truck turned off the asphalt onto the track for Ait Tazigout, I've been traveling into the desert and *away* from roads. How could I have been disoriented long enough to make a complete circle? "I don't understand."

Jamila sits next to me. "Not really a road. Along here is only the *piste*, the dirt track for 4x4s and motorcycles. Did you have an accident?" she asks softly. "We found you rather far from the *piste*. The men have been out all morning, searching for your vehicle. In case you were not alone when you crashed." Then, with a frown, she chides, "It's very dangerous to drive in the desert at night."

"No, I ... I don't have a car. I walked."

Her eyes briefly widen, then Jamila pats my hand and looks away. She thinks I'm delirious.

I reach out to grasp her hand. "My sister, Fay ... is she here?"

"So there *was* someone else in the car."

"No, she was here. Visiting. Someone here."

Jamila purses her lips and gives my hand a gentle squeeze. "I'll go tell the men to keep looking for her."

She doesn't know who Fay is. This isn't the right place.

The girl returns a few minutes later with a bowl of soup and holds it in front of me, but my hands still quiver. Hardly any liquid remains on the spoon by the time it reaches my mouth. The spoon clatters into the bowl.

Jamila picks it up. "Let me help you."

The first swallow soothes my scratchy throat. A second swallow, a third—the liquid slides in slow motion into my stomach. Nothing has ever tasted as good as this simple chicken broth.

A fourth swallow. I have to rest after that one.

I can't do it anymore. I can barely sit up in bed. I don't have enough strength to hold a spoon. *This is the end of the line.* I failed. Fay isn't here. She might be near, but I'll never be able to find her on my own.

I don't know exactly where this place is or where their dirt track leads, but there was cell phone reception in Zagora when I called Gil. Or perhaps Jamila knows of a *téléboutique* closer. I have to get help.

So a few sips of broth later, I ask, "Can I get to Zagora from here?"

"To Zagora? Is that where you were traveling?" Once more, Jamila shakes her head in consternation. "That's so far. The only road to Zagora has to go around by way of M'hamid because of the desert and the mountains in between. A few tracks cross the empty country, but they're not safe for the Jeeps or trucks, even for rally cars. And really, the only people who journey through the black desert these days are those who wish to avoid the border patrols. It's extremely hazardous. Anyhow," she says with another solicitous pat, "you're too weak to travel. If there's someone who will be worrying about you, though, we can try to get a message through today."

"Telephone?" A geyser of hope wells up.

"My husband can make a call from the *téléboutique* in M'hamid. He's leaving for a village near there soon to fetch his cousins who are coming for Eid al-Adha."

The consulate will be best. Jamila's husband can explain where I am. Let them come and get me. I can only hope someone will listen to me this time, and we can finally find Fay. And go home.

A peremptory knock at the door. Jamila's face brightens. "Perhaps they've found your car."

My stalker from Ouarzazate enters.

CHAPTER TWENTY-ONE

"You!" the man yells.

He crosses the room in a few quick steps and jerks me to my feet. The blanket falls away, revealing my dirty corduroys and fleece. My knees buckle as my inflamed ankle gives way, but his grasp doesn't slacken and the fall almost wrenches my arm from its socket. I gasp from pain and surprise.

Jamila shouts at him, not intimidated in the least. Not that it matters. The man drags me from the room, my feet gouging furrows in the dirt. He drops me on my stomach by an olive-green Land Rover and puts his foot on my back. Two camo-garbed soldiers come running. After a brief consultation, he has them lift me into the back of the Land Rover. One impassive soldier sits on either side, squashing me in the middle.

My stalker jumps into the driver's seat and executes a tire-spinning U-turn. I've heard people say they were so scared they couldn't scream—and always dismissed it as hyperbole. *Of course* you'd scream and yell, make as much racket as you could in a threatening situation. But when I open my mouth, I can't make a sound, can't even whimper, and I'm shaking so hard only the pressure from the soldiers' bodies keeps me from toppling to the floor.

The man drives no more than thirty minutes before we enter a massive walled fortress, with armed guards controlling entry and high

barbed-wire walls all around. A military post. If *this* was Fay's destination, it seems that, just when I've given up hope of finding Fay, the
people she came to see—her captors?—have found me.

A paunchy man dressed in khaki with military patches at the shoulder emerges from a two-story dun-colored building and comes over to
the Land Rover. My stalker, today wearing a similar uniform, jumps
out of the driver's seat, salutes, and addresses him in a gravelly smoker's
voice. *"M'sieur le commandant, ici Capitaine Mamoud Benkerine, à
votre service."*

He explains that his patrol assisted villagers at Ksar al Rima who
were scouring the dunes near the *piste* because they'd found a woman
lying unconscious, possibly the victim of a car accident. "We found no
one else injured, nor did we find evidence of a vehicle that had broken
down or crashed, so I entered the room where the woman was recov-
ering in hopes of learning more. I recognized her immediately as the
woman I followed in Ouarzazate. This time I took her into custody. As
I am reluctant to overstep the bounds of my authority in this matter, I
hereby hand her over to you."

"How is it that you failed to prevent her from arriving? It was a simple
job—one woman." The older man's voice is a hiss of restrained menace.

"She was neither logical nor straightforward in her thinking,"
Captain Benkerine says. "Fortunately, we had installed a tracking
device. When she bolted from Ouarzazate after our failed attempt
to extract information from her at her hotel, we kept her under loose
surveillance, there being no time to set up a secure stop such as we used
in the mountains east of Marrakech last week."

I've closed my eyes against a pounding headache. My mouth is slack.
The men's voices rise and fall in waves as my head throbs, but I hear the
captain explaining that when I drove toward the border, they immobilized my car to keep me from reaching this place until, as Captain
Benkerine concludes, "you've dealt with the problem here."

"Yet here she is." The softer the older man's voice, the more ominous it becomes.

I'm still too limp to move, but as my head clears, my thoughts also grow clearer. These men are behind the mysterious Mohammed *and* the attack at the hotel.

Benkerine stumbles through an apology, then says, "In the morning, when we returned to monitor the situation, we found she'd already taken a truck out of town, a truck that would eventually reach Taghabene and the people who delivered her friend to us. So I drove directly there and paid two men to watch for her and get rid of her for us. They were supposed to take her into the mountains and see that she never returned. I expected them to throw her off a cliff. Instead, it appears they merely took her deep into the desert and left her there."

Ahmed did more than that: he directed me *away* from here. His directions, north and over the pass in the mountains, were perfect for reaching Jamila and her family, whereas the Land Rover drive took us the opposite way—due south, the direction of Ahmed's original path from Taghabene. Whatever his original instructions or intent, Ahmed was keeping me away from here. He tried to save my life.

"Was this all she had with her?" the commandant asks. My backpack, which the stalker picked up at Jamila's.

"Yes, sir."

"Come with me."

The soldiers' voices fade into the distance. The two men hemming me in relax perceptibly. Like Dorothy spinning toward Oz, my life has spiraled out of any understanding. Based on what the men said, Fay's mission never had a chance. Those men of Mohammed's village who were paid to *get rid of* me had *delivered Fay* to this place. Fay. Is she . . . ? Oh, dear God, what if she's dead.

A door slams. Footsteps. The men are returning. Phrases from the soft-spoken commandant: ". . . too compromised here . . . a transfer . . . do it tomorrow. I'll handle it from here." The man in charge turns to the soldiers in the car. "Take her out back."

They're going to kill me, too. I writhe, contort myself, but there isn't any space in the cramped back seat to wiggle away. One man pulls; the other pushes. The soldiers each hold tight to an arm as they propel me, my feet barely touching the ground, along a manicured path. I don't have the energy to resist.

The men march me around the big building where the Land Rover stopped. Last night when I collapsed in the dunes, I was too disoriented to fully grasp what was happening to me. But now—now with each step they take, I concentrate, memorize, absorb, appreciate: the single orange flower with long curving petals on a straggly vine, the rasp of the men's breath, stones marking the side of the path, smelly exhaust from a ragged unmuffled motor, a black-and-gold-striped lizard scurrying away from our footsteps, sunlight warming the back of my head. It seems important that I do this even though soon there will be no *me* to remember these things.

We go behind a garage housing half a dozen other vehicles, past a vegetable garden with rows of tomatoes and peppers—toward a barred enclosure at the back corner of the compound.

"You hold her," one man says. "I'll get the door."

A jail? Not a firing squad?

The second soldier moves behind me and squeezes a sweaty hand on my other wrist. Twisting it to agony, he wrenches it behind my body and uses the leverage to push me to the side of the path. His comrade raises a stout wooden plank from slots in the doorframe and hefts it to the side. The door creaks open. They push me in without another word. The heavy bar thuds back into place when the door slams shut. My ankle collapses once more, and I fall to my knees.

*   *   *

Fay sits on a bench in the sparse shade of a single spindly tree, her arms circling her body as though she's cold, looking abnormally pale, with blank red-rimmed eyes.

Fay's alive.

Two women sit opposite her on a seat built into the side of a stucco wall. One fans herself with a bunch of leaves; the other holds a young child on her lap. The child jumps off and flees when he sees me. Fay jumps up, too, but she runs to me and bends down, enveloping me in her arms.

"Oh, Julie, Julie." She hugs me so hard it hurts my wrenched shoulder. "I am so incredibly happy to see you, but not here—here, it's—I'm sorry." She's sobbing. Hot tears land on my cheek and trickle down my face.

"Fay, what *is* this? Where am I?"

Where am I? The second time today I've needed to ask. The visceral fear of death consuming me just a second before brings panicky, angry words simmering just below the surface.

Fay sniffs in little hiccupping breaths. She keeps hold of my hand, but sweeps her other arm in an arc toward her companions, two Moroccan women, who stand shoulder-to-shoulder in the hot sun. "Julie, I'd like you to meet my mother-in-law, Lalla Yasmin Ohana bint Mohammed, and her daughter, Gil's sister, Nadia. The little boy is Nadia's son, Hamid."

"What?" That doesn't explain anything. I struggle to my feet, bringing Fay along with me. Only Fay, her hand hot and dry, seems real. The other women shimmer like a desert mirage. Gil's *mother*? His *sister*?

"I didn't think Gil had a family."

My focus remains on Fay, and I speak in English, but it's the older woman who answers. "Gil has more family than he realized." Her English is accented, hesitant. "It has taken many years to get a message out." With her eyes shut tight, the small muscles of the woman's cheeks ripple as a battle of conflicting emotions rages across her face. "We sent so many little carrier pigeons out into the world. It has been torture, never knowing if any would ever come home to roost. Hope. Hope is all that sustains us here."

"Where is *here*?" I shout.

The older woman answers again. "This is an army barracks, head-quarters of the tenth division. It has been our prison, mine and Nadia's, for the past fifteen years."

The younger woman murmurs something to her mother and leaves the patio for the interior of a small house.

"Nadia has to see to Hamid. He isn't used to people."

This feels more than anything like one of those horrible nightmares with just enough realism to give a veneer of authenticity to the most terrifying parts. I blink, but when I open my eyes, the mirage remains unchanged. I'm awake and these strangers have form and substance. I'm locked up somewhere in the Moroccan desert with my sister and three Moroccans. With Gil's family.

"Will somebody *please* tell me what's going on?" My raw throat burns from the force of the shrill words. "All I know is that you, Fay"—and, God help me, I pull my hand from her grasp and push her away—"lied about this trip from the start. You brought me to Morocco with you as . . . as a decoy. 'See, everybody, I'm just an innocent tourist seeing the sights with my innocent sister.' Except you weren't. You came here to . . . to meet these women."

Oddly, Fay shakes her head—no—but I'm on a roll.

"The problem was, you kept me totally in the dark. I *didn't* know what you were up to. I *was* innocent of any involvement. And then that man started following me, and they might have killed the poor woman in our hotel room." I stop for breath and run my hands over my cheeks. "There's only so far you can push me, Fay."

"But I thought—"

"*You thought*. You thought *what*—that I'd be perfectly content to sit around and wait for you? Thought I wouldn't worry about you? For crying out loud, I'm not a fucking pet rock—I'm your sister."

"I really am sorry, Julie. Gil said it was safer this way, and besides, you—"

"Gil said. *Gil said*—give me a break! You didn't *want* to tell me, couldn't figure out a polite way to say you were using me, didn't want to give me a chance to say no. Well, screw you." I jab Fay's chest with my index finger. "You've gotten us into one hell of a mess and you had better fucking get us out." I pause and take in a wobbly breath.

In a normal situation, I would've stopped then and, after I caught my breath, apologized for losing my temper. But nothing about my life has been normal since the moment Hamza, shivering on the sofa in the hotel lobby in Ouarzazate, told me I'd narrowly missed being knifed.

Fay has collapsed onto the bench, huddling next to the older woman. "Oh, Julie, I wish I'd told him no." Fay claps a hand over her mouth and turns to Yasmin. "I didn't mean that. I didn't mean I wish we hadn't come."

"It's all right, my dear. I understand you're thinking only of your sister when you say that." Yasmin touches her right hand to her heart. This time the gesture is an apology. To me, she says, "I, too, am sorry you've come to such grief on our account. However grateful we are to Fay— and to my son for sending his lovely and resourceful wife—yet we never wished to endanger *her*, either. You have my most sincere apology." And turning back to Fay, "My dear, she deserves a full explanation."

CHAPTER TWENTY-TWO

Yasmin and Fay clamber to their feet. Yasmin takes my elbow and pulls me close. Her hand is misshapen and leathery, and she smells musty, like old paper. She clutches me inflexibly between two pincers, as a bird's claw would hold its prey, and we shuffle three abreast to the back of the little patio and through a large arched doorway. The inside is simple in the extreme—one room, perhaps twelve feet square, with whitewashed walls. The only light comes through the open door and from a high barred window with a partial view of the water tower at the back corner of the base. The floor is tiled in a yellow and blue grid. Folded rugs on one side. Nadia and the little boy, Hamid, sit together on the rugs; she's singing softly to him. There's a table under the window and two chairs. A cardboard box on the floor contains fabric, perhaps clothing. Nothing more.

Lalla Yasmin catches my gaze. "This was once a place to offer hospitality to visiting dignitaries. As you perhaps observed, there is not a great choice of hotels in the area." An elfin smile lights her face. "So when they brought us here, first they said, 'You will stay in our guest house, as our guests.'"

She'd lowered the timbre of her voice to mimic the tones of stodgy male officialdom, then goes on in her regular melodic soprano. "And so I said, 'I want you to release my daughter. She is innocent of any wrongdoing. I want to write my son in America and my brother. I want a radio.'"

Switching again to the lower pitch, Yasmin continues, "And the commandant in charge at that time said, 'Lalla, you are alive by the great mercy of the king. He has given you this gift; however, his benevolence does not extend to communication with the rest of the world. You will spend the rest of your life meditating on the words of the Prophet, most particularly his admonition concerning guilt: *A believer's soul is attached to his debt till it is paid.* Your family's treachery has incurred a debt, one you must pay for in your way as your husband did in his.'"

Lalla Yasmin sighs and lifts her open hands to the sky. "So, having been well schooled in my youth, I asked the commandant, 'What about the Prophet's lesson about struggle? When Mohammed was asked the best type of jihad?'—this word means *struggle*," she interjects for my benefit—"he replied, 'Speaking truth before a tyrannical ruler.'

"The commandant slapped me—hard—and told me to consider myself fortunate that he did not have the ear of His Majesty, for such was blasphemy."

She shrugs. "That was the first of many small defiances. Not a one, I might add, was successful."

The whole time she's talking all I can think is, *They've been here fifteen years? I'd go crazy.* I'm already half crazy with fear. Her stories about this prison, coming on top of all the bewildering events of the two—no, three—previous days since I fled the hotel, leave me dizzy. It's too much to absorb.

Lalla Yasmin still has a tight grip on my arm. Perhaps she feels me sway for she says to Fay, "Help me get her down on the rug, my dear. Your sister isn't well."

In one corner, rugs are arranged in a loose semicircle on the floor and up both sides of the walls, forming a sort of bolster pillow. I sit gingerly and stretch my legs out in front of me. My ankle is still strapped in a now-filthy makeshift splint.

"Oh my God," Fay says. "What happened?"

"Old news." I swat away her question with a weak backhand. I don't want to talk about my injury; I want Fay to draw me a detailed picture of exactly how we've ended up at the headquarters of the tenth division of the Moroccan Army.

But Yasmin takes charge. She nudges another rolled rug under my leg to elevate it and unwinds the makeshift bandage. My pen clatters to the floor. She removes shoe and sock to expose my ankle, which throbs as blood rushes into it. Purplish bruises have formed along the outside, but the swelling is receding. It doesn't feel as bad as it looks.

"A sprain?" she asks.

At my nod, she tosses my dirty T-shirt aside and removes a strip of cloth from the cardboard box. Yasmin has taken off my sneaker, which I was afraid to do in the desert for fear I couldn't get it back on, so she is able to work the wrapping under and around my foot and lower leg in a figure-eight, making a much more secure binding.

"Are you hungry, Julie?"

Mainly, I'm exhausted and disoriented and frightened, but all I've had to eat or drink in the past day is the little bit of soup Jamila spooned into my mouth. I can't see any food in the empty room, though.

"Don't worry." Yasmin pats my hand. "Adequate supplies are normally provided, but the past few days have been anything but normal. Still, a little fresh food remains. Fay," she says, "fetch me the orange."

Fay stands and stretches to her tiptoes to take a single orange from the sill of the high window. They might have been saving it for a treat, but the thought of the tart-sweet flavor makes my mouth water. Yasmin pulls her long skirt around herself gracefully, settles on the floor at my side, and feeds the orange to me in sections.

When I finish it, she gets slowly to her feet. "Stay here and rest. Fay can keep you company while Nadia and I prepare dinner. Our kitchen, such as it is, is the shed at the back of our patio. There's no light in our house, save that from the perimeter lights coming in through the window, so we'll eat in perhaps two hours, before the sun goes down."

Nadia and her son moved to the table when Fay and Yasmin escorted me to the pile of rugs. Now they're flicking a crayon back and forth across the table like a game of Ping-Pong. When her mother calls out that it's time to start dinner, Nadia scoops Hamid up in her arms and the three of them exit through the arched doorway.

Aside from letting my head loll against the wall, I don't move; I don't think I *could* right now.

I've found Fay—in a manner of speaking. The little I know makes it clear I was right not to involve the police but also that, on my own, I had zero chance of rescuing her. But when she wrote me that note, Fay really thought she'd be back in two days. *Time for answers.*

"You talk," I tell her. "I'll listen. Start at the beginning and don't leave anything out. It's way past time for me to hear the whole story."

Fay sits beside my rug. Her teeth nibble the inside of her cheek, a delaying tactic I remember well from childhood beating around the bush.

"I suppose I should begin in the autumn of 1990."

"They've really been here for *fifteen years?*"

"Almost." Fay crosses her arms over her chest. "In 1990, Gil had just graduated from law school at Penn and moved to DC to begin a research fellowship when he heard that his entire family—father, mother, sister, and brother—had been executed for treason."

"Ohmygod." Fay is two-for-two with blockbuster disclosures right out of some wild foreign-intrigue playbook. Like anyone who pays attention to the news, I've heard awful stories—and they make me angry, but they've never . . . well, never affected me, my life.

"Gil was totally blindsided. His father had been an advisor to the king, a lawyer and a confidant, high up in the palace hierarchy. But they were all dead, and Gil couldn't get any answers. Whispers reached him—traitorous Ohana and his family silenced, watch out—but no concrete leads. Eventually, Gil gave up trying."

An overwhelming tragedy like that, I think, couldn't help but mess Gil up. Perhaps the taciturn and rather severe man my sister fell in love with was once a sunnier person.

"Flash-forward to 2004, to the beginning of last summer, a few months before I began enticing you with this trip." A tiny glimmer of her old self surfaces in Fay's self-deprecating grimace. "Out of the blue early one morning, the phone rang when I was getting out of the shower." Fay describes the scene in such vivid detail that I feel like I'm present—how she dressed and walked into the bedroom, saw Gil sitting on the bed, the look on his face—wonder, doubt, exhilaration, confusion, dread—all at the same time.

"When I asked him what happened, Gil said the man who called claimed to be a soldier in the Moroccan Army, stationed at a post near the Algerian border. In addition to his regular patrol duties, he was responsible for securing under house arrest two women and a young child. The soldier became friendly with the prisoners. And the older women pleaded with him to contact her family. That's when Gil started crying."

Fay breaks off the narrative and stands to pace, tension apparent in every muscle of her clenching fists and stomping feet. "It turns out that although Gil's father and brother *had* been shot, his mother and sister were alive, being kept captive. The men shot—bang, bang—just like that." Fay fires a pretend gun with an outstretched index finger. "And fourteen fucking years later, Gil finds out his mother and sister aren't dead after all. They were, in the expression used at the time, 'disappeared.'"

CHAPTER TWENTY-THREE

Fay stops pacing, hangs her head. Her shoulders hunch toward her ears as she hugs herself once more. "Gil's mother had promised the soldier money for delivering her message. That was Mohammed, by the way—and he had also indicated a willingness to arrange their escape." She pauses, grimaces. "In exchange for a rather considerable sum, even by inflated New York standards."

Fay goes on at length about their initial worry that it was some sick scam. Mohammed was able to relay stories about Gil's childhood, though, incidents only his mother would know. And for every question Gil asked—like the name of their first doorkeeper in Rabat—the man came back with the right answer. "So eventually he convinced Gil. But Mohammed could only call when he was away from the base. Weeks would pass without any word at all. Poor Gil was all over the place emotionally; he had to rescue his mother, but he couldn't enter Morocco safely."

Fay's recital is so remote from *any* context I've ever had about her life, about Gil, or about their life together that bright flashes like fireworks erupt in my peripheral vision and my ears ring with the rhythmic dinging of low blood pressure. Executions and treason and disappearances—fifteen years of confinement—and reappearance and rescue plots. I keep blinking to clear my vision.

Fay runs her fingers through her hair and then sinks to the floor. Sitting cross-legged beside me again, she explains that after hearing about the deaths of his immediate family, Gil went to stay with his nearest living relative, an uncle living in London. He was so furious, Fay says, that he was ready to rush back to Morocco to avenge their deaths—no doubt a shortcut to his own death—but the uncle talked him out of it. "Gil returned to the States a very angry young man." Fay sighs heavily. "He's been busy 'avenging' in his law practice ever since."

"Gil's *Moroccan*?" That's the next thing I need to get straight on this disorienting Alice-in-Wonderland day. "The only time I remember asking him about his family, he mentioned that uncle in London and then deflected the conversation into a story about riding double-decker buses, leaving me with the impression *that* was his background."

"Yeah, he doesn't open up about himself very much, does he?" Fay combines a quick up-and-down quirking of her lips with an eye-roll. "He totally remade himself, the classic immigrant. Most people probably imagine he is Gilbert Ohana of the Irish O'Hanas. But his name, Gil, is actually short for Gildun, and his father's family name, Ohana, is one of the most common Berber last names."

This has become a seriously down-the-rabbit-hole conversation. "Oh" is all I can manage.

"Lalla Yasmin's family was very prominent in Rabat, but even with their connections, Gil couldn't ask for help. The only way they could remain safe was to denounce their relatives, so that's what they did. They thought they were dead anyhow. Some of them *might* have been secretly sympathetic, but Gil decided he couldn't take that chance."

Fay's nervous energy has her picking at lint on the red-and-gold-patterned rug next to her and rolling the bits around in her fingers, in much the same ineffectual way I plucked the threads of the embroidered pillow while listening to Hamza's tale of the men who came in the night.

She ticks off Gil's other inquiries—quizzing US State Department people he'd worked with, talking to his uncle's Moroccan contacts. No one could find out anything. Plus, Fay tells me, even though Gil has become a US citizen, Morocco still claims him, so people in our government said they couldn't guarantee his safety.

"After that, Gil investigated traveling on a false passport." Fay's pinched lips and narrowed eyes show what she thought of *that*. "Finally, he asked me—no, Julie, he begged me—to help him. I didn't take his last name. He believed, and I believed him, that I would fly under the radar and be safe." Fay looks down at her hands. "I'm sorry."

Sorry.

It's like reading in a foreign language I'm just beginning to learn. I can only decipher one disconnected word at a time during Fay's recital. Her lapsing into silence gives me time to process what she said.

Sorry. What an unbearable situation—and one with haunting similarities to our father's final illness. Dad needed a bone marrow transplant, and we all volunteered to be tested. Neither Fay nor Greg nor any of our cousins were compatible. I was.

The following week, I found out I was pregnant with Alex. You can't donate stem cells while pregnant, and Dad wasn't going to last nine more months without help, so they resumed testing—more cousins, aunts, uncles. Then they searched the national registry. Nothing. I was ten weeks pregnant. Steve and I talked; we cried; we agreed I would have an abortion to save Dad's life. We could get pregnant again, we rationalized. I was Dad's only chance.

He had a massive heart attack the night before I was to go in for the abortion. Alex's full name is John Alexander Welch, Anglicized from his grandfather, Jean-Alexandre Lariviere.

I can't imagine my life without either of them.

So I get it. Gil, unable to rescue his mother and sister. And Fay, unable to say no to her husband if she believed she was his last resort any more than I could say no to my father. But for me, it was an out-of-options last resort. Surely, in this case, there were alternatives to putting Fay in harm's way.

Like . . . "Why didn't you bring it all out in the open? Tell the newspapers. Give interviews. Expose the facts to public scrutiny in the States, in Europe, if not in Morocco itself. Demand their release. Alert Amnesty International. Wouldn't that have given Gil a good shot at getting them free?" I don't add *without putting us in danger.*

"It would have been more likely to get them killed or at least hidden deeper." Fay drops her head and buries her face in her hands. "Gil heard horrible stories of people who managed to get word out that they were being tortured, only to have their torture end—at the hands of a firing squad." She crosses her arms again. "Dead prisoners tell no tales."

The little boy has been peeking around the door while Fay talks, scooting on his bottom to inch closer. Hamid is maybe three or four years old, with a mop of long, dark curls, but skittish and way too skinny. Every time Fay pauses, he freezes, only moving again when she picks up the story.

"It's nice that he's getting more confident," Fay says, with a tiny nod in his direction. "This is the first time he's left his mother's side since I was thrust into their midst."

Since Nadia has been locked up here for fifteen years, I'm not sure I want to know the answer, but . . . "What's the deal with him, Fay?" I ask, keeping my voice quiet.

"I don't know. He was, obviously, born in this prison. His father is 'no longer here.' That's all they've told me." Fay chews on her cheek a second. "Listen, while we've got a minute alone, I need to tell you that Nadia, his mom, is nuts." A small shrug. "Not a medical diagnosis, I know, Julie. But she's up; she's down. Wild, wild mood swings. She's convinced I'm their savior one minute. She . . . God, she started hitting me last night when—out of the blue—she seemed to register the idea that I was as much a prisoner as they were. And she's strong, too. It took both her mother and me to subdue her." Fay shakes her head. "She hasn't had much of a life, poor thing. She was only, like, twenty or something, studying chemistry at the university, when her father suddenly became an enemy of the state and was shot—right in front of her—along with her older brother."

"Am I ever going to find out what her father did that was so awful?"

"Let's leave that story to Yasmin, okay? She's a fabulous storyteller. I ought to go out and see if I can help with dinner, if you don't mind."

Fay unfolds her legs and rises but, having thought of the similarities between Fay's dilemma and my crisis over the bone marrow donation, I have one more thing to get off my chest. "Fay, wait. Before you go—I'm sorry I laid into you like I did. I understand better now. You really were stuck between a rock and a hard place. But I trusted you. You should've told me what you were up to, given me a chance to say yes or no."

Fay's eyes fill with tears. "I deserved everything you said—and more. I let Gil's ideas get in the way of my own good sense. He was wrong to ask me to betray you. And I was wrong to agree. Keeping a secret from you was too heavy a burden. And left you without . . ." She sniffs, and teardrops snake down her cheek.

Tears of regret or not, I plow ahead. I *have to* because I would never in a million years have made that awful decision without talking it through with Steve. And I would never have done it if we hadn't both— however sorrowfully—agreed.

"It left me completely at a loss, Fay. Worried and confused at first. Then frantic." Despite the fatigue, my body twitches uncontrollably. I can't even think about the last few days of increasing desperation without reliving my distress. My voice rises. "And eventually, because I *didn't* know any better—because you *didn't* tell me what the stakes were, didn't tell me where you were, who to call if there was a problem—I ended up here. Where I can't do a damn thing." Fay is sobbing now, so

I try to soften my harsh words by adding, "At least I found you, but it was only dumb luck."

"No, Julie. *Luck* had zero to do with it." Fay smears the tears with her palm and launches herself toward me, smothering me in a hug. "*You* were the person I wanted with me. I told Gil I'd only come if I could get you to watch my back. Then, when you agreed, Gil swore me to secrecy." Fay pulls away. Her lips quiver upward like she's trying to smile, but her eyes are red-rimmed and filled with unshed tears. "So unnecessary. He doesn't know you like I do."

I am about to erupt with a tirade about her choices, but Fay has already reached a breaking point. I settle for the least bitchy thing I can think to say. "What the fuck did he think I was going to do—drop a dime?"

"He was afraid to trust anyone besides me." Fay's repeating herself instead of answering my question. "Anyhow, all I was supposed to do was meet with Mohammed and his army buddies. Pay him for delivering the message and firm up plans for the rescue—if we could agree on what to do. The whole thing should've only taken an afternoon in Ouarzazate, an afternoon when it would be simple for you and me to be doing separate excursions. But after we'd already made our reservations, Mohammed said the dates conflicted with a major holiday, and the men needed to be home in their village, so I had to go to them instead." She shakes her head slowly. "Really, I wanted to tell you so many times, but I'd promised. When things started to go wrong—shit, from the minute that policeman motioned us over—I should have said something. I don't know why I didn't," she finishes lamely.

"Because you have worse tunnel vision than a kamikaze pilot," I snap, no longer able to hold back. "I'm not saying that single-minded focus is always counterproductive, but this time it sucked. When we were picking up our stuff the police left blowing across the road, instead of giving me that bogus shit about not knowing why we'd been targeted, you could've come clean. Or if, instead of holding it all in when you were worrying about your errand Friday morning at Ait Benhaddou, you told me then. Think about it. We could have driven right back to the airport, changed our flight, and been sitting in a café in France right now."

"And Gil's family would still be prisoners."

"I hate to be the one to break it to you, but not only are *they* still in prison, so are we." I look around at the bare room, the barred door beyond the patio. "And, with us here, I can only imagine their situation is worse now than before you interfered."

Fay takes a deep breath. I can almost see a speech-bubble *"But"* forming above her head.

I cut her off. "You know it's true."

CHAPTER TWENTY-FOUR

I lie alone in the dim room, listening to the murmurs of voices nearby. Rays from the setting sun creep up the wall, illuminating section by section all the little cracks and irregularities. I can see where it was once painted blue. The twelve-foot-high ceiling gains a sunbeam—revealing brown bundles of rushes and spider webs. Caught in a web. Damn it—Fay ran right into their trap, and then I fell into it, too.

Before she left the room, Fay lifted her gaze to the tiny high window, neither an acceptance nor a denial. "I had to do something." Then she pivoted with a jerk and glared at me. "*You* would've."

I knew without her having to say it that Fay was thinking about Dad, too, but she didn't give me a chance to reply before stomping out. So I haven't told her that, given what I've heard so far, I would've said no this time.

Just as well.

People say it's harder to forgive people close to you than an enemy—the betrayal factor. You don't expect your enemy to tell you the truth or look out for your welfare. But your family . . . I sigh. *Family is complicated.* In keeping a promise to her husband—in his belief that it would safeguard me—Fay had to rationalize not telling me the truth. And the confluence of those conflicting decisions has left us in mortal danger.

The tangled knot in the center is Fay's acknowledgment that Gil doesn't know me the way she does—enough to trust me. Nor do I know Gil the way she does—enough to trust him. A cliché in the repertoire of my sports-crazy brother, Greg, comes to mind: *offsetting penalties.* This time, I think, it's *mutually assured destruction* instead.

All the locks, all the guards, all the guns. The desert, the mountains. Home is so far away.

*　*　*

It's twilight when the women bring a large dented pot inside. Without enough chairs to go around, Yasmin asks Nadia to unfold a couple of rugs. These she arranges into a comfortable nest on the floor around me. We sit in a circle—Fay to my right, then counterclockwise, Yasmin, Hamid, and Nadia, on my left side. They made a rustic vegetable stew, mainly potatoes and carrots in irregular chunks, skins left on. We serve ourselves from the pot with big spoons.

Yasmin tucks her long skirt and sits on her knees. As she talks, her expressive hands constantly touch Fay, smooth Hamid's hair. She begins by apologizing for the simple meal. Even under the warped circumstances, it's only polite to say, "No, no, it's delicious."

The stew, if not exactly delicious, is substantial and nourishing. "How do you get your food?" I ask.

According to Yasmin, *something* gets delivered every couple of days—whether it's a pot of soup that only needs reheating or a bucket of vegetables or fruit or, very occasionally, meat. "And never fresh meat unless it's a chunk cut off a goat they slaughter. Ah!" Yasmin claps her hands. Hamid, startled, leaps into his mother's lap, overturning her spoonful of stew. "Tonight's the start of Eid al-Adha. There'll be mutton tomorrow."

All over Morocco, families are gathering for a meal of thanksgiving. *And I'm in a locked room somewhere near the Algerian border.*

Yasmin cocks her head to one side. "I'm surprised they didn't send any over tonight, though." She hasn't even finished her sentence when the obvious conclusion—retaliation for the current trouble—washes across her face. Yasmin erases her brief grimace and, making light of our simple meal, tells her first story of the evening: how their rudimentary kitchen had been whittled away to nothing.

"You see," she says, with one of her puckish smiles, "to cook properly one must have all sorts of dangerous weapons. In the beginning, when Nadia and I thought it was only a matter of a time until His Majesty relented, we gave our jailers no trouble—on the contrary, we offered to cook and to clean for them. We made ourselves useful."

Yasmin squints at us in the twilight, something she would do often in the course of the evening, and spins a tale right out of Scheherazade, complete with different voices for the various characters—how she and Nadia ingratiated themselves with the soldiers who, at first, considered them a novelty and gave them the run of the place as long as they obeyed the rules.

With a ragged sigh that's almost a sob, Yasmin admits it was easy for her to be docile because she was still in shock from the death of her husband and son. Nightmares kept her awake in the dark hours, so she'd collapse in the shade in the afternoons, crying and praying. And then crying some more.

"But Nadia was restless," Yasmin says. "She used activity, not prayer, to relieve her anxiety. One day she simply walked through the gate into the desert. After that, they put the bar across the door to our residence. We were caged except when there was a soldier willing to watch us as we walked."

Lalla Yasmin readjusts her legs with a wince of discomfort and resettles herself on the tile floor. "So I wrote a letter to King Hassan. Those were days when we still had paper and pens," she adds in her everyday voice. "It was a birthday greeting to Hassan, and as he shared a birthday with Nadia, I asked him to release *her*, at least, an act of benevolence to commemorate her twenty-fifth birthday. When the commandant refused to send the letter, Nadia flew into a rage and attacked him with a paring knife. And there went the kitchen."

I'm counting up years on my fingers. "Her twenty-fifth birthday? So you had been here for . . . four or five years then?"

"Yes. That was the summer of 1995."

*   *   *

After we scrape every last bit of food from the big pot, Nadia takes it outside to clean and doesn't return. Instead, she paces on the concrete patio, swift pent-up strides that take her from one side to the other in a flash.

Lalla Yasmin leads Hamid to the pile of rugs in the corner to tell him bedtime stories, leaving me alone with Fay.

Yasmin's elaborate tales at dinner were a welcome respite from my all-encompassing hopelessness. Either she's a born storyteller, I think, or she's a genius, having created this . . . this amazing fictional reality to stay sane during fifteen years of solitude.

But I've still only heard part of *Fay's* story, and it's time for her to finish telling me the truth. "What the hell happened Friday afternoon?"

"Okay . . ." Fay laces her hands behind her neck and stretches her elbows wide, takes a deep breath. There's nothing to distract us, but she's clearly playing for time. It comes out in fits and starts: driving to the village, meeting Mohammed's friends, the former soldiers who agreed to help with the escape. "They were polite," Fay said, "but evasive about the rescue. At the time, I put it down to cultural differences, but in hindsight I should have guessed something was up."

She's dancing around the point instead of zeroing in on it. Fay must know her recent lies will be a harder sell than Gil's heartbreaking family tragedy. I wiggle my fingers—hurry up.

Mohammed wanted his money right away, Fay told me, but because she was already nervous, she said he couldn't have it until they brought her back. "That's when Mohammed changed tactics. *Yes, tomorrow we make plans. Now we have tea*—Berber whiskey, he called it. They all laughed."

"So *then* what happened?" Fay's revelations are giving me a sick feeling in the pit of my stomach.

"When I tried to beg off, they seemed offended. I knew it was traditional hospitality, so . . ." Fay runs her palms roughly over her cheeks. "So we all sat around, and they filled my glass several times. They talked for *hours*. I kept nodding off, figured it was just the long day."

When Fay speaks again her voice is an octave higher from the pressure to get her words out. "The next thing I knew it was daylight and I was waking up in the back seat of a car, with Mohammed's two friends in the front. Tied up. They just laughed when I yelled and tried to get free."

Drugged Friday night. Saturday morning . . . "Where'd they take you?"

"Here. To an office at first." In a hushed monotone, Fay tells me how a uniformed man took all the cash, badgered her for hours, and searched through everything she brought.

But they had Fay and lots of money. "So what else was he looking for?"

"He wanted the cheat-sheet Gil wrote for me—contact names and phone numbers, the location of the camp, and names—his mother and sister, the man in charge here. Thank goodness I didn't bring it, but apparently when I was woozy, I told Mohammed about it, and the man refused to believe I didn't have it."

"Was your list written on a piece of legal paper with words in Arabic script?"

Fay leans forward; her eyebrows draw together. "Yes."

"I found it after you left, in the pocket of your sweatshirt."

Fay's hand claps onto her mouth. "You didn't bring it, did you?"

I have to think whether I'd stuck it in my backpack—it's been a confusing couple of days. "No, the paper's in your suitcase, in the trunk of our car."

Fay gives her forehead a histrionic swipe. "Whew."

"Why?" I ask her, not sure what the big deal is.

"The people here are looking for confirmation of who got involved in the rescue attempt." The *a-ha* expression that spreads across Fay's face is the equivalent of a light bulb flashing over her head. "But *you* found it and that's how you found *me*."

Meanwhile I, too, am putting two and two together. "Is that what the police were looking for on the road the day we left Marrakech?"

"I think they were after the money which—especially taken together with that list—would constitute proof I planned to engage in an illegal activity. I was also worried the policemen might stuff contraband in my suitcase. I've heard that crooked police will compromise your luggage with drugs and then use that as an excuse to take you into custody."

"So, that's why you insisted we travel with only a carry-on bag." Events tumble into place. "And you *wore* the money inside your quilted jacket. What the hell were you thinking?"

"Really, Julie." Fay goes on the defensive again. "I thought we were both adequately protected. Remember I even insisted we buy our plane tickets separately so you wouldn't be connected to me? And how we only put your name on our hotel reservations?"

My evil eye stops her equivocation.

It's true, though, that Fay has remained Fay Lariviere through two marriages, while I switched from Julie Lariviere to Julie Welch the second I married Steve. And after her ugly divorce a few years back, Fay vowed forevermore to keep her finances separate.

Saturday night, Fay was in their custody, and they were sure she didn't have the list on her. But I was followed Saturday morning. And evening. Nothing much happened until Sunday, though, when keeping an eye on me turned into finding out what I had and what I knew—it turned into the attack on the wrong woman at our hotel.

"One thing I never found out," says Fay. "Was the man who brought me here really Mohammed, the soldier from the fort who'd befriended Yasmin? Did he trick us? Traded a reward or promotion for double-crossing Gil? Or was the real Mohammed found out somehow? I mean, should I be worried about what might've happened to him or pissed that he betrayed us?" Fay's voice has drifted off into a dim, faltering whisper. I desperately want to console her, but telling her everything's going to be all right would be *me* lying to *her*.

Tadefi, the hotel maid from Ouarzazate, knew the man Fay left with as Mohammed, but I don't tell Fay this. As my nemesis, Mr. Ray-Ban, said, "There are lots of Mohammeds here." It's as common a boy's name in Morocco as Tom or Jim is in the States. Although I'm guessing she and Gil have been played, the last thing Fay needs now is the despair of believing this has been a setup from the beginning.

Anyhow, nothing I say or do at this point will make one single bit of difference.

CHAPTER TWENTY-FIVE

A few minutes later, Yasmin tiptoes across the room and pulls up a rug next to us. "Hamid's finally asleep."

With the setting of the sun, the air has turned chilly. We huddle together on piles of rugs, a couple of soft kilims around us for warmth, and Yasmin talks long into the night. She weaves stories of her early childhood in a harem—which, she explains, merely means a cloistered existence—in Fes, about the war years when she was evacuated to her grandparents' farm in the mountains, and about her adult life in Rabat as the cosseted young wife of a senior government official.

I finally learn the terrible crime of her late husband. Qasim was a lawyer who, in the mid-1980s, represented some imprisoned Saharawi, residents of the disputed Western Sahara. He became convinced their cause should be taken to the United Nations and spoke out in favor of the UN plan for a cease-fire and open elections in the Western Sahara—even though the king was opposed.

Yasmin looks away for a few seconds, tears pooling in her eyes. "When the king heard about it, he flew into a rage. And with the absolute arrogance of his absolute power, Hassan ordered his guards to eliminate the family. Killing Qasim and Nabil was a . . . spasm, a hiccup, a vicious angry moment with dreadful consequences he did not stop to consider. He swatted out the life of my husband and my son like you would step on a bug and with as little concern."

A flickering smile, like a memory of a long-ago summer day, crosses Yasmin's face. "Ah, but for him, the trouble escalated after they were shot because, you see, he stopped short of ordering my death. His wife Latifa is my cousin. I've always believed he knew the queen would never have condoned it—yet I knew what he had done."

Yasmin has moved close to me, and we sit with the intimacy of two old friends having a heart-to-heart chat. "And the final irony—the king agreed to the UN-backed cease-fire leading to an election not six months after he murdered Qasim for suggesting it."

"But Hassan's not king anymore." I'm thinking about the ceremonial Mohammed the Sixth portraits displayed everywhere.

"No, he died in 1999. When I heard about it, I thought *now perhaps his son will bring us home.* We used the last of the gold balls from my necklace to pay a soldier who was being transferred back to Rabat to deliver a note to Mohammed—now the king, but once a little boy who ate too much cake at Nabil's birthday party and was sick in the toilet. I don't know if the soldier ever delivered it." Yasmin shrugs with her entire body, a sinuous movement under her shapeless garment. "If he did, King Mohammed did nothing."

Lalla Yasmin's stories fill the air with a kaleidoscope of shifting images. They are peppered with little flecks of hard shiny anger, occasionally masquerading as wit. Nadia, on the other hand, speaks not a dozen words all evening. She's silent and watchful in the murky reflected half-light, a lioness, curled up with her hand on her son's chest. It rises and falls regularly in deep child-sleep.

Fifteen years.

Fifteen years ago, Steve had just finished grad school. Our children were in the future—our family's future of toddler playgroups and back-to-school clothes, of birthday parties and bike-riding and T-ball and sleepovers, vacations at the beach, ice cream.

All the milestones, the memories, the photographs.

Memories flow in both directions, I think. When my dad got sick, one of us would sit with him whenever we could and he'd talk about growing up in a small town in Quebec. Later, when he became too weak to talk much, Fay compiled a slideshow of family photos on her computer. Then it was *our* turn to reminisce—about Scout, our rescue puppy, who loved to bring home squirrels; about the "surprise" birthday party for Mom—that she knew all about because Greg and I asked her to make the cake; about Fay dropping her camera on the helicopter ride over Miami Beach.

Fifteen years. If Nadia was twenty-five in 1995, that makes her only a few years younger than me. Locked away without cause for half her life. Without her father or brothers. Without a future—except Hamid, and I shudder to imagine how she conceived a child in this prison. No wonder she stayed silent.

Disoriented and uncomfortable on the lumpy rugs, fearful and too exhausted for normal slumber, I lie awake for a very long time. Cool air seeps in through the open window. Yasmin is still talking when I drift off into an uneasy sleep.

CHAPTER TWENTY-SIX

Friday, January 21, 2005

The opalescent sunlight of early morning finds us all outside on the benches. Nadia and Hamid, first up, have made tea. Birds twitter in the scraggly little tree. Hamid breaks off the stale end of his bread and scatters the crumbs. The birds chatter; several drop to the ground and peck in the dirt. Fay says something about being almost out of food; Nadia suggests Fay go ask for more if she's so hungry. Perhaps hoping to end the bickering, Lalla Yasmin says, "Julie, I've been wondering how you found us here."

I'm finishing the story—whisked from Jamila's to the stockade—when I realize what I overheard the day before. "Oh no!"

Everyone turns in my direction.

"That soldier who brought me here was talking to the man in charge when we first arrived. They said this location was compromised and they intend to move you—move us—to another place today."

Instant panic. The questions fly at me: Where are we going? When? Who's taking us? Do they know you heard them say this? Will they let us keep our belongings? Why now?

I'm sure the answer to "why now?" is because first Fay, and now I, have breached their security. Yasmin's message has reached the outside world, and the men must suspect others will follow. Mohammed told Gil where his family was imprisoned, but without our presence in the garrison and absent any new "Mohammed" inveigled into carrying a message, our trail will disappear. *We* will disappear.

I tell the women I think no one realized I was listening. I had my eyes closed; the young soldiers saw me limp and obviously in pain. Possibly, they didn't even know I could speak French. As to the rest—I shrug and repeat the bits I heard.

The women rush into action. From hidden cubbyholes come small treasures, things I would never think twice about—a few crayons, a letter, a broken butter knife, keys.

From a hole dug alongside the pit toilet, they remove a cloth bag. Nadia shakes the dirt clods off. As they work, Yasmin calls to me and Fay to prepare. She pulls out an old cotton robe, now sun-bleached to an uneven gray and consigned to the rag bag, and rips off wide strips. "Wrap one of these around your body, just under your breasts, and put inside it everything you care about."

I pull on the collar of my turtleneck and wrench the leather pouch from around my neck aghast that, with one yank at the slender cord, those men could have removed my only chance of survival. My heart pills are in it, along with my passport, fingernail clippers, the pen I'd used as a splint, a spare lipstick, and my emergency stash of money. The rest of my money, along with everything in my backpack—gone.

I count twenty-one pills, a sobering deadline. I turn out my pockets and recover the curving bit of ostrich shell—a talisman for cunning and endurance, Ahmed said. I add it to the pile. The total of my possessions doesn't even make a bulge when I bandage the pouch with everything in it around my midsection.

Fay is traveling lightest. Like my backpack, her purse and red tote bag were confiscated on arrival. From a pocket on the inside of the patchwork vest she's wearing over a now-filthy blue sweater, she extracts only a few hard candies and her miniature sewing kit, a thin plastic oval.

"How'd you manage to keep that?" I ask, thinking of how my pouch was spared only because my turtleneck covered the strap completely.

Fay grimaces—and adds a quick eye-roll. "The man was so interested in my boobs when he patted me down that he didn't bother much with my waist. He, you know, ran his hands down pretty quickly to get to other more, um, interesting areas."

Gathering and concealing, careful to eliminate any sign of disturbance, amounts to thirty minutes of frenzied activity. Then we sit on the benches once more. The sun is blazing now; the birds have flown off. I'm oddly numb; I should be in problem-solving mode, I think. Or praying. But the small part of my brain that's still functioning refuses to focus. I watch the door.

No one says a word. Even Lalla Yasmin is out of stories.

They come about an hour later. Marching footsteps stop outside the closed gate. The hinges of the heavy door squeal. It swings open. Eight unsmiling men in uniform enter.

"*Mesdames.*" The commandant makes a stiff bow. "Your stay with us has come to an end. You will be leaving immediately for new accommodations. These men are instructed to bring you without delay to the transport van."

Lalla Yasmin peppers him with questions, the same ones she posed to me, but the senior officer turns on his heel and, barking a command to the others, walks away.

Two soldiers block the arched entrance to the little house and one stands by each of us. The men avoid eye contact. One soldier grabs Hamid from Nadia and walks toward the gate. "Come with us."

"*Maman!*" Hamid cries.

Nadia darts after him, screeching, and pounds on his back. Another man pulls her away and slams her into the wall. Her hands stay out of the soldier's grasp long enough for her to claw his face, howling all the while. When he restrains her hands, she head-butts him, thrashing this way and that as she struggles for an avenue of escape. The soldier, nose dripping blood, finally wrestles her against the wall and lashes her arms to her sides with a length of cord. Even then, she kicks and shrieks as he frog-marches her outside.

Nadia's stream of invective echoes. And any remote chance of compassion vanishes with the soldier's bloody face. With Hamid screaming for his mother at the top of his lungs, they propel us single file, each in the uncompromising grip of a soldier.

While Nadia continues to writhe and curse impressively, they load us into the back of a work van. No seats, just burlap sacking on a hot metal floor. They slam the doors shut.

Through a small metal screen separating our space from the front compartment, I see two burly armed men with a satchel between them. They turn on the radio and speak quietly, so we can't hear them. Yasmin unties the cord binding her daughter's arms and calms Hamid. Nadia, her rage spent, lapses into toneless humming.

The van's motion has finally shaken me into motion, too, with fear and morbid curiosity struggling for primacy. Although our bouncing along on the rough *piste* makes it difficult to remain upright, by peering through the little screen, I can tell we're running along a wide and nearly featureless plain with tall, spiky mountains far off on the right and lower, smoother, browner ones on the left. After traveling a while on the *piste*, we stop at a mud-brick café standing alone by the side of the track. The soldiers return to the van with Cokes, and we're on our way again. Now there are more signs of human habitation: scattered dwellings, goat pens, people working in fields, flags flying on hilltops.

"The big question," Yasmin says, "is which direction they'll take when we get to a paved road."

"What do you mean?" asks Fay.

"A left will take us back toward the Algerian border." Yasmin gestures with one hand. "Probably to another garrison much like the one where we were. But if the driver turns right, we could be in for a long ride." She shakes her head slowly. "They could drive just about anywhere in the country—north to the imperial cities of Fes and Meknes, west to Marrakech or Casablanca, south to Agadir and the Western Sahara. There are," she says, "prisons everywhere, police everywhere, army everywhere."

Before we learn the answer to Yasmin's question, we stop again. The driver announces that we'll be let out. The guy riding shotgun fiddles with the lock at the back and flings open the door. We're in an enclosed courtyard. Scarlet and magenta bougainvilleas twine in the pillars all the way up to the top level and arch over the interior, creating dappled shade. The cobbled floor is liberally scattered with blossoms. A pile of rolled prayer rugs lies off to one side. There's a distant sound of running water. A telephone rings; a rumbling male voice speaks in French. It looks like an elegant private residence.

But it isn't. Out of a side door come four uniformed men. Our desert soldiers who, an hour earlier, seemed so dangerous, look amateurish next to these trim, taut, red- and blue-garbed policemen.

"Moroccan Security Service," Yasmin whispers. "Paramilitary police. Not good."

It's not an instant disaster. We're escorted into the building and, blissfully, one by one, to a toilet. But when we return to the courtyard, the van and our soldiers are gone. In their place is an olive-green truck and a lone policeman. He's a big man, but not soft, imposing in his impeccable uniform and standing immobile, save for his eyes, which dart speculatively over each of us in turn, strafing our bodies, while his meaty hands knead his thighs.

The amorphous sensation of helpless dread circulating through my body transforms into a lightning bolt of terror.

According to Fay, the man who interrogated her when Mohammed brought her to the barracks had demanded she tell him who knew where she was. "I lied, Julie." Fay laid icy fingers on my arm. "I named everyone I could think of. I was so scared I would have said anything, named *anyone*, to appear connected to the outside."

With instant insight into her desperate need to name names of *people who knew where she was*, I long to run at the policeman—to beg him, promise him *anything*—if he will please, please, please open the door and let me walk out. I don't, of course, and he neither moves nor speaks but continues his appraisal.

Another man in the same red-and-blue, this one carrying a straw basket, joins him. The second policeman jerks his head in Lalla Yasmin's direction and grunts, "Hey, you!"

Yasmin, with her frail build and wispy white hairs straggling out of her faded headscarf, looks over, startled.

"Yes, you. Come here, you old bag of bones, and make yourself useful."

Even I, newcomer and foreigner that I am, can tell the difference between the stolid desert soldiers and these cold and menacing strangers.

Lalla Yasmin doesn't move, a rabbit caught in the headlights of a car, frozen by terror into a potentially fatal immobility. Her eyes widen; she rocks experimentally as though her feet might be glued to the floor. Fay and I have the same idea: we close in on either side of her and, each taking an elbow, we walk across the cobbles to the policeman. When we get close, he tosses the basket hard at Yasmin. She opens her arms just in time to catch it.

"Lunch," he growls, a bad-tempered man of few words, but still preferable to his ominously silent companion.

In helping Yasmin, we left her daughter exposed. The first policeman refocuses on Nadia, who's hugging Hamid close. He smiles, exposing sharp white teeth. "Such a beautiful daughter you have—oh, not a girl?" He shakes his head in mock disbelief. "Ah, well, it's better to take care of that confusion right away." He advances on her swiftly. I hold my breath, anticipating another outburst, but Nadia stands her ground and looks him in the eye.

"Your little boy is too pretty." An ugly smirk pinches his cold, impassive glare. "When you get where you're going, he'll need to fend for himself." He snatches Hamid in one fluid move and, before any of us can react, brings up a knife from his pocket and slices off a handful of curls. Hamid's neck is bent backward by the pressure of the blade on his tangled hair. He screams.

"*Tais-toi!*" The angry shout brings results. Hamid sniffles, but stops crying. The policeman flicks the knife closed once more and, with his free hand, squeezes Hamid's cheek—hard—before dropping him to the ground.

Nadia pales, accentuating twin spots of red that flame on her cheeks. Miraculously, she maintains her composure. She even avoids a rush to Hamid's side. Instead, with solemn gravity, she lowers her head. "Please permit me to carry our lunch. My mother is elderly, and the years have been hard on her."

When he doesn't respond, she walks, without interference, over to Yasmin and takes our lunch basket from her. "Please, sir," she asks, "could you tell us where we are going?"

He sniggers. "We're taking you down south to the camps where women like you earn their keep on their backs and where they'll cut off the rest of this one's pretty-boy curls and teach him to be a man."

A third man, this one silver-haired and self-important, comes into the courtyard. "What are you waiting for?" he grumbles. "*Allez-vous-en.* They're expecting you by five."

CHAPTER TWENTY-SEVEN

Nadia's composure slips the second the door to the truck rattles shut behind us. Unlike her incoherent screaming fit earlier, this time she speaks passionately. "We have to get away. Today. You heard what he said—they're taking us to the Western Sahara, to a prison camp. If they get us that far, we'll never get out." Her voice cracks. "Never. I'll kill them. I'll kill them all before I let Hamid walk into that place."

She turns angrily on her mother. "*This* is what your bright idea has provoked. Your precious Gildun," she jeers, "who was going to save us—hah! He's no more use than any of the others. My father's bad judgment cost me my youth and now yours is going to cost me my life."

"Now, Nadia—"

"Don't try to placate me. Ever since the day they shot him you've been making excuses for him."

"I was proud of him, Nadia. I still am. Your father dedicated his life to his country. Speaking truth to tyrants is seldom rewarded. But," she agrees, "it's true—we're suffering the consequences of his actions."

"My father gave his life for nothing. His country dishonored his memory. And we're on our own, as we have been all along. No one can save us." Nadia flings out her arm, striking Fay in the chest. "And these women, what a joke! Bringing money to strangers. Believing their stupid stories like gullible children. What have they done except ruin everything? You thought they could rescue us? Can't you see how idiotic that was? No one can save us," Nadia repeats, "no one but ourselves."

She falls silent then, snatching up Hamid who's been cradled in the crook of his grandmother's arm. Fay and I keep quiet. I feel sick at heart. Nadia is, in most respects, correct. She's ignoring the fact that now her brother knows they're alive, but that isn't likely to help if they're being held incommunicado in an unknown location.

If *we're* being held. If *I'm* being held. No one will know where I am.

I think I prefer my early-morning numbness, when the events of the day had yet to unfold. It's too painful to think about Steve and the kids. Or Mom—me and Fay missing, her not knowing what happened. And I have twenty-one days until—I enforce a full stop on my thoughts.

I can't let it happen.

The brakes squeal. The truck rolls to a stop, then turns right. Definitely not back to the border but onward, as the policeman said.

We can't see much in the dim interior of the truck, and we can't see out, either. The window on the rear door is painted over, but a narrow swath of unpainted glass runs along the bottom edge. By putting my face up against it, I have a peephole-sized view of a world of dust and rocks. Although the truck is barreling along a paved surface, it still kicks up plumes of sand as we speed along. Looking up, blue sky; looking out, barely discernible shapes that must be mountains. Once, I see a white 4x4 speeding in the opposite direction. Another time, we stop, the sand settles, and the driver comes around back and rattles the door. I freeze. Nadia stops her dissonant murmuring and sucks her breath in a squeaky whistle, but he must have been checking the lock. He stays next to the door for a while, pissing copiously onto the asphalt.

We eat sandwiches; the back of the truck heats up; Hamid closes his eyes.

After an hour or so, the driver down-shifts. The truck rumbles over a series of bone-rattling bumps and takes a hard left.

Yasmin stiffens like a bloodhound on the scent. "I think we just turned off the highway to Marrakech. They must be taking one of the roads that goes south through the Souss Valley."

South. We sit side by side, each alone with our thoughts.

I voice one of mine. "How far is it to this camp?"

"I don't know." Yasmin shrugs. "Somewhere in the Western Sahara. Remote."

"Well," I say, "in that case, we can't possibly arrive there by five this evening, can we?"

"You're right, Julie." Fay jiggles my arm. "That man who rushed us out the door said they expected us by five."

"So where are we stopping tonight?" Nadia asks.

No one speaks for a long time.

"We're going to play a game," Fay says when she breaks the silence. "Pick one thing you saved and tell how you can use that to escape. Concentrate. Don't worry about being totally logical. This is a good time to be creative." Dubious looks all around. "Come on," she urges. "Anybody? No? Okay then, I'll go first. I have a little sewing kit."

"Scissors?" Nadia, intense and focused, comes on board quickly.

"Technically, yes," Fay says, "but they're less than two inches long and not strong at all. I have two needles and black, white, and green thread." Fay looks around for a reaction, but no one says a word. "So, perhaps we could braid enough strands of thread together to make it stronger, then tie it across a doorway and trip up our captors."

"Then stab them with the scissors," says Nadia.

Yasmin and I exchange looks over her head.

"Satisfying. Definitely. Who wants to be next? Julie?" Fay raises her eyebrows in a mute pleading question.

"Ummm, I have a lipstick. It's bright red. If I could get my hand outside, maybe I could write a message on the outside of the truck, ask for help. And I have a pen, too—no paper, though."

"Okay, thanks, Julie. Lalla Yasmin, what do you have?"

"A small amount of cash we could use to buy things, but perhaps more importantly, I have a ring—gold and silver with jade, very valuable. It's the last thing I have left from my husband; I've kept it safe all these years. I don't know if we can bribe these men with it, but I'm willing to try."

"Thank you, Lalla," says Fay. "Nadia? What about you?"

"I have a knife." Nadia bares her teeth. "And I will use it."

"Okay, round one: sewing stuff, lipstick, a pen, a valuable ring, and" —with a nod toward Nadia—"a butter knife. Back to me," Fay says. "I have a few hard candies. That's a tough one, but I suppose if you spit one into a guard's face, it would sting, maybe distract him for a minute."

Nadia's cackle chills me.

Yasmin adds, more sensibly, "Plugging holes—if there's a hole we need filled."

Murmurs of agreement.

"Wait!" I say. "If you suck on the candy, it'll get sticky, and we have my pen and thread, too. So attach a candy to the thread. Then, if we can just come up with something to write on, we could hold the thread and use the candy to lower down something light, like a piece of paper asking for help."

"Clev-er," crows Fay. "Julie again."

"Fingernail clippers. No clue. Much like your scissors, they have sharp edges but not much strength."

"Okay, let's pass on that for now. Lalla Yasmin?"

"I have keys; they were the keys to the pantry of my kitchen in Rabat. I know, I know—it's not likely they'll magically open a door, but I've used them to gouge wood. They made some of the cubbyholes in our room in the desert."

"So they could be a tool to dig or possibly to poke or pry something." Fay nods approvingly. "Nadia, how about you?"

"My mirror, which I kept in one of those cubbyholes *maman* mentioned. I don't want to lose it, but if we break it, it will be sharp." Her face twists into a fierce scowl. "We could slice their—"

Fay interrupts, possibly to derail Nadia's intensifying bloodthirstiness. "Hey, can't you make a fire by concentrating the sun's rays with a mirror? Does anyone know how to do that?"

"Is it a flat mirror," I ask Nadia, "or curved?" I demonstrate with my hands.

"Flat, yes, a little rectangle for seeing my face." She blushes.

Ignoring this as-yet unexplored aspect of Nadia's personality, I ask, "And does it enlarge your face so you can see more clearly?"

Nadia shakes her head.

"Probably won't work then. You need a concave mirror to catch and focus the sun's rays, that or a magnifying glass."

I return Fay's look of incredulity. "Greg showed me how to do that when you were still playing with Barbie dolls," I retort. "He was good for a lot of Boy Scout shit—making fires, purifying water, edible mushrooms."

"Okay, I bow to your superior knowledge," Fay says. "We'll save Nadia's mirror for other things. Back to you, Lalla."

"I'm wearing all my clothes. Two kaftans, many scarves. I think the extra clothing will be helpful if we're able to get away."

I feel, just for a second, a frisson of hope. "Right, Fay and I would be dead giveaways in our pants and sweaters."

Nadia joins in. "My under-robe is old and faded, but it will do for one of you. The person who wears it will look like she's in cast-off clothing. She can be the servant." *Nadia unbending?* "She'll have to carry our belongings." *Nadia actually teasing?*

A nervous laugh rolls around the enclosure.

Lalla Yasmin cuts her amusement short and waggles her index finger at Fay. "You're so fair, my dear. You must be completely covered up, showing only your eyes. If you wear one of my kaftans, hunch down a bit, and shuffle your feet, you could pass for an old country woman. But we'll have to alter a head-covering so it doesn't give you away. Your sewing kit, Fay. Let me do it now." She unwraps her *hijab* and removes a gray-white inner scarf.

"So I get to be the servant," I say.

Lalla Yasmin nods with make-believe elegance. "Fortunately for you, my dear, there won't be much for you to carry."

Fay pulls up her sweater to unwrap the cloth around her belly. She takes out a needle and the white thread and hands them to Yasmin. Then she spreads the remaining pieces of the sewing kit in her hand. "I can't come up with anything else right now, but we seem to have made progress with our disguises for *after* we get away."

Fay's channeling our energy toward action is a massive improvement on the sick despair I was feeling. Years ago, when she pulled the fire alarm at that Mardi Gras party to give us time to sneak away, she couldn't know ahead of time if her idea would work. She simply took the simplest, most immediate action she could imagine. Whether *this* exercise ultimately bears fruit or not, she's doing her best to do exactly what I told her: *get us the fuck out of here.*

"My turn again," I say. "But first, I want to remind you that we all have other gifts—not the things we have, but who we are. Fay, you've always been clear and logical, a good problem-solver. I appoint you *our* commandant."

My lingering resentment toward Fay for getting us *into* this mess is a waste of time and energy. Instead, we need to work together to get us *out* of it. We have to get home together. Home to Steve. To the kids. Home to Gil. And, having come this far and stirred up this mess, it's time to get Gil's family home to him.

"Okay," I continue. "I have a little money too. I can add that to the pot. The only other thing I have is the bottle of pills I take."

"What medication?" Nadia asks.

"I take atenolol."

"What for?"

"I have a cardiac arrhythmia. The technical name is Long QT syndrome." I translate that into everyday speech. "The wiring in my heart is screwy; electrical impulses fire in a really disorganized way. Untreated, my heart rate speeds up too fast and eventually goes out of control."

"What happens if you don't take your medicine?"

"It starts out like a panic attack. Adrenaline floods my system. I get short of breath. Chest pain. The longer it goes uncontrolled, the worse it gets."

"And what happens if you take too much?"

I shake my head slowly. "I'm not sure. Atenolol is what's called a beta-blocker. It lowers my heart rate and evens it out by blocking the action of adrenaline in my sympathetic nervous system."

"Couldn't you guess?"

"I've never taken two at the same time." I think for a minute. Years ago, my doctor told me that someone else he was treating with beta-blockers had the bright idea that, if one tablet per day was good, two would be better. So I got the don't-do-that lecture.

"From things my doctor said, an extra dose would probably cause fatigue and dizziness, blurred vision, and shortness of breath. Then, because the medicine depresses your heart rate, if there was *more* drug working its way through the bloodstream, you might end up with bradycardia—that's a seriously low heartbeat—and *that* can lead to fainting or even heart failure." My last words trail slower and slower as it dawns on me what Nadia is asking.

"This is the key," Nadia says. "We have to find a way to get your pills into their bodies. How many do you have?"

Just *thinking* about giving up my lifeline elevates my heart rate. "Twenty," I lie, knowing I have one more than that.

"How many people would that knock out? How many could we disable, like giving them a sleeping pill?"

"I have no idea."

CHAPTER TWENTY-EIGHT

The truck bounces along. Lalla Yasmin fits an old-fashioned *niqab*-style veil for Fay, although the few exposed inches of her face still look awfully smooth and rosy for an elderly woman. Conversation falters as we each gaze into a pool of our internal reflections. Hamid continues to nap. The air becomes stale and hot.

"We're definitely southbound," Yasmin says. "The road toward Marrakech would have been winding into the mountains by now."

Meanwhile, I rack my brain for anything else I can remember about overdosing on a beta-blocker. I take a single hundred-milligram pill every morning. Rarely, like that panicky night at the hotel in Ouarzazate when Fay didn't return, I break a pill into bits and swallow a piece to lower my stress level. I've always assumed the dosage has more to do with the severity of the condition, not the body mass of the patient. I don't know whether my remaining pills would have any effect on our captors. If they'd incapacitate them. Or if they would kill.

Lalla Yasmin's wistful voice breaks into my thoughts. "Sometimes, they used to bring us couscous on Fridays."

"Couscous on Fridays?" Fay echoes.

"Yes, it depended on which soldiers were working in the kitchen. Often, though, they would send over a plate of Friday couscous."

"Is there something special about Friday?" Fay asks. "Gil never talked about that."

"It's a tradition here. On Fridays, shops close early and families gather together to eat couscous as a group. Now, here it is Friday afternoon—and the second day of Eid al-Adha. I wonder if there will be sheep's head couscous for dinner tonight."

Friday first makes me think of Izri. Since he hasn't heard from me, this is the day he's supposed to notify the consulate—although it's probably too late to do any good. My trail will end at Taghabene. Ahmed might've taken pity on me, but I doubt he admitted that to Mr. Ray-Ban or the others. And if Gil ever finds someone else to reach the base Mohammed told him about, we'll be long gone.

But *Friday* jogs another memory, too. "I heard about couscous on Fridays at a restaurant last week. The owner's wife told me the best couscous always comes from the kitchen of a Moroccan woman and Fridays are the days she makes the most elaborate couscous. In fact..." A risky idea takes shape, and I slow my words so much that the women are staring at me. "*In fact*, Fatima said to me, 'Next Friday, wherever you are, you must eat homemade couscous.'" I look around. "Do you think these new guards know your routine at the barracks?"

"Probably not," Yasmin says. "Army. Police. Totally different branches of security."

"What if we offer to make couscous? Last night you said you and Nadia cooked for the soldiers when you were first sent to the base."

"But that only lasted—"

"I know, but *these* men don't. If they think they can get a good home-cooked meal on a Friday evening, we might just get our chance."

"Will we even be in the kind of place that has a kitchen?" Fay asks. "They might stick us in a cell and lock us in."

"Then we use candy and string and the knife." Yasmin's smile doesn't reach her eyes. "But prisoners are often responsible for their own food in this country. Qasim, when he became incensed about the shameful situation in the Western Sahara prison camps, told me in great detail about the conditions in those places. Those without resources died of starvation. Or they died for their shoes or for sitting in the shade when someone larger or more ruthless desired it."

Nadia has shifted gears since her explosions of the morning. No more blindly lashing out. She's committed to escape and immediately grasps the idea. "So we'll go in assuming we have to make their dinner, not like we're accustomed to being locked away. And we make them a delicious and very relaxing couscous. Oh, Julie." Her massive exhale becomes a whoop of joy. "Let's try it."

* * *

We have about ten minutes' warning. The truck slows and turns onto a local street. The piping sounds of children calling alert Hamid. His eyes crinkle in confusion. He's four years old, I've learned, a year younger than Molly—a boy who's never seen another child. I can't fathom the unimaginable weight fifteen years of isolation has meant for Yasmin and Nadia, but for Hamid, it has been forever.

Fay takes charge. "Are we agreed to try to get away tonight?"

"I think this is our best opportunity," Lalla Yasmin says. "Unless they plan to keep us here"—her expressive hands indicate *wherever here is*—"for some days. We'll likely be at the camp in the desert with one more day of travel. Two at the most. We can't wait for rescue. In the desert, it will be impossible to escape; here, we have a chance."

"Nadia?"

"Yes." Firmly.

"Julie?"

I'm in way over my head. While I'm grateful to Fay for guiding our energy into actual plans, I'm just plain scared. I don't want to die. A slow death of starvation or abuse is dreadful to contemplate, but if I give up my atenolol and we don't reach safety within a day or two, my heart will begin to pulse out of control. Although the last time it happened was decades ago, I still remember the uncontrollable pounding in my chest, my heart quivering and rippling, the waves of nausea, and finally unconsciousness.

"Julie?"

Yasmin stares solemnly. It's so easy to read the progression of her thoughts in the flicker of her eyes. She understands the magnitude of what they're asking, but she also knows her daughter has reached the breaking point. Nadia herself gapes at me in wide-eyed horror. Her life of deprivation and powerlessness, bottled up for so many years, is about to boil over. She would die and take Hamid—and the rest of us—along with her before she'll allow him to arrive at the camp.

There's only one thing I can say. "Yes."

CHAPTER TWENTY-NINE

We lurch out of the truck, stiff and disoriented. The first thing I notice is how sweet and fresh the air smells, so unlike our stinky sweaty selves. We find ourselves in an enclosed courtyard, similar to the one where the desert soldiers deposited us in the morning—a two-story cinderblock square about forty feet across, long ago painted in drab browns and greens. Where there were lush scarlet bougainvilleas in the morning, however, here are only bedraggled dusty bushes. The ground isn't cobbled, merely packed dirt. A disused octagonal fountain, now littered with empty soda cans and candy wrappers, occupies the center of the courtyard.

There are doors on each wall. I imagine offices behind the doors, desks, filing cabinets. Interrogation rooms. Cells. I look up at the second floor. After hours in the dim van, the square of bright blue sky blinds me. My headache comes back instantly. Nadia, however, goes right to work.

She bows to the men. *"Assalamu alaikum."* A slight change in her demeanor—a curtain dropping behind her eyes, a vacuous set to her mouth, the submissive tilt to her head—transforms her into a deferential underling. A placidity I would not have thought possible stills her body. Only her hands, clenching and unclenching behind her back, betray her. Ignoring our police driver and his assistant, she unerringly isolates the boss of this place, an older man in yet another uniform, this time khaki. "We ask your permission to clean our hands and pray before beginning to prepare your meal. The drive here has been long and hot, but we know you must be getting hungry."

Lalla Yasmin hangs back with us. Sweat has dripped down the side of her face etching rivulets of dirt onto her wrinkles; fuzzy white hairs escape from her headscarf. Fay stands between us, her hands clutching ours for reassurance.

At Nadia's words, a glance travels between the police drivers and these new soldiers.

"Colonel Adnane?" inquires the big policeman, the one I instinctively fear.

The old man Nadia spoke to clicks his heels together and bows perfunctorily. "*À votre service.*"

The policeman says indifferently, "Use them however you wish, Colonel. My orders are to leave them with you overnight and return to load them into the truck at first light. Meanwhile, you might as well enjoy yourselves. Dinner . . . and anything else you desire. I may return later myself." He pokes his companion in the ribs. "Eh, Abdul? What do you think about that?" Turning back to the colonel, he says, "Have a nice dinner. Perhaps you'll see us later."

The chill begins at *use them.* The curl to his lips when he said it left little doubt what he meant. I'm shaking so hard I have to lean against the truck for support. Fay has gone completely white. She moans softly. "It'll be okay," I say under my breath. "We'll just have to make sure our plan works."

Dinner turns out to be the easy part. There *is* a sheep's head, a second-day-of-Eid delicacy that leaves me nauseated, and enough vegetables to make what Yasmin says is the ultimate festive couscous.

From the top shelf in the kitchen, Yasmin pulls down a huge pot that she separates into bottom and top sections. It's like a double boiler except the upper pot's base isn't solid. Instead, it's pocked with small holes like a sieve.

"It's a *couscoussier*," Yasmin says when she sees me looking. "The vegetables cook in broth on the bottom and the steam rising up cooks the couscous grains in the upper chamber."

Nadia channels all her anger and her fears into the peremptory manner of a woman trying to get dinner on the table in time. She bosses us all around—you chop the carrots, you cut the zucchini and cabbage. To her mother, Nadia says, "Get the spices together for the sauce, but don't make too much. We'll keep the drug as concentrated as possible."

There's not enough room in the kitchen for all of us and someone has to keep an eye on Hamid, who's spied, of all things, a kitten. Where Fay and I reduced him to a mute shadow hiding behind his mother, the tiny fur-ball draws him like a magnet. The kitten, a calico with a creamy face and black and orange whorls over her back, delights in the game. She stays in one spot, twitching her long tail, until Hamid draws near. Then, with a come-hither toss of her head, she bounds away, Hamid in hot pursuit.

I become the designated babysitter so his mother and grandmother can concentrate on the meal. In his quest for the kitten, Hamid guilelessly pries into every nook and cranny. Moroccans, everyone says, love children and freely indulge them. These soldiers permit Hamid, a little boy with a lopsided haircut, to wander about the courtyard pursuing a cat from one hiding place to another, clearly not a threat to anyone.

Hamid dances around wide-eyed and grinning, like my kids on Christmas morning. The kitten is probably the most fun he's ever experienced in his young life. For Hamid, today has meant more attention, more people, more *things* than he's ever seen at once. More firsts: his first look outside the locked room he knew as home, his first car ride, his first flush toilet, his first pet. Probably his first haircut, too, but with a young child's resilience, he's shaken off his agony of the morning. Where I might expect him to be bewildered—I am—or scared—we all are—he remains secure in the cocoon of love around him. Hamid has no idea what's in store for us. And none of us has the slightest intention of letting it happen.

I limp along in Hamid's wake. It's been forty-eight hours since the camels spooked me. This morning, Yasmin unwrapped my ankle and helped me bathe from a bucket of warm water before reapplying the bandage. The swelling has receded, but it's still stiff and sore. I should wait one more day before doing range-of-motion exercises, but thinking about what lies ahead has me attempting calf stretches and heel raises.

Meanwhile, I study the details of the barracks as best I can. There are no windows to the outside, and the exterior door is secured from the inside with a heavy metal bar. When it lies across the door, no one can enter, a system more designed for keeping people out than holding them in. A speaker mounted to the side of the door serves as an intercom; anyone wanting to enter has to call to have the bar taken down. Next to the entrance on both sides are small, open storage rooms. One has taped boxes stacked in wobbly columns; the other contains cleaning supplies and a haphazard assortment of gear, most of which looks broken and discarded. The gray steel door on the left side of the courtyard opens into an office—desks, phones, and filing cabinets. Opposite the main entrance and open to the courtyard are a kitchen and dining area. The door on the right side of the patio is secured by a padlock and chain. Rows of weapons are visible through the wire mesh of the barred window set in the door. From each of the two rear corners, a flight of stairs leads up to the second floor, broad shallow steps of green and white octagonal tile fashioned into an intricate design.

One flaw with our plan is executing it so promptly. It isn't exactly a *flaw*—escaping immediately is crucial—but we haven't yet learned what sort of secure accommodation has been arranged for us.

What's upstairs? Bedrooms? Barracks? Jail cells? I want to get up there to see. Not alone—but if *Hamid* becomes curious, perhaps the men will go along. Maybe I can tempt the kitten to run up the stairs.

My babysitting role doesn't call for me to come too close to Hamid, but I get a chance to put my plan into action when, skipping after the cat, the boy falls and skins his knee on the hard-packed earth. He howls. Acting like it's the most natural thing in the world, I hobble over to Hamid. "*Pauvre petit, viens avec moi.*" I pick him up and carry him into the kitchen.

Over his sobbing, I whisper to Nadia that I want to look around upstairs. "Can I have a scrap of meat? I'm going to toss it as high up the stairs as I can. If I can entice that kitten into running up there, Hamid and I will follow and I can look around."

While Nadia chops off a few pieces of gristle, Yasmin says to me quietly, "I've ground the spices I need. In a minute I'll add them to the hot vegetable broth to make the sauce. We should put your pills in soon to give them time to dissolve. There are eight men stationed here, so that means about two and a half for each man."

"Oh." I squeeze my arms around my midsection. Too late to save out the pills I need for myself. Nothing I can do about that now, so I slowly untie the fabric that conceals my belongings. I bring out the bottle, twist off the top, and dump the pills into my palm.

All of them. Twenty-one round tablets and the piece left over from the night Fay didn't return.

Yasmin stares at the tiny white lifelines in my palm. "Have you taken what you need for yourself?"

"I took one at noon."

Two by two, she scoops the little pills from my palm to hers. "... sixteen, eighteen, twenty."

One pill and the piece remain in my hand. "Twenty for the sauce," Yasmin says. "I can't imagine one more or less will make much difference with these men, but it might for you. Keep these. You'll be saving our lives; we need to take care of you. In two days, we'll be somewhere where there's a doctor or—"

Yasmin doesn't complete the thought. We'll be safe or we'll wish we were dead.

Hamid is becoming restless. He wiggles free from his mother, and with a kiss, she sends him back out to the courtyard.

But it's all for naught. Although I get a chunk of meat onto the stairs and the kitten prances up to sniff, the second Hamid follows her, an older fellow who's sitting on a low step wrestling with something mechanical shoos him away. A second try has the same result. He's not permitted upstairs.

* * *

The muezzin begins his hi-fidelity call to prayer—*Allahu Akbar, Allahu Akbar, Allahu Akbar.* Dusk is approaching. The square of sky visible overhead fills with the cries of birds. They swoop and whirl above us before going home to roost. From the kitchen come smells of roasting meat. Almost time to eat.

The soldiers line up in the courtyard. Six men, many of whom followed us with their eyes and undoubtedly harbor carnal fantasies, stand shoulder-to-shoulder, heads bowed. At an unseen signal, their hands move to their ears, palms forward; then they place their folded hands at their bellies. They murmur as they bend forward, hands to toes, and then stand tall once more.

I slink into the dining room, a long narrow space next to the small kitchen. On one side are a dining table and chairs; on the other, sofas and easy chairs are grouped around a television set. Fay is setting the table. Only six places. "Nadia said there'd be eight men at dinner. What about the other two?"

Fay's free hand latches onto my wrist. "They just told me one man is sick today and won't be coming down for dinner. He's upstairs sleeping—their barracks *is* up there. The other man had two days off for Eid. He's on duty early tomorrow morning, so he'll be returning tonight, but he's not back yet." Our eyes meet briefly, anxiously. What if the sick man doesn't eat? What if the off-duty man shows up to find his comrades drugged? Not having any real idea of the strength required to knock someone out, I waver between hoping twenty pills will be powerful enough to knock everybody out—and fast—and hoping we won't actually kill anybody.

Yasmin eases over behind me and says quietly, "The way things usually work, Julie, the men will sit at the table and, unless they lock us up first, we'll stay in the kitchen to eat. Nadia has saved out a platter of food for us and a little sauce, not the doctored kind. That way, if they finish all their sauce and complain about not having enough, she can pour them the rest of ours. That will mean, of course, they've taken all of the drugs already."

I nod to show I understand.

"What did you discover upstairs?"

"Nothing." I try to be as quiet as she is. "Every time Hamid started up the stairs, a soldier sitting on the steps yelled at him. Do you think there are cells up there?"

She gives a listless lift to her shoulders. "I don't know, Julie. If we're locked in, we have one set of problems. If they keep us out here with them, we have another set. The soldiers here are lonely and bored—and that *connard* of a policeman not only put the idea in their head, he gave his blessing."

We glance over at the six unknown men rolling up their prayer rugs. Nadia walks out of the kitchen. "Dinner is served."

CHAPTER THIRTY

They lock us up.

As soon as Nadia announces the meal, the old guy in charge rattles off something fast in Arabic. The soldiers come to attention. Two stand guard around Nadia and me, while the others round up Yasmin and Fay. Fay is loading our plate of couscous. Yasmin returned to the kitchen to get our sauce bowl and a pitcher of water. More words fly through the air. The sauce is in a small plastic bowl, but they confiscate our forks. And the pitcher. Glass—also a weapon.

Nadia, her cheeks flaming red in what I know to be anger, stomps her foot.

Her mother intervenes before Nadia's temper throws a monkey wrench into our plan. "Please, *m'sieur*. It's been a long and dusty day. Can you find something to hold water for us?"

Meekness works better, but clearly the men are in a hurry to get to their own meal. The soldier dispatched into the kitchen returns with another plastic bowl into which he unceremoniously dumps the contents of the glass pitcher. The men form a square around us and, with Colonel Adnane leading the way, march us up the stairs by the kitchen and then along a wide passageway open to the central courtyard on one side. The interior wall is divided into three jail cells with doors of metal grillwork. We halt in front of the last iron-barred door. The colonel removes a large old-fashioned key ring from a hook on his belt and applies it to the door. It screeches open with a long ear-splitting reverberation.

"*À plus tard, mesdames.*" He bows us into our prison. *See you later.* We shuffle one after another into the empty room. Fay stumbles and falls sideways into the door, catching herself on the bars.

The men retreat down the corridor. While it appears they'll leave us alone for now, *à plus tard* expresses a different sentiment than *à demain*—see you tomorrow—and doesn't calm my fears. The noise of chairs scraping along tile and the chink of glasses being filled filters up from the courtyard.

"I managed to keep a few things," Nadia mutters with a contortion of her mouth that might be a tense grin. She lifts her skirts and pulls out a sharp knife and two forks.

Friday couscous—Fatima from the restaurant in Ouarzazate had it right: Nadia and Yasmin have created a meal fit for kings. I only wish the knot in my stomach could relax enough to enjoy it. Nadia passes the forks to Fay and me. She and Yasmin serve themselves and Hamid with small bites rolled around in their fingers. Perfectly cooked vegetables and a bite or two of mutton on a bed of fluffy round pale-yellow grains. The rich broth from steaming the vegetables and meat is seasoned with cinnamon, saffron, ginger, and coriander.

Our cell is ten feet square and totally empty except for a bucket in a back corner. No blankets; no light; one barred window high on the wall. Through it, wispy gray ostrich-tail clouds float by in a sky that has lost all its color. Soon it will be dark. The moon will rise later, I think, since it came up in the late afternoon and was high overhead when I went to sleep in the hut, three nights ago in the black desert.

Fay jumps up and peers through the bars the second our food is gone. "I can only see three of them. I can't tell if they all sat down to dinner."

From the bars on our cell, at the front left of the building, a sideways squint downstairs brings the closer end of the dining table into view. "They're eating hearty," she says with grim pleasure.

"Now, I suppose, we wait," Yasmin says.

"*Now*, we ought to refine our escape plans," says Fay, "so we can be ready when the time comes." She turns to me. "Do you have any idea how long this will take?"

"Fay, I don't even know *if* it will take. This is all wild guesswork on my part. Educated guesswork—but I've never set out deliberately to push the limits."

"Well, for my part," she says, "I stuck a hard candy into the door latch when we came in to keep the lock from going all the way in."

"That won't work," says Nadia.

"What?" It's a challenge to Nadia, not Fay asking for clarification.

"When the key turned, it shot a bolt out. The bolt might not be in all the way, but until the key turns it in the other direction, that piece of iron will hold in the position it's in now."

The truth of what Nadia said sinks in slowly. Our fanciful, brave talk of the afternoon now seems silly. We're going to incapacitate, perhaps kill, six—or seven or eight—men. And when morning comes, if not before, the police will arrive and—*Don't go there. They haven't returned yet.*

We still have time, time to concoct another plan, time to improvise. But no matter how hard I struggle to imagine a clever scheme that will free us, the voices of the men intrude.

Listen to the men downstairs.

"Nadia?" I ask. "Can you understand what they're saying down there?"

She takes my place at the door followed by Hamid, who's clutching at her skirts. "I can only hear the loud man sitting with his back to the opening. I think he's the same one who was harassing Fay in the kitchen. They're talking about a football match. I think it might be on later."

"What happened?" I ask Fay the second Nadia stops talking.

She shakes her head quickly, mouths *don't ask*, and looks away.

We have to get out of here.

"You know, that gives me an idea," Nadia says, "a dangerous idea, but it may be the only remaining way to get the door unlocked. The man from the kitchen—the one who was ogling Fay—his libido is tormenting him. What if we call to him and get him to come up here?"

"Absolutely not." Lalla Yasmin's eyes open wide. "You must not do that."

"We need to get that door open somehow."

Yasmin responds with a jerk of her head toward Hamid. "You cannot allow the little one to witness—"

"It's *Fay* he fancies."

"Nadia Ohana, I'm ashamed of you! She's your *sister*," Yasmin hisses. Then she switches to Arabic, which they've refrained from using as a courtesy to us. The women erupt into a protracted argument, all the more violent for being conducted in harsh whispers. Fay listens in wide-eyed panic, her head swiveling between the two.

After a few minutes, Nadia throws up her hands and turns her back on her mother.

"I reminded her that the key to unlock the door was in the hands of the commanding officer, *not* the underling whom she wished to entice," Yasmin says.

Thank God.

Nadia, having given way with ill-concealed bad grace, paces around the small enclosure. Every eighth step or so brings her to a wall or to the bars.

"Shhh," Fay whispers. "Someone's coming upstairs."

Like a game of Statues, we freeze in place, hardly daring to breathe. One man comes up the steps on the other side and walks along the far-side corridor to the middle door. He enters with a tray. They fixed a plate for their sick comrade. If he's awake to eat, that's one more taken care of.

A sudden burst of music and blaring voices. The men have turned on a radio or TV. When I take my turn at the door, the chairs at the dining table are empty. The men are on the other side of the room—invisible to us—where the sofas are. Flickering lights play on the dining room wall; they're watching television.

The TV show continues, a comedy judging by the raucous laugh track. The men have stopped speaking, or else we can no longer hear them over the noise of the television. The off-duty soldier hasn't rung to have the door unbarred. The sick one is still in his room, but we don't know if he's eaten anything.

Nadia elbows me out of the way, an exhausted Hamid clinging to her like a limpet. He's whimpering and pulling on his mother's hand, trying to get her attention, something he's not accustomed to lacking. "No noise from them?" Nadia asks me, ignoring Hamid's snuffles.

"Not for maybe ten or fifteen minutes."

"How long, do you think, since they ate?"

"Forty-five minutes, give or take."

"Hmm."

I know Nadia's going to ask me yet again if I don't have *some* idea how fast the pills would take effect when Hamid trips on her foot and goes sprawling—his head and one arm ending up outside the bars.

For a second, he's too surprised to cry out. We all stare at him, speechless. The bars are adult-sized. Little Hamid fits between them. His face scrunches up, and his mouth opens wide; he's going to let out a howl of pain and frustration. Nadia pulls him back inside and presses him close to her. "Sh—sh—sh—" She's hugging and rocking. His cries disappear into her breasts. We four women sit silently in a circle that evokes last night's dinner.

"Nadia," says Yasmin, "this decision is yours. But Hamid is the one who can get us out of here."

Nadia wraps her arms more tightly around Hamid. "I need time to think."

CHAPTER THIRTY-ONE

amid's sobbing tapers off. He relaxes in his mother's arms, and eventually he sleeps. The last of the light fades from the sky. My friends' faces blur into the fuzzy chiaroscuro of old photographs. No one speaks.

Downstairs, aside from the laugh track and flickering lights from the television, all is still and silent. Then there's a resounding clunk, like a heavy weight dropping, and the unmistakable crash of glass breaking on tile. Fay's hand reaches for mine and squeezes it. When the echoing aftermath dies away, everything is quiet again.

"Here's what we'll do," Nadia says. "Hamid needs to sleep for a while. He's too tired to help us now. While he's sleeping, Julie and Fay, you put on your robes and hijabs. Take turns, so that one of you is always keeping a lookout downstairs and on the door of the room where the sick man is. *Maman*, see if you can come up with something to quiet the door hinge noise and listen in case someone starts talking. I'll think of how to explain to Hamid about getting the key."

* * *

In the end, she makes it into a game. Nadia wakes Hamid and suggests they play *cache-cache*, what French-speaking children call hide-and-seek.

She has him close his eyes, and she hides one of his crayons. There's no good place to hide it in our barren cell and, even though the light is dim, Hamid has no trouble finding the crayon.

"This isn't much fun for you," she says after a few lightning-fast finds. "It would be so much better if we could play somewhere else. Don't you think so, too?"

Hamid agrees enthusiastically. Then Nadia has *a great idea*—in the breathless way of cajoling mothers worldwide: "Why don't we play *downstairs*?" Nadia pauses a beat or two while Hamid absorbs that possibility, then muses aloud, "I wonder if that kitten is still down there."

Hamid's face glows in the low light. "Can I play with the kitty again?"

"Before we look for the kitty, we'll play *cache-cache* one more time. Are you ready for a really hard game of *cache-cache*?"

"Yes, *maman*."

"In this hard kind of *cache-cache*, there are two different rules." Nadia tickles his nose with her index finger. "The first rule is to be very quiet. Can you do that?"

"Quiet, like the little cat," he whispers, down on all-fours and squirming like he could twitch his tail.

"Good boy, Hamid. That's exactly right. The second rule is to come—quietly, like the kitty—back here as fast as you can as soon as you find the hidden prize. But—" Another tap on the tip of his nose. "It doesn't count if you make any noise at all. Okay?"

"Yes, *maman*." He's jiggling and twisting, ready to be off.

"Let me tell you what the prize is. It's a large ring with keys on it." She picks up Yasmin's keys, the ones they rescued before leaving the desert compound, and shows them to Hamid. "Keys like these, like *mémé*'s, and some that are even bigger."

He nods his head solemnly.

"Now. The last thing. Because this is a hard game in a new place, you get one special hint. Here's the hint: the ring with the keys on it is on the belt of a man sleeping downstairs in the big room next to the kitchen."

Hamid thrusts his thumb into his mouth.

"It's okay, my dear, because they're all sleeping now. The noise in the room is coming from the box with pictures that move. I've told you about *les télévisions*, don't you remember?"

His thumb doesn't leave his mouth, but his mouth opens and his eyes grow wide. Although Hamid is clearly still anxious, Nadia's stories about the box with moving pictures must've been intriguing.

"But it's best to be sure about the men," his mother adds, "so peek around the corner first. Like a little cat." She tousles his curls. "And come right back here to *maman* if they're awake. Can you do that?"

He vigorously bobs his head up and down.

"Do you want me to explain the game one more time?" Huge shake, no. "All right then," Nadia says. "I'm going to count from the time you leave. Let's see how long it takes for you to find the key ring and bring it back."

*   *   *

How long is exactly two hundred and fifty-four of the longest seconds of my life. Hamid padded away so quietly that his footfalls were imperceptible after a few seconds. We stood on the locked side of the bars, powerless to come to his aid, and watched Hamid disappear down the shallow steps, his distorted shadow dancing high on the wall. An interminable lacuna until the shadow reappeared downstairs in the dim light of the courtyard. His tiptoeing to the open archway and stealthy glimpse inside. The prancing, catlike steps as he skipped into the lion's den. That's when I closed my eyes and said a silent prayer.

Hamid's feet come to a sliding stop. He holds up the ring and says in a triumphant stage whisper, "How fast was I?"

He wiggles inside the bars and presents the key ring to his mother. "I didn't see the kitty. I want to play again so I can look for the kitty."

Nadia soothes Hamid with the promise of another game. "Later," she explains, "once we get out of this room." And Fay and I get to work on the cell door. I angle my arm outside the bars and insert the key. Because of the awkward angle, I need Fay's help to hold it firmly in place while I twist. The lock gives way with an impressive thwack. The combined pressure of my weight and Fay's leaning against the door causes it to jerk outward. In a slapstick moment, our heads clunk as we spontaneously pull back to keep it from squealing all the way open.

Earlier, Yasmin and I greased the accessible parts of the hinges with my lipstick. Now that the door can move, I swiftly work in the rest of the lipstick while Fay swivels the door back and forth in tiny increments. It's squeakier than we hoped, but a vast improvement. When it opens wide enough for us to pass through, we tiptoe out, keeping to the shadowed inner side of the passageway. Nadia holds Hamid, who's fidgeting, trying to get down to search for the kitten.

Born of a dreadful curiosity, we each take a turn peering into the dining area. The table is a jumble of dirty dishes, cigarette butts, and half-finished glasses of tea. The couscous platter sits empty in the center. The men moved across the room to the sofas and easy chairs by the television before succumbing. Most collapsed with their heads lolling on couch cushions, their mouths hanging open. One toppled from his chair and is curled into a ball on the floor. I was expecting snores, but under the chatter of a news program now airing, all is deathly silent.

Nadia doesn't stop at the doorway. She hands Hamid off to her mother and walks over to an easy chair. The man who sat by the door at dinner, the one Nadia said had bothered Fay, is sprawled with his head sideways at an awkward angle and his right hand extended toward the floor. There's a pile of ashes on the tile floor inches below his drooping fingers where a burning cigarette must've slipped from his hand. Nadia looks down at him, her face an expressionless mask. Just as I form the mental question *what the hell does she think she's doing*, Nadia moves her hand to her pocket and brings out the sharp knife she stole from the kitchen. She raises it.

Her mother is at her side in a flash. I don't believe Yasmin says a word, but with a smooth motion, she whisks the knife from Nadia's uplifted hand at the same time as she presses Hamid into Nadia's other arm. Like a sleepwalker abruptly wakened, Nadia looks confused, but she allows herself to be led out.

Fay is examining the keys Hamid took. "No car keys," she mutters. "Let's see if they keep them in the office."

Fay and I go through the door on the left. Three desks. Phones. Filing cabinets. Nothing as obvious as a peg on the wall with keys dangling. Nothing useful in the unlocked desk drawers. Fay tries the commandant's keys. The third one she tries gets us into the locked drawer. Still no car keys.

By now, I'm bouncing from one foot to the other; it's all I can do not to run out the door.

"Maybe they don't have any vehicles?" Fay massages the back of her neck.

"More likely they're locked in a nearby garage with the keys kept there, ready for use." I pull Fay from the room. "Listen—we need to get out of here. Keep the keys. Maybe one of them opens a garage outside."

"Good call."

And so off across the dusty courtyard to the front gate we troop. We remove the iron bar, open one side of the big double doors, and walk out. Since we can't replace the bar from outside, Fay wedges a few stray rocks at the bottom to keep it from swinging open.

I take a deep breath, then exhale and tip my head back to look at the stars. Free.

Crunching footsteps come up the path.

CHAPTER THIRTY-TWO

A khaki-uniformed man carrying a small duffel bag materializes in the gloom. He's broad-shouldered, with a bulbous nose and closely cropped hair. All this I see in the split second before he calls out, "Who are you? What are you doing here?"

"Run!" Yasmin barks, and we scatter.

I haven't gone far before I realize Yasmin stayed behind. I turn. The knife flashes—once, twice. The man falls, slow-motion, in a heap at her feet, his pale shirt already discolored with a spreading stain. Yasmin looks down briefly, the knife she took from Nadia a bloody extension of her hand, and then drifts toward the inky wall shadow where we clustered. "The returning soldier," she mumbles needlessly. "He would not have let us go." Then, looking directly at Nadia, she adds, "It's far better that this be on my conscience than on yours." And she walks on, away from the building, away from us.

We stagger after her. The army post occupies the end of a short street, no more than a truncated alleyway. Yasmin comes to a standstill at the cross street. Not knowing anything about this place, the rest of us glance at one another with indecision.

Wherever we are, the town is shutting down for the evening. Across the street, a shopkeeper cranks down the aluminum awning. Next door, a waiter stands motionless in a café doorway, arms crossed and hands folded into the crooks of the opposite elbows, a blue and white striped towel draped over his shoulder. Four old men remain on the café's patio, coffee cups and cigarette packs littering the table. They're playing a board game and are so close the thwack of the tiles they slap down sounds like gunshots.

Nadia, Fay, and I instinctively move back a step into the darkness. Lalla Yasmin, her pale cheeks shining in the glow of a streetlight, stays rooted where she stopped, so Nadia reaches out and pulls her back. The street is empty save for a group of adolescent boys roughhousing in a park, standing on stone benches and jumping down on each other.

Behind us, the soldier is a darker lump on the dark ground. "None of those gates in the walls around the barracks are wide enough for a car to go through." I keep my voice in a low whisper. "So their vehicles—if any—aren't around here."

"We'll have to keep going on foot." Fay's whispering, too. "I'm almost positive the last turn the truck took was a left. We only drove a short distance after that before the driver got out to ring the buzzer." She gestures off to the right. "So the main road is probably that way. What do you think?"

I don't remember, and Nadia says she doesn't, either. Yasmin's eyes are dilated, her face ashen, and her breathing shallow and rapid, like she's gone into shock. I can't keep my eyes off her bloody robe and the knife, which still dangles from her hand.

I wish I knew the words to console Yasmin, but she's departed for a star light-years away, and I'm reluctant to intrude.

But *Nadia* isn't. With tenderness I've never before witnessed, she curls her free arm around her mother's neck and hugs her close. Cheeks touching, their closed eyes brim with unshed tears. Then Yasmin weeps in earnest, and the tension drains from her body. She leans into her daughter, taking huge gasping sobs. Nadia murmurs quietly. When the two women break apart, the knife is in Nadia's hand. She heaves it over the wall and wipes her hands on the insides of her loose kaftan sleeves.

Fay takes a heaving breath, like she's just finished a 200-meter free-style. "Let's get away from here as fast as we can," she says. "We'll turn down this street, the way we think leads to the highway. Perhaps a shop sign or direction markers will give us an idea where we are. Keep your eyes open."

We slip along silently, walking two by two. I'm cold with dread. I keep replaying the scene in front of the barracks: the man appearing like a ghost in the mist, his loud ringing voice when he confronted us, the look on his face—yes, he *would* have stopped us—the knife, the blood.

The soldier's challenge was probably loud enough to have been heard inside the army post. If the sick soldier didn't eat his doctored couscous, he might already have come downstairs to see what the shouting was all about.

Yasmin is soon out of breath, and we stop to let her rest. Even though we're horribly conspicuous on the almost-deserted street, I'm glad of the break, too. My ankle aches, and the flapping robe makes my progress awkward. And Nadia, with Hamid squirming in her arms and begging to be let down to find the kitten, must be exhausted. When we stop, she perches him atop a retaining wall—but keeps tight hold of him. By then, we've passed most of the businesses and are in an area of urban housing.

We're free, yes, but I don't know how long our freedom will last unless . . . I tell my companions what's topmost on my mind. "We need to get out of town. Before anyone comes looking for us. Walking toward the highway is a sure way to call attention to ourselves. Yasmin is already wiped out; Nadia can't carry Hamid all night. I don't know how long I can keep putting weight on my sore ankle. And someone is bound to spot us. Even if they don't, what the hell are we going to do when we get to the highway—hitchhike?" I shake my head. We need to scram, preferably in a nondescript car. "You stay here and stay out of sight. I'm going to look for a car."

"What did you have in mind?" Fay might as well have asked, *What the fuck are you talking about?*

"I was thinking that, in a sleepy little town like this, some people probably leave their cars unlocked. Maybe even with the keys in them."

"What if there's a *gardien*?"

"A *gardien* is good—as long as he hasn't come on duty yet or is patrolling elsewhere. When people think they're protected, they get careless. The moon's not up yet, so it's pretty dark out, and I'll be discreet, don't worry."

It takes a few more minutes of convincing. The absence of reasonable alternatives works its magic, however; so, leaving my companions in an alley tucked behind a barrier of packing crates, I set out on my mission.

We've reached a hilly area of narrow attached houses fronting streets lined with parked cars. I hope I look innocuous in my faded robes, a gimpy servant woman shuffling along the sidewalk—not a threat to steal a car. If I can't find a car with keys, I *could* try hot-wiring one, although what little experience I have with that is a dim—and embarrassing—memory from my long-ago teenage past.

I go up one street and down the next, crisscrossing the neighborhood. The fancy Mercedes and BMWs are not only locked, they have glowing lights indicating equally fancy security systems. The trucks and vans and mid-size cars are not always locked, but I don't spot any keys. I stop at likely vehicles and pretend to rest—only half of it is pretend—feeling around on the tops of the tires, in wheel wells, and inside bumpers to discover the hiding place of some lazy soul who's simply left his keys in a handy spot.

If I can't find a car to drive in the few streets remaining, I'll have to go back to one of the unlocked sedans and pray that I remember the trick to hot-wiring. Finally, though, I locate an old blue truck near the top of the hill with the key lying on the dashboard. It's rather dilapidated, with one headlight taped together and rusted-out floor panels, but the tires look fine and the lights in the closest houses are dark.

A wider circuit unearths the *gardien*, a man with a watch cap jammed over grizzled hair, limping like me while he ambles along, peering into windows and stooping to pick up roadside trash. His route includes several streets.

"Found one," I tell my friends after I trudge back down the hill to them, "but I need help. The parking space is so tight I'll have to go back and forth a few times to angle out of it."

Even though he's had a couple of naps, the long and confusing day—topped off with the loss of his kitty—has sent Hamid into a downward spiral. His lower lip juts and one foot keeps poking his mother in the stomach as she tries unsuccessfully to keep him quiet.

"Hey, Hamid, if I can borrow your mother for a few minutes, we're going to take a ride in a truck. This one's going to have the top open so you can see the stars. Want to go for a ride?" Hamid blinks a few times and an almost-smile blossoms—interested enough, I think, to proceed. "If you stay here with your grandmother, we'll go get the truck for you."

That has to be the other part of the plan because Yasmin isn't in any shape to be walking around. She holds out her arms, and Hamid settles onto her lap. Fay, Nadia, and I return to the truck, timing it to arrive after the *gardien* passes by and turns the corner.

"It's too dangerous to start the truck here because it'll take a while to wiggle it out of this space," I whisper. "I don't want the *gardien* to turn back to check or the owner to glance out his window when he hears the engine starting. We'll roll it down the hill first."

For once grateful for the periodic screwups that defined my teenage years—like a dead battery at three in the morning when I was supposed to be home, sleeping in my own bed and not out with a jug of wine and some sketchy friends—I release the hand brake and turn the key to *on*. With the clutch depressed, I put the truck into neutral and cut the wheel sharply. It takes four back-and-forth maneuvers with the others pushing, first in one direction and then the other, to clear the parking space and get the truck out into the street. Once free, I point the truck down the hill, gaining speed as I descend. Close to the main street, I hit the brakes to let my friends catch up.

"Stay out of sight in the truck bed until we're out of town." I tear off the uncomfortable scarf and cover my short hair with an old St. Louis Cardinals baseball cap that was sitting on the gearshift.

I start the engine and cruise into the alley behind the row of stores where we left Yasmin and Hamid. Nadia jumps down to take Hamid from her mother and lifts him over the tail gate. She and Fay help Yasmin in. After they clamber into the back, I put the truck in gear again and drive onto the main street. All is still tranquil, and I pray no alarm will sound until we're far, far away.

The built-up area becomes suburban—bigger residences surrounded by razor-wire fences, many with their own personal *gardiens* hunched on upturned crates against the wall, keeping watch on the street. Watching us as we pass. And the unknowns pile up again: If the watchers know the man who owns this little truck . . . if they wonder where he's going . . . if they see the cap and assume the owner is driving. Or if—already—they know I'm an impostor.

CHAPTER THIRTY-THREE

I drive on. Houses become more widely spaced; then empty lots predominate. After a few miles, I reach a larger road. We didn't see any road signs in town, but here at the crossroads an arrow pointing to the left says *Treyfia 13 km* and one pointing right *Mrimina 46 km*.

Geez. A highway, directional signs, our own transportation—*I wonder if I have a road map in here.* I riffle through the glove box, but our luck doesn't run to that much of a miracle. I hop out of the cab, and we have a conference at the back of the truck. "Anybody know where we are?"

Nadia and Fay both shake their heads.

"Yasmin?" I touch her shoulder to get her attention when she doesn't respond, careful not to stare at the red blotches dotting her kaftan. She's been our unofficial geographer all day, and I hope she can give us a clue to our whereabouts.

"Lalla Yasmin," I repeat. "Do you have any idea where we are?"

I'm about to give up hope of her answering—we'll have to wing it—when she begins a tentative recitation, slowly gaining steam. "Well, the town the army people drove us to this morning must've been M'hamid. That's where the soldiers from the outpost go on their days off. It's the only place that fits. We took the highway—that would've been the N9—north from there but turned off onto one of the roads that run southwest to the coast."

"And then we drove—what?—a couple of hours?" Fay asks.

I shrug. My watch, attached to the strap of my backpack, disappeared when the soldiers took it.

Yasmin seesaws her head. She might be listening to an inaudible melody. "You know, when I was younger, there was talk of building a road through the mountains to the Western Sahara, but planning stopped because the rough terrain would've made it exorbitantly expensive. Instead, they widened and improved the existing road, which runs along the coast."

Fay picks up the thread when Yasmin falls silent. "So, since we were heading for the Western Sahara, they were most likely driving toward the coast. If so, it doesn't matter, then, exactly *where* on the road we are. Driving west should get us to the Atlantic Ocean; east, back to the desert. Next question—which way should we go?"

If I expected dissension or even discussion, I would have been flat-out wrong. As one, the other women opt for the coast. I understand their reasoning: inland means being hemmed in by mountains and desert, being trapped between a closed border and the Atlas Mountains. The Atlantic coast, on the other hand, is dotted with cities and towns, full of tourists and modern amenities—like telephones, I'm thinking—and it's home to several international airports *and* to the American consulate.

The rental car, however, with my spare bottle of atenolol and the rest of our possessions, is tucked away in a remote village on an unmarked road between the mountains and desert. *First things first.* It will probably be faster and definitely less conspicuous to get a new prescription in a big coastal city than to try retracing my steps to Izri's village.

"Let's hit the road." I'm all at once in a furious rush to be away. "See the moon? It's rising now. So, if that's east, it would put *west*, the coast, in the direction of Mrimina. Let's give that a try first."

"When we get moving," Fay says, "there should be those white kilometer markers by the side of the road. I've seen them on all the other highways. That'll tell us how far it is to more distant points and, if they're counting down, we'll know we're going the right way."

"So what cities on the coast should we be looking for?"

"Agadir," says Yasmin promptly. "Or if we've already traveled farther south, there are Tiznit and Guelmim."

"Let's go," I repeat.

When I pivot to get back in the driver's seat, Fay tugs my arm. "Wait. Want to flip a coin to see who takes the first turn driving?"

That's a sweet reminder from Fay about our shared past. While I'm sure I look as bedraggled as she does, I'm a much better driver, so I say, "Nah, that's okay," making an effort to sound less bone-weary than I am and to disguise the nervous quaver in my voice. "I'll drive. Who wants to come inside with me and navigate?"

Nadia gives a minuscule shake of her head and tips it slightly toward her mother. Lalla Yasmin is once again standing apart, looking disoriented. Nadia steers her mother toward the truck bed. "We'll watch the stars together."

* * *

After Nadia, Hamid, and Yasmin pile back into the truck bed, I accelerate onto the highway. In the blackness of night, all I can see is the narrow lane illuminated in the headlights' glare—a dark ribbon unfurling ahead with a white line running down the middle.

Fay has scooted as close as she can to me, and I'm glad for her warmth. Both our bodies are shaking. Too much adrenaline is coursing through me—decisions made, roads not taken, the terrors of the day, the body in a heap on the ground—but too little atenolol remains. I don't dare take any of it now.

"You and me on the road again, Julie," Fay whispers.

I don't know what road she's remembering. I remember an unmarked road somewhere near Austin that led to a honky-tonk where we boogied arm-in-arm in our matching red dresses. I remember the sandy track to the ocean in Belize and how our swim fins kicked in rhythm when we dove the reef that day—but we've never been *anywhere* like this road before.

I'm still lost in that reverie when Fay yells, "Stop. There's a marker."

I'm a hundred yards down the road before I can slow the truck. I reverse until we get back to the marker and train the headlights on faint black lines on white stone: *Agadir 388 km*. Whew. My breath catches; my eyes fill with tears. *We're going in the right direction. One hurdle down.*

"You ought to slow down," Fay says as I wrench the truck back onto the highway.

It's a crucial reminder. I don't want to jeopardize our escape, but creating distance between us and the dead soldier consumes me.

"W-what in the world are we going to do?" My voice quivers. "Yasmin just stabbed a man, for crying out loud. I stole a truck. If anyone spots us—or sees this truck and knows it's been stolen . . ." I give up trying to formulate the complete thought. Fear is rendering me inarticulate.

Fay links her arm through mine like the night we danced in our red dresses. "You're doing great. Driving toward the coast is the only thing that makes sense. I'll call Gil when we reach Agadir. Have him set wheels turning to get us to safety. Or—if it gets to be morning and there's a place with stores open before we hit the coast, I'll call from wherever and we'll drive on. But at the rate you're going, that won't be an issue."

Another pointed warning. I ease back the pressure on the accelerator. Then I see the man walking up the path, the look on his face, the thud when he fell, the blood on Yasmin's hands. Fear wins; my foot presses down harder again.

We check the markers twice more to be absolutely certain we're going west. Keeping the truck pointed at the road's center line provides the mental focus that keeps my panic at bay. As Fay said, we're doing the only thing that makes sense. We're free, we have transportation, and I'm going to get us to Agadir as fast as I can.

Then what?

I think about what Fay said earlier. "What can Gil do from the States?"

"Well, we don't have money or credit cards, and we're going to have to run under the radar. Gil's in a far better position to organize, make calls, reservations—whatever it takes."

"Whatever it takes. I like the sound of that."

Fay angles her head to look out the back window.

"How're they doing?"

"Lying on their backs, holding hands. I think Hamid is asleep again, but Nadia and Yasmin seem to be hypnotized by the stars whizzing by." Fay's voice becomes husky with emotion. "I promise you, Julie, I'll do everything I can to get you home safely."

"Them, too," I say. If Yasmin and Nadia are recaptured, their lives will be forfeit—or will become a living hell. And I refuse to think about what might happen to Hamid. They *cannot* remain in Morocco. Having come this far, Gil's family needs to go home to him and heal.

Fay nods. "All of us."

I'm still driving too fast. The headlights of the truck are stuck in low-beam and the highway is narrow with eroded edges and steep shoulders. Hairpin turns through rugged mountain passes alternate with boring stretches of lumpy valley.

We're heading for the coast, for airports, for home.

I found Fay, we got away from our captors, and we're going home.

We fly past sleeping Mrimina in the blink of an eye. All quiet. Then the markers count down the miles to Tissint. Tissint, when it flashes by, is bigger; the mountains higher and nearer. No activity. The Big Dipper rises over the mountains and pirouettes. Orion flickers on the other side.

I drive for two hours before the truck runs out of gas.

CHAPTER THIRTY-FOUR

We stand in a circle by the side of the road.

"We have to hide the truck," Fay says. "If the police make a connection between our escape and the missing truck, I don't want them to know we continued on foot from here."

I lean against the truck's still-warm hood. When the engine started sputtering, I managed to pull to the side of the travel lane before it died. All around us is lumpy scrub desert. "How can we possibly hide it in this empty countryside?"

But, once again, Fay is creative—and self-effacing. "Let's reverse Julie's coup in getting the truck in the first place. We'll push it to the top of this hill and run it off the road, down into the brush. If they don't see the pickup, fine. But if they do, they'll have to go down and investigate. It'll buy us more time."

Three exhausted women and a little boy propelling an unwieldy truck uphill proves much harder to accomplish than Fay envisioned. The fat crescent moon, surrounded by a halo of fuzzy clouds, casts a diffuse light over the harsh terrain. While we strain and push, Fay steers the truck close to the edge. She jumps out of the cab at the brink and provides the extra bit of force that sends the truck crashing down the scarred, scrubby incline. It flips over with a satisfying bang and settles upside down in a stony crevice. If anyone in pursuit spots it, it'll take serious time to scramble down the rocky hillside, determine the truck is empty, and scour the area for us.

Traffic has been sporadic all night. We walk along the road, dropping into a gully that runs alongside when we hear the thrum of approaching vehicles, mainly overloaded long-distance trucks. The kilometer markers to the coast count agreeably downward—*Agadir 223 km, Agadir 222 km*—but precisely what lies between here and there, none of us has any idea. There are no towns or villages worth signposting on this lonely stretch of highway.

It becomes too dark to walk when the moon disappears behind the mountains. We've been trudging along a stretch of highway bordered on the left by a dry riverbed. Between the sometime-river and the road, a slender line of reeds sucks water from damp rocks. We make ourselves as comfortable as we can in the shelter of the reeds. Nadia finds a small pool of water and helps her mother wash the bloodstains from her dress. Then we nap until peachy light from the rising sun sets us in motion again. The morning light makes clear what we assumed in the dark: the landscape is entirely empty of signs of humanity. In many ways, it's like being back in the black desert, although the rocky countryside here is pink and there's a real road, not that I know what's around the corner. But this time I'm not alone.

Saturday, January 22, 2005
Agadir 216, Agadir 215. The sun rises higher and warms us. Dark bobbing shapes loom in the distance. Crows, I think, when I first notice them. As we draw closer, the forms resolve into a group of a half-dozen black-robed women ambling along the road, a gaggle of young children in tow.

"They've seen us," Yasmin says. "I don't think we have anything to fear from them, but it's time for you to get into character." Meaning me and Fay. Looking at Fay she says, "Your *niqab* is awfully ragged, but I doubt they'll be impolite enough to say anything. Just remember, you're an old woman, a pious widow who's taken a vow of silence. That's an unusual thing to do, but we can't pretend to be local—I don't have any idea where we are or what language they speak."

Then Yasmin bends down to speak to Hamid, explaining to me and Fay that she's telling him to keep quiet around the new people.

Nadia looks us over with a sour expression. "For heaven's sake, try not to show your soft little American hands. Here, rub this sand into them. That's more like it. Julie, you obviously can't talk either. And walk behind us. Let me see . . ." She has us turn around. She resets Fay's face-covering. Poor Fay is already grumbling. "I can't see anything."

Lalla Yasmin becomes our spokesperson. The rest of us lag behind while she goes over to greet the women. Returning, she says quietly, in French, that the women are mountain nomads journeying to a Saturday market to trade their handmade silver jewelry for blankets and food staples. "They speak a variant of Berber that's only used in the southern mountains," Yasmin says, "so it was normal for us to switch to Arabic, the market language. I told them we were hoping to get a bus back to Agadir after visiting a cousin with a new baby. They said lots of buses run along this road on market days."

And so we join their group.

"Safety in numbers," Fay mutters from behind her veil. It's true. The second we become part of the nomad group, we become invisible.

The women are simultaneously waiting for a bus and hoping for a lift to save money. They laugh and chatter as we amble along the road, their black dresses edged with a line of bright sparkles, their voluminous head coverings caught up in a wide belt at their waists. They have babies on their backs, one hand for a toddler, another to keep their long scarves in place, and a third—or so it seems—to steady the baskets balanced on their heads. Fay and I keep back; I link my arm through hers (no red dresses today), a lowly maid in charge of guiding an old lady. The children, including Hamid, run in circles kicking around a soccer ball.

Then an empty cattle truck chugs over the horizon. The women jump up and down, pumping their arms; the truck stops. We all climb aboard.

In less than thirty minutes, we're lost in a sea of veiled faces at the weekly market at Irherm, a nondescript jumble of brown houses straggling up the side of a brown mountain that rises up on the side of a brown riverbed. Famished, we fork over some of our precious cash for market food—roasted fava beans and corn—and meander with the same rhythm as genuine shoppers.

On a morning when I should be feeling triumphant—Fay and I are together; we've rescued ourselves and her new family from a desperate situation—instead, a heavy mantle of gloom weighs me down. We have miles to go before I'll consider us safe but no transportation and hardly any money. On the one hand, the market is a godsend. The constant activity shields us from the spotlight, but the crowded streets also mean little chance of stealing another car. And I need to get to Agadir before my pills run out—tomorrow.

In an effort to give myself a little wiggle room, I've taken only the broken piece today—this morning, while we were walking along the road. I'll leave the last whole atenolol for . . . afternoon? Evening? Tomorrow morning? I don't know how long I can hold out.

In the window of a café at the edge of the market, we see a placard identifying it as the bus stop. The posted fare to Agadir is fifty-five dirhams for adults, half-price for children. Fifty-five dirhams is about what I have—not quite seven dollars. We also see two *téléboutiques*, but both have long market-day lines straggling out the door so we walk on.

Because most rural women don't know French, we've been speaking little and then only in whispers. Fay suggests a walk to discuss our next moves. We take the road out of town up to a hillside tomb where we're alone and we sit, confident in our isolation, with the valley spread out at our feet.

"Money is the first thing," Lalla Yasmin says. "What do we have left?"

Pooling all that remains, we count one hundred and twenty-two dirhams—about half of what we need for bus fare into Agadir.

"Next," Yasmin says. "Do you think we can get through to Gildun from here?"

"Let's try." Fay pulls off the tight headscarf and lifts her hair away from her neck. "We're stuck here for now. We don't have enough money for a bus, and any truck driver who might give us a ride won't be leaving town until the market closes. I *really* want to hear Gil's voice and let him know that we're together and safe."

Safe? Good lord, Fay. I mean, okay, it was amazing how we all pulled together to get out of that cell and get away from town, but now we're on the run with personal enemies of the king. We incapacitated—possibly killed—a half-dozen soldiers last night. We're practically penniless in a small town in the middle of nowhere. And I have exactly one atenolol remaining. My despair intensifies.

Their chatter takes on the muffled echo-y quality of voices overheard in a distant corner of an empty train station. In my funk, I hear them hashing out plans to go into town to use the phone, thinking that the waning of the market will ease up demand on the town's phone capacity.

Then the conversation turns to how to proceed *after* alerting Gil.

"But without money or identity papers, we're going to need help to stay hidden for a while," Nadia says.

"I have relatives in Agadir—my cousin Hachim and his wife. They were close friends. Once upon a time." Yasmin's smile wavers, and she looks down at her feet. "I don't remember their address or phone number, but if we can find them, perhaps I could persuade them to let us stay while Gil is arranging things." Her next words show she's thinking along the same lines I am. "But—say we get to Agadir, say Hachim and Badra agree to hide us for a while and let us use their phone to stay in touch with Gildun—*then what*? How are we ever going to get past the long reach of the king's talons?"

Fay, oddly, began to smile a minute earlier when Nadia first brought up lack of money and papers. "I have a surprise," she says. "I brought a little gift for you, something you were supposed to get *after* your successful escape. I think this qualifies as the right time." She clears her throat with a theatrical flourish. "Do you remember what I'm wearing underneath this charming robe?"

"Your jeans, a filthy blue sweater, and a patchwork vest," I say.

"Correct." Fay nods. "And sewn inside my vest, which happens to be another Fay Lariviere original, I have three passports—one for each of you." She beams at her Moroccan family. "Gil had them made—don't ask me how! I was supposed to leave them with Mohammed, sealed in a package, without telling him what they were because Gil says bootleg passports are worth a lot of money. But Mohammed double-crossed me first, and so I still have them. As soon as we can get you to an airport, you are *gone*!"

Lalla Yasmin breaks out crying. Nadia hugs her mother, then—amazingly—Fay, while Hamid stares blankly at this incomprehensible display of female emotion.

They have a million questions, first being the one Fay told them not to ask.

"No, no, I don't know how he did it. And no, they aren't legitimate, but they're good. Gil says they're called one-use passports. Once they're in the system, they'll get digested and eventually spit out as fake. But all we need to do is get you to the States. We can deal with the rest from there."

"How did Gil know what we looked like?" Nadia asks.

"He didn't." Fay ducks her head and lets a curtain of hair fall around her face, almost concealing her embarrassment. "He started with the assumption that you'd had a . . . well, *difficult* number of years and would have aged without the benefit of healthy food or cosmetics, so he hired an artist and showed her the last photographs he had of you.

"Anyhow, the artist 'aged' you from those pictures, and Gil found models who resembled the drawings. From what I remember of the passport photos, they're pretty accurate. For Hamid, Gil said children grow so fast that a toddler photograph seldom looks much like the live four-year-old wiggling in line. He was confident an immigration agent wouldn't notice any discrepancies."

Lalla Yasmin is still too overcome to speak. She smiles through her tears and pats Fay's hand incessantly.

"I'll show them to you when we reach Agadir. For now, let's leave them hidden where they are."

"What about *your* passport, Fay?" Yasmin asks.

Fay swings her head slowly. "It was in my suitcase, so wherever Julie had to abandon the car, that's where it is."

"Oh no!" cries Yasmin. "We have to go get it!"

CHAPTER THIRTY-FIVE

"I'm a lot safer than you would be." Fay's words sound a lot braver than her hunched-over body language indicates. "All I need to do is lie low until you're in the States with Gil, beyond the reach of the king and his security force." That gnawing-cheek action again; Fay's nervous, all right, but hiding it well from the others. "Besides, your new passports give you different names; ours don't. And since they know our names, traveling with us would be dangerous. Without us, you'll be three anonymous French-Moroccan travelers. Oh—did I mention your passports are French?"

That was a smooth change-of-subject maneuver, but Yasmin isn't swayed. "Still, we shouldn't leave without you, my dear. After all you've done for us, I want you to be home safe with your husband, with all of us—not in danger."

"One step at a time, Yasmin. Maybe Gil will come up with something."

As a measure of the buoyancy having passports has wrought, there's nodding acceptance of Fay's suggestion by the Moroccan women. We'll cross that bridge when we come to it.

"And *your* passport, Julie?" Yasmin asks.

"I still have mine." I tap my chest. "It's in the security pouch I kept around my neck. Now it's bundled out of sight, wrapped in that piece of fabric. The soldiers took my backpack, but they must've assumed I didn't have anything else."

Thank God. Or I'd be dead by now.

"Now the phone?" Nadia suggests.

Since her meltdown leaving the desert barracks, Nadia has been alternately sullen and withdrawn or efficient and hyper-focused. When the door to her adult life slammed shut just as it was beginning, Nadia—no longer a child, not yet a woman—was stranded in limbo. The farther we get from captivity, the steadier and more competent Nadia is becoming. Freedom is finally giving her a chance to grow up.

"Yes, and that's your job," Fay says. "Neither Julie nor I can pass as local. You'll need money for the call."

"And Gil's number, too."

We opt to wait up here, away from people and in the shade of the tomb, for Nadia's return. Hamid petulantly agrees to stay and keep us company, but only if he can play *cache-cache* again.

*   *   *

Nadia returns within the hour with bad news. "The *téléboutiques* here aren't equipped to make direct international calls. We'd have to set up the call, pay for it, and wait for the connection to be established. The man said it could take more than an hour."

Fay is already shaking her head. "No, that's too risky."

We all reluctantly agree with her that we'd be too exposed, so that's out for now.

"While I was waiting, I spied a stack of phone books on the counter," Nadia says. "I might've located your cousin Hachim, *maman*." She pulls out a slip of paper. "There were two listings with the same name, but with two different addresses and phone numbers, so I copied them both down."

Yasmin stares for a minute at Nadia's paper. "Let's . . ." she says, and then more decisively, "No, I think it will be better to simply arrive at their doorstep and beg for their hospitality, hoping they'll be too kind-hearted to turn us away in person."

"There's one bit of good news, though." Nadia pulls Hamid onto her lap and snuggles him. "I heard a news broadcast in the *téléboutique*. There's no mention of escaped prisoners."

Our luck is holding so far.

"Let's go to Agadir *now*," I urge. "Use your cousin's phone and stay out of sight until Gil can arrange to get you out of the country."

"That's going to be a problem." Nadia rests her chin on top of Hamid's curls. "The eastbound bus will be leaving in about forty minutes, and we don't have enough money for our fares. There's not another bus until morning."

"How about hitching a ride with a truck driver? We could offer the rest of our money?"

Nadia shakes her head. "The market has wrapped up, and most of the trucks have loaded. We can't get back to town in time."

"There must be another way. An unlocked car, perhaps?" I suggest. "Or someone with a car?"

"And extra room for five?" Yasmin's words are a gentle rebuke. "Five rather smelly individuals?"

"Well, shall we go into town and see what turns up?" I, too, am feeling slightly more optimistic since Fay has, metaphorically, pulled three passports out of her hat. Agadir is less than two hundred kilometers away. There's a road. Trucks. Buses. One way or another, we *will* get there. We're well on our way to making Gil's family whole again. And even though getting home to my family still seems a bridge too far to envision, it's a bridge that might soon be coming closer.

Crowds of people milling around make trying to skip out undetected in another vehicle highly unlikely. What *does* turn up, however, when we arrive in the main square is a tourist couple with a toy poodle and a video camera. And a big SUV. The man is filming the chaos of the winding-down market, obviously going for "local color" as he focuses on the piles of vegetables, worn faces of the old women, rambunctious children playing with a partially deflated soccer ball in the street. The woman hangs back near their shiny Toyota Land Cruiser, holding a beribboned, rhinestone-collared little dog tightly on a leash.

I haven't seen a mirror in days, and I'm dressed in Nadia's faded inner robe. Yasmin's comment about our personal hygiene didn't penetrate my skull. Disheveled and probably stinking to high heaven, I make my way over to the woman. *"Excusez-moi, madame, mais nous avons eu un petit problème et on a besoin de . . ."* She doesn't even let me finish. As soon as she registers that I'm speaking to her and have used the words *problem* and *need*, her eyes go wide with alarm. She yanks the little dog's leash and takes her husband by the arm. They leave me staring after them.

Yasmin hugs me tight. "Thank you for your willingness to try, Julie, but I think we have to resign ourselves to a slower, but more certain approach to get our bus fare. And you and Fay are not suitable. I'm afraid I must do this."

I lift my eyebrows.

"Begging," she says simply. "A tired old woman at the close of market day—oh, yes, that *is* who I am today. Vendors who make a good profit will give me charity before going home. It's our way. The ones with little money will give me a bit of food. So one way or the other, we'll eat tonight and, I hope, leave tomorrow. What time is the bus in the morning, Nadia?"

"Seven o'clock."

"And how much do we need to buy our tickets?"

"About a hundred and fifty dirhams more."

Yasmin sucks in her lips. "Well, then, I know what I need to accomplish. Now, we should find a comfortable place to pass the night, but not one so comfortable that we oversleep and miss the bus." She crinkles her lined face into a generous smile. "I need sleep. I also need to bathe, but that can be accomplished outdoors if we find a good spot."

Yasmin turns to Nadia. "We passed a river on the outskirts of town when we were coming in on the truck. It was off on the right. Water was flowing, and trees lined the edges. That place may be too visible to prying eyes, but while I make the rounds of the market, take Fay and Julie with you and see if you can find a secluded spot. Come back at dusk and find me here."

CHAPTER THIRTY-SIX

We find the river and follow it downstream until it becomes a nightmare of clambering up hillocks and down ravines. Finally, Fay calls a halt. "We'll never be able to get back here with your mother after dark," she tells Nadia. "We have to look in the other direction."

Back over the same ground. Nadia tries to make it a game for Hamid, but two days on the run has sapped his energy and dulled his curiosity. He whines for his mother to carry him, which she does with ill grace. Upstream, north of town, on a grassy height of land screened from view of the road, yet easily accessible, we discover a grove of olive trees at the water's edge, a perfect campsite.

Nadia tips Hamid to the ground and, with a grin of pure delight, strips off her headscarf and plunges into the river fully clothed. She has to coax Hamid to join her—another first for him. Fay and I wade in as well. The cold mountain water jolts my system but we jump around beating our hands against our grimy clothes—to clean them and to try to get warm. I unwrap the fabric encircling my belly and scrub my whole body until it stings, rubbing off the dust and dirt. When we reassemble our clothes, I put the pouch back around my neck for convenience, and we sit in a patch of late-afternoon sunshine to dry.

Nadia, looking more relaxed than I've ever seen her, casts a maternal glance at Hamid who's picking up stones and looking for bugs underneath. "I'm sure you're curious about Hamid, about his father," she says. "It really goes back to that time my mother mentioned, when I walked out the front gate. I didn't mean to make trouble. But *maman* was so grief-stricken. I tried to comfort her, but there was nothing I could do. My brother Nabil was the light of her life. And my father, he had always been her protector. *Maman* was not used to being self-sufficient in those days."

Nadia, like her son, begins to pick up the pebbles scattered at the edge of the stream. After a quick peek at Hamid, she continues in a lower voice. "I was company, yes, but sometimes I got the idea she'd rather be alone. I was, perhaps, a reminder of her loss."

As she speaks, Nadia takes one stone after another between her palms and inspects each before setting it back onto the ground. "At first, our main punishment was the unimaginable isolation. We weren't mistreated, just discarded and forgotten. And so every day, for years, I just...walked...all day." Nadia forms the larger rocks into a tight circle. "One day *maman* woke up crying again and it was summer, hot with a fierce wind and the sun like a fire overhead, so bright I wanted to close my eyes and...and I began to wonder how long it would take out in the desert before the heat melted me, like a candle that has burned itself out. I would prefer that, I decided, to living the way we were. So I walked out.

"I wasn't thinking clearly." Nadia's rueful smile doesn't reach her eyes. "Obviously. And with that walk, the last of our freedom disappeared. We were locked up inside the little room for days at a time. Occasionally when they brought our food, one of the soldiers would stay long enough to allow us to walk around outside the house—but it was random. Days, weeks, would go by that they'd shove a basket of vegetables at us and barricade us in again."

With each sentence, Nadia's stone pile grows taller, becoming an elaborate cairn almost a foot high, smaller stones nestling between the larger ones.

"Then, five years ago, a soldier new to the base started bringing our food. And he was often willing to take time to watch us. His name was Amir." This time Nadia's smile transforms her gaunt face. "He liked to talk, and he was curious about me, about who I was *before*. He told me about his life, too. His brothers and sisters, his dream of studying pharmacy. We often walked alone because *maman* wanted only to sit and grieve. One day Amir touched my cheek and told me I was beautiful. He was . . . it was what I had always dreamed of."

Nadia selects a perfect egg-shaped stone and rolls it between her hands. "I soon became pregnant with Hamid, and yes, silly me, I really thought that would make a difference. I was so happy to be carrying his child. Then I told him." Nadia lays the rock atop the cairn but doesn't let go of it. She pauses, takes a deep breath.

When she resumes, her voice is brisker. "I see now it was an impossible situation for him. I never saw him again. He was gone from the outpost within the week. For many years, I believed he loved me and would come for me as soon as he could arrange it—my version of 'Gil to the rescue.'" Nadia flings the stone into the river. "Hamid is the very image of Amir. To this day, I don't know what happened to him."

*   *   *

The market day was profitable, according to Yasmin. She's stiff and looks the part of a destitute beggar. Now that we're clean and rested, I realize how scary I looked to the couple with the car in town. We count up her take. We made our bus money with a little to spare—along with carrots, tomatoes, and green peppers for supper. Nadia is delegated to take a few dirhams to buy bread in town.

She comes running back to us with news. "The TV had a story about escaped prisoners from Foum Zguid—four men armed with knives who *may* be disguised as women and may try to commandeer a car."

Yasmin puts her hand on Nadia's sleeve. "What about the men?"

Nadia's eyebrows pinch together; she wets her lips. She doesn't want to answer, and I know I don't want to hear what she has to say. "Two died," she mutters. "One was stabbed; the other poisoned. We're considered dangerous."

Yasmin sags against the stone wall. Nadia goes over and puts her arms around her. "*Maman*, you saved our lives." She leads her mother off to our camp. Fay takes Hamid's hand and follows.

I remain where we were standing, too dizzy to trust my balance. Two dead. One dead because of *me*. My heart beats painfully fast. *Because of me*. I scoop the pouch from under my robe. Bring out my bottle of atenolol, now empty except for a single pill, which I drop into my hand. Because of this. My breath becomes ragged; I'm hyperventilating.

Because of *this*. I break that last pill in half, and swallow one section.

CHAPTER THIRTY-SEVEN

Sunday, January 23, 2005

We wake at first light with the birds and the roosters and the morning call to prayer, muted by our distance from town. We saved a piece of bread and a carrot for Hamid. No food for the rest of us. After washing our hands and faces, we make our clothing as presentable as circumstances allow and hurry into town.

The bus to Agadir is idling in the main square in front of the café, debris from market day swept into heaps in corners where scrawny dogs prowl. A tubby man in a long white robe occupies a rusty iron chair near the door of the café. He's sipping tea from a glass. Thick mist obscures rooftops; condensation drips rhythmically onto the cobbles.

The bus driver sits at the wheel, cigarette in one hand and newspaper in the other. The engine heat has warmed the interior to stuffiness, and cigarette smoke further fogs the air. Nadia has wrapped an unresisting, sleepy Hamid onto her back using a strip of cloth torn from the end of her scarf. Yasmin takes the lead, holding out exact change. The driver counts it, looks us over, and pockets our money. We're on.

In the next fifteen minutes, an assortment of drowsy locals board—men with bristly mustaches and hollow eyes, women dressed in their finest to go to the city, an ancient man with an equally ancient leather

suitcase. Then the driver beeps the horn twice, looks around for strag-
glers, and jerks the bus into gear. The bus stops at every small town and
many crossroads, eventually filling to capacity.

Our group is squashed in two rows on the left side, Fay and I each
in a window seat, farther from scrutiny and less liable to be spoken
to. We keep quiet—using either French or English would mark us as
outsiders and draw attention to us. Nadia and Fay take turns holding
Hamid who, after two strenuous days, seems content to cuddle. I
hoped to wait until later in the day to take my last section of atenolol,
but by the time the roadside markers count down to 87 km—almost
to the city—I'm light-headed and my heart is racing too fast for further delay.

The bus enters Agadir from the south, on a broad highway that skirts
the ocean. From the brown-gray-black-tan-ochre inland landscape,
we emerge into full tropical sunshine, blue skies, dazzling turquoise
water, blinding white high-rise hotels, red tiled roofs, sunlight glinting
off huge plate-glass windows, high-end boutiques, airbrush-nippled
mannequins displaying all of their naked ivory curves. Even I, after
only a few days wandering in the wilderness, succumb to culture shock.
Yasmin looks stunned. Nadia squeezes across Fay, pressing as close to
the window as she can, the very picture of a wide-eyed country bumpkin on her first trip to the big city.

The bus station in Agadir is a whitewashed building beside a large
expanse of packed dirt. The bus rounds the corner and, before it even
comes to a stop, people rise to gather boxes and string bags, hoist babies.
We have arrived.

Now we have to get to Yasmin's cousin's house—not knowing which
of the two addresses Nadia found is the correct one. "Let's try this one
first," Yasmin suggests, pointing to the top address. "Something about
it looks familiar."

The first person Lalla Yasmin asks, a street vendor selling peanuts from her basket, gives us directions and says it's only a fifteen-minute walk.

It isn't even that long before we stand at the outer gate of a seaside villa. "I'm certain this is the place," Yasmin says. "See the design of sunbursts on the wall? I've been here before. You were, too, Nadia. When you were young, perhaps six or seven, we came here for the wedding of Hachim's brother Yousef. You played out in the driveway with cousins from Fes you'd never met before. Do you remember?"

Nadia slowly swivels her head. "No."

Lalla Yasmin gives a faint sigh. "Oh, well, let's ring the bell and see what happens."

A woman slides open a panel in the gate and casts a dubious glance that encompasses our threadbare clothes. She asks what we want with frosty reserve. Yasmin greets her with Arabic flourishes. First, Yasmin makes sure her cousin Hachim Alfasi, son of Sidi Rachid, whose brother was Mohammed, is indeed the master of the house. Then she identifies herself as Lalla Yasmin, daughter of the same Mohammed who was brother to Sidi Rachid. I guess they play do-you-know enough for the maid to be convinced to open the gate and let us in.

In a hushed undertone, Yasmin says, "I told the maid we'd met with an accident outside of town, which is, for the most part, true."

The stout maid, in a Western-style black dress and short white headscarf, leads us to a round, glass-topped table on a patio. This is no traditionally built riad enclosing a central courtyard, but a sweeping modern house curving around an oval swimming pool. The walls and gate are at the outer perimeter of an expanse of lawn and flower gardens. Bees drone in the heavy sunlight; a gardener clips the hedge. On the upper floors, green-striped awnings shade windows that are open to catch the sea breeze.

The maid brings us lemonade and a plate of cookies and goes off to inform her master.

The shit, so to speak, hits the fan within a few short minutes. A puffing, red-faced man storms out onto the patio. Black trousers and fancy dress shoes show under the pale wool djellaba he's just pulled over his head.

"Who are you? How dare you take advantage of my hospitality. My cousin is—" He stops and stares.

"Hello, Hachim. Yes, it really is me, Yasmin. It's been a long time."

"My cousin is dead." But he seems less sure than a minute before.

"I assure you, Hachim, that I am not. And may I present to you my daughter Nadia, who is also not dead."

He looks from one to the other, panic overspreading his face as he realizes the implications. "How do I know you are who you say?"

"Because I was at this house, sitting in a chair much like this, only it was smaller and less comfortable than this one, painted white with cushions of purple and gold silk, when your wife came out and announced that the cook had dropped an entire tray of couscous on the floor. How is my dear cousin Lalla Badra, by the way?"

"You can't stay here. You have to leave now. If they catch you here, my family will never recover. Leave."

Lalla Yasmin bows her head. Under the table, her fingers intertwine. She isn't giving in; she's steeling herself for what comes next. "Cousin Hachim, we have nowhere to go. I am begging you, on the memory of your father and of my father, to allow us to stay here overnight and make some phone calls. We need to arrange passage out of the country. I promise we will go as soon as we can."

"No. It's too dangerous. If it *ever* became known I helped you, they could take away everything I have worked for my entire life. They would destroy me!"

"Like they destroyed me?" Yasmin asks sadly. "I'm sorry you don't have the strength to honor your family obligations. The daughter of your father's brother stands before you with nowhere else to go. After all, the Prophet has commanded *whoever believes in God and the Last Judgment, let him honor his guest.*"

Hachim shakes his head. "Leave now or I will—"

"Call the police? That would be awkward. Let us stay."

"No! No, I'll give you money. Money for a hotel." He glares at her triumphantly.

Lalla Yasmin must realize this is as far as she can budge him. "All right," she says. "Money *and* a ride into town to a hotel. We're at the end of our strength, and none of us has eaten today." She flicks her hand across the table, causing the little plate of cookies to skitter to the edge of the table and bobble there. "Except for your delicious tidbits."

Hachim nods his agreement. Now that the deal is set, he takes charge. "I need to finish dressing," he says, "and I'll give you what money I have. Wait here."

He returns in short order. He's run a comb through his sparse black hair and doused himself with cologne. "Unfortunately, I'm short of cash this morning." Hachim quiets Yasmin's protest with a dismissive wave. "If you will kindly allow me to continue . . . I took the liberty of calling the Hotel Kamal and reserving a room for you. For one night. The reservation is in the name of my company, Al-Mogador—can you remember that? Al-Mogador—and the room is paid for. For one night only," he repeats. "Then you must go."

He's walking, speaking to us over his shoulder. We follow him to a gleaming silver Mercedes sedan and pile in. While he weaves through traffic, he takes out his wallet and inspects the contents. He pulls out a wad of cash that looks pretty substantial to me. Handing it to Lalla Yasmin, he says he hopes she understands he has his sons and grandchildren to protect. At first, I think Hachim has mellowed. Until he adds, ". . . unlike the way your husband failed completely to protect you and his children."

Lalla Yasmin sinks back in her seat, flattened by her cousin's words. After a moment of silence, she asks again, "How is your wife, Lalla Badra? You haven't told me."

"She's dead. Like you were. You should have remained so."

CHAPTER THIRTY-EIGHT

Hachim squeals to a stop a block away from the hotel. After pointing it out to us and repeating the name on the reservation, he reaches across Yasmin to open the passenger-side door. "From Allah we come and to him we shall return," he mutters. Possibly he thinks of it as a prayer, but it sounds like a curse to me. The second the car doors close, he roars off.

The past forty-eight hours, culminating in the painful visit with her cousin, have aged Yasmin. Her face is gray, her expression bleak. Since Fay and I—obvious foreigners dressed in tattered Moroccan clothes—would be conspicuous the second anyone got a close look at us, it falls to Nadia to collect our room key. Her light blue kaftan is the most presentable anyhow. She's never checked into a hotel before, so we coach her on what to say and do.

"And if Hachim lied about a reservation to get rid of us faster," I tell her, "just say you must've gotten the hotel name mixed up and walk out."

We wait for Nadia on a bench across the wide boulevard from the hotel, drooping in the heat that radiates from the white buildings and metal surface of the bench. We've *almost* made it to safety. And we have money, stuffed deep in the pocket of Yasmin's robe. "We can count it in privacy later," she says.

Hachim did what he promised, and Nadia has no difficulties check-ing in. "I told the desk clerk our story about being in a traffic accident and needing a quiet place to rest and recover while our car was being repaired," she says. "I was nervous, but he probably thought I was still upset from the accident."

To avoid strolling up the circular drive, past the uniformed door-man, and through the ornate front doors like a troupe of beggars, we scout the rear of the hotel and find an open door. That's how we walk the last long steps to our refuge. From the wide boulevard, to a side street, to an alley with dumpsters, to the back door, to a narrow stair-way of cracked tile and peeling wallpaper, along a carpeted hall, up one more flight to the room.

Soft beds, towels, television, telephone—my God, a telephone right in the room!

Calling Gil is at the forefront of everyone's mind. *He* is the one who will make arrangements to get us out of here. And getting home trumps everything else.

Almost everything else. I'm already a little shaky again. Of course, I could be shaky from no food or shaky because of seeing a man killed, shaky from stealing a truck or from a week of terror—but an upsurge in adrenaline has begun bombarding my oversensitive receptors. Now that we have an anonymous hiding place for making plans, *my* first task is stabilizing my heart rate.

I think longingly about my spare bottle of pills, tucked in the side pocket of my suitcase, in the trunk of a disabled rental car, in a dusty village on the other side of the mountains. Too bad it's so far away and probably irretrievable. As soon as the phone is free, I'll call a doc-tor about getting a new prescription. It's Sunday, though, and I don't know if that's part of the Moroccan weekend. If I can't reach a doctor, I'll head for the nearest hospital emergency room. Either way, I worry about the risk of exposure—not to germs, but to officialdom in an office or busy public hospital where regulations might demand a passport be presented before treatment, exposing my identity and possibly alerting the authorities to our whereabouts.

I suggest Lalla Yasmin take the first shower, but the prospect of talking to her son is far more enticing than washing off a layer of dust. Since setting Gil's wheels in motion is the first order of business, I commandeer the bathroom to give them privacy.

I close my eyes and hold my face to the warm spray coursing down my body. I slather soap all over and work it into a white lather. Arms. Belly. Breasts. Legs. Feet—my poor feet. Even clean, they're in bad shape, with cracked skin and bruises, covered with cuts. At least my ankle is no longer tender to the touch, and the remaining swelling has subsided. I clean my hair with a mini hotel shampoo of overwhelming floral fragrance. Finally, I'm clean and dry, but with only my dirty sweater and pants and Nadia's cast-off kaftan to wear, I return to the living room wrapped in a huge fluffy towel.

The call to Gil is just ending. Everyone's sniffling. Nadia holds the phone to her ear, beaming while tears trickle down her cheeks. Fay gets on for a minute after Nadia says goodbye. Her conversation is a series of agreements. "Yes ... okay ... sure ... we can do that ... yes, I understand ... okay, I'll wait. Love you, too. Bye."

Fay turns to the Moroccans, grinning from ear to ear. "Gil's going to check for flights right now. Apparently, the Agadir airport is small and most international flights are vacation-package charters, but if he can get you on one, he'll book it. More likely, you'll be flying from Marrakech, which is closer, or Casablanca, which is bigger. Once Gil gets the flight lined up, he'll rent a car for us. He's going to use his law firm's credit card to get everything squared away so we don't need to show ID or license—which, of course, we don't have. He said for corporate clients a rental firm will deliver a car and leave it with the keys, ready to go. He'll try for flights tonight, but says, considering where we are and driving times, it'll probably be tomorrow."

The Moroccan women take over the bathroom then, with much animated chattering, and coach Hamid on the intricacies of the shower.

Fay grabs my arm, lips tight. "I didn't tell them the rest of it. Gil's obviously known *something* was up since Monday when you called his secretary to say I hadn't returned. He said he tried your phone a hundred times. No answer, of course." Fay flashes the ghost of a smile. "On Friday, though, Gil got a call from someone who said he was a neurologist at a hospital in Casablanca. He told Gil I'd been attacked and seriously injured in a robbery, had just regained consciousness, was in pain and asking for him in my lucid moments. He suggested Gil get on the next plane. Said the hospital could arrange someone to meet him at the airport."

"Oh shit. They're trying to lure him back."

"Got it in one."

"But what—"

"Because of all the money I was carrying and your call alerting him to my absence, a mugging was a distinct possibility. Fortunately, Gil had the good sense to call the hospital back—call their listed number, not the number the so-called doctor gave him. They *do* have a Dr. Benabbou on staff, but he's on vacation in Portofino with his family."

"So Gil knew he was fake."

"Yeah. But . . ." Fay's eyes fill with tears. "He also knew that meant something had happened to me, and he was frantic with worry. And guilt—kicking himself for sending me here."

What a mess. I understand better now the tough spot Gil was in—needing to rescue his mother and sister while knowing their peril would only increase if he called official attention to their plight. He must've been desperate to use Fay . . . and me. And at *that* thought, my brain explodes again: *Asshole, how could you?* But it sounds like Gil realizes how foolhardy he's been. Against long odds, Fay and I have gotten us this far. Now Gil had just better pull out all the stops in getting us the hell out of Morocco.

"The fake doctor called him back early the next morning— yesterday—to find out his plans," Fay says. "Gil claimed he'd be on the first flight that had an available seat, said he'd call when he boarded."

"He can't really do that!"

"No—and besides—Gil wants *us* out, too. Like *now*. We've stirred up a major hornet's nest."

"But your passport..."

"I told him." Fay kneads the back of her neck. "We'll have to lie low until I get a replacement. I don't know how long that takes, but I'll call the consulate in a minute."

"The sooner the better—find out what kind of red tape is required for a new one, where we have to go, how fast they can process it."

"We have to keep the line open for Gil. Let's see what he comes up with first."

CHAPTER THIRTY-NINE

Gil is efficient. Fifteen minutes later, a call from him results in reservations for three on the following day's Air France 12:55 p.m. departure from Marrakech, nonstop to Paris, and then on to JFK. *And* he arranged for a car to be dropped off at the hotel within the hour.

"How far is it to Marrakech?" I ask Fay.

"About two hundred and fifty kilometers."

Before I can make my fuzzy brain focus on the math, Fay adds, "Gil suggested we use back roads, though, not the major highway where it would be easy to set up a roadblock. So, figure on at least four hours instead of the three it would normally take."

"We'll have to be out of here at dawn."

"Yeah, or leave later this afternoon and cover part of the distance today."

I look around the luxurious hotel room. *Leave this afternoon?* Yasmin finished her shower and collapsed on one of the king-size beds. She's already snoring softly. Nadia and Hamid are curled up on the sofa in cushioned comfort, mesmerized by the TV.

"We should all rest for a little while." Fay hands me a stack of money. "Here's what Hachim gave Yasmin. Why don't you see how much we have to work with?" Then, finally, Fay takes her turn in the shower.

I count the dirhams. And count. And count.

When Fay comes back into the living room, she tosses Lalla Yasmin's former inner robe onto the bed. "There's no way I can put this on again." She plops next to me to tie her sneakers. "But since I can't go shopping naked, my jeans and sweater will have to do one more time."

"Almost two thousand dirhams," I say.

Fay's brow crinkles as she tries to puzzle out what I'm talking about.

"What Hachim gave us." I hold up the cash. "Over two hundred dollars."

"Holy shit, how much does he think a hotel room in this town costs? I'm taking some of that money to buy us all new clothes for our trip home."

Seeing Fay again in her American clothes brings back a vivid memory from our arrival in Morocco. "Go tourist," I say.

Her brow furrows again. "Huh?"

"Don't you remember all the women who lined up for the bathroom on our flight from Madrid to Marrakech?" I ask. "How each one entered the cubicle as the tourist or student or businesswoman who'd been unremarkable in Europe and emerged a properly attired Moroccan woman, covered from head to toe?"

Fay's face brightens in understanding. "Oh, yeah. That woman across the aisle from us—the one in the red tank top who was telling me about zip-lining in the Canary Islands. When she sat down in her black gown and veil right before we began our descent, I almost told her she was in the wrong seat."

"Once they changed their pants and T-shirts for kaftans and headscarves, they were unrecognizable. I'm sure the same thing works in reverse," I say. "I mean, here we are on the coast in a tourist hotel. We're driving them, now supposedly French citizens, back to Marrakech. Put them in Western clothes. Earrings. Makeup. Total camouflage."

"Good call. Hang in there. I'll be right back."

She leaves in a rush. And finally, the phone is mine.

Fay's need to call the consulate about her passport reminded me that, even though the consulate office is in Casablanca, someone there should be able to give me a referral to a discreet medical facility here in Agadir. So I phone the consulate and who do I get but my old friend Sam Monatti. He is, I now realize, the low man on the consular totem pole, condemned to having his weekends and early mornings interrupted by distraught tourists.

"Hi, this is Julie Welch. We spoke last—"

"Omigod. Julie. I'm so glad you called." Definitely a change in attitude.

"Yes, I've had quite a week. I found my sister, but the problem is—"

"No, listen. A Moroccan boy has called here a dozen times—well, I exaggerate, but he became very concerned about you when you never returned to pick up your car."

Izri, bless his heart. With all the turmoil, it slipped my mind that I asked him to notify the consulate.

"He insisted that you were in trouble and kept pestering us to do something. He also said he's had your car repaired and wondered what he should do with it."

Izri has the car.

It's fixed.

I get the glimmer of an idea.

Sam keeps talking. "He left a number for us to call—or for you—I'm sure he'd prefer to talk to you. It's his landlady's phone or something. I'm not sure. He was talking really fast."

Coming from speed-talking Samanotti, that's hilarious. "Give me the number please. I'll call him now."

"So what happened to your sister?" he finally asks.

I make up something lame on the spot—turning Fay's rendezvous with Mohammed and his friends into a story about a rug salon in an out-of-the-way village and the sketchy taxi driver who took her for a ride, then relieved her of her belongings. I mention specifically that Fay's passport and a vital prescription of mine have been stolen.

I get, in return, the phone number for a good private clinic—after first listening to his harangue about the crowded conditions and inefficiencies in Moroccan hospitals. Because I'm already skittish about hospital bureaucracies, Sam's suggestion is welcome.

He also promises to expedite a new passport for Fay. When he starts to detail what Fay needs to bring, though, I rush him off the phone. "I'll fill you in on the rest later. It's been a crazy week. I'll call back after I talk to Izri." *Or not.*

First, I call the clinic. Voicemail: *Closed for a staff meeting from two until four. Evening hours until eight.*

Damn.

The clock on the bedside table reads 2:48. I'll call Izri while I wait for it to reopen.

"Izri is in his room," says the woman who answers. "He's studying and doesn't want to be disturbed."

"It's Julie Welch."

She drops the phone yelling for Izri to come downstairs and to be quick about it. The American lady is calling.

CHAPTER FORTY

"*Allô,* Julie! I'm so glad you called! I worried for your safety when the army men arrived looking for you. Are you okay?"

"Hi, Izri. I'm glad to be talking to you, too, and, yes, I'm okay." The catch in my voice might be obvious, but he can't see me, and I'm not telling him about the tears blinding me.

"Where are you? Did you find your sister?"

"It's a long story, but, yes, I finally located Fay, and we're together now in Agadir."

"Agadir?" he asks, as though Agadir were in a distant galaxy.

I give Izri a more accurate version than what I told Sam at the consulate, but gloss over Fay's absence as "helping some people out of a difficult situation."

Fantastique. Incroyable.

His praise brings more tears to my eyes. "Thank you," I say, "for calling the consulate."

"But you asked me to call, Julie. I promised. Oh—about your car. Sidi Abillou, who drives the taxi, got the parts that were needed on Thursday, and Omar replaced the missing wires. It was, as he said, five minutes' work."

Izri gives a careful recitation of how he spent the money, apologizing for the extra cost of having to sweeten the disposition of the auto-parts store owner to persuade him to open his shop which, along with pretty much everything else in Zagora, had been closed for Eid al-Adha.

"When you didn't come back for the car and the man at the consulate didn't know anything, my brother suggested that he drive it back to Ouarzazate when we returned there from our village after the holiday."

"Oh, that's wonderful." *Fantastique. Incroyable.* The glimmering idea grows bright. *Thank you, God, for Izri and his sensible brother. Now we have a chance, an honest-to-goodness chance.*

"You have the car with you in Ouarzazate?"

"Yes, it's right outside our door."

Deep breath. "Listen, Izri. I have a big problem. We left our suitcases in the car, and we really need them. I wonder if your brother would be willing to drive the car to Marrakech tomorrow. With you perhaps? To meet us there and deliver the car? I'll pay for your return in a *grand taxi.* I'll—"

"But you're in Agadir?" It's still farther than the moon.

"Our friends need to go to Marrakech, so we're driving there tomorrow. Driving a different car," I add for clarity.

"My brother isn't home now, but I'll tell him it's important. His work isn't very busy this week. We'll bring the car."

"Please be sure to tell him I'll pay him and pay for all your expenses." I hope I'm not laying it on too thick, but I have to make sure the brother-who-can-drive won't decide to go to work first and deal with the car later.

"Where can we meet you?" Izri asks. "My brother has traveled to Marrakech for his boss. He knows the city a little."

The airport itself would be too big and confusing and, besides, I doubt the wisdom of hanging out in such a security-conscious place. Still, it should be a location clearly identifiable and easy to reach. "Oh"—thinking back to our cab ride when we first arrived in Morocco—"I know. There's a stretch of nice hotels and cafés on the boulevard that leads to and from the airport. One place is the *Café*

Excelsior. It has a big sign and blue awning and lots of tables outside. I don't know the exact address, but anyone local can tell you where it is."

We settle on meeting at nine thirty the next morning. With long drives to Marrakech for all of us, that's the earliest we can reasonably arrive—and also just about the latest time to rendezvous, get organized, and still get Gil's family to the airport on time. I give Izri our number at the hotel and ask him to call if there's any problem bringing the car. He reassures me, but I still worry that his brother might have other priorities on a Monday morning.

"*À demain.*" See you tomorrow—this time it's a promise, not a threat.

I sink back into a soft yellow chair and watch the slow, rhythmic undulations of the Atlantic Ocean. I checked the clock when I got off the phone with Izri. Still more than half an hour before the clinic opens. I'm not going to bother calling the consulate back since Fay won't need a new passport any longer.

Except for low chatter on the television, it's quiet in the room. Nadia is still glued to the television. Hamid is making a cave from pillows and comforters on one bed. Yasmin is sleeping in the other. Fay will be back soon with clean clothes for us all. Then, tomorrow, Monday, we'll retrieve Fay's passport and my pills and take the Moroccans to the Marrakech airport.

If only *we* could get on a plane, too.

Staccato images of our escape intrude, quick pop-pop-pops— Yasmin's resolute face when I handed over my pills, the silent comatose men, the knife flashing, the lump on the ground that was once a man visiting his family for Eid-al-Adha. We've committed horrible crimes in the name of rescuing Gil's unjustly imprisoned family, crimes I'll carry with me until the day I die. I only hope Fay and I can also find safe passage out of here.

In an odd way, the long view through the window of the ocean disappearing at the horizon makes my family feel more inaccessible than when

I was lost in the desert or walking through the brown hills of southern Morocco. Then, it was easier to imagine them just around that proverbial corner—down the road, out of sight. But here, the empty distance stretches farther than I can see. And there's nothing as straightforward as a bridge spanning the vast ocean, no direct path leading on to the people I love.

I pull the pouch from around my neck. I open it and stare at my passport. The phrase *safe passage, safe passage* repeats in a loop. I dump the rest of the contents into my hand. *Safe passage.* Technically, we'll be able to leave once Izri brings the car with Fay's passport. It would be foolish, though, to call attention to ourselves by using our previously booked return tickets. Anyhow, that flight isn't until Thursday.

I want—we need—to get the hell out sooner than that, but *our* passports are in our real names. And as Yasmin so poetically put it, how can we elude the long reach of the king's talons?

The timing of those calls from the fake doctor to Gil worries me, too. The first call must've happened right after we left the army outpost in the desert, when we disappeared from the last place he knew to look for his mother. But *Saturday's* call came after we escaped from that cell. The police know we'll be trying like crazy to get out of Morocco. And they must suspect we'd contact Gil.

So call number one was probably to tie up loose ends—lure Gil to Morocco and silence him, in other words. Call number two, though, was an attempt to kill two birds with one stone. They still wanted Gil, but now they also might be using Gil to find us.

How would they do that?

The pretend doctor wanted to know Gil's arrival information. That way they could detain him the second he arrived. But Gil must've seemed awfully vague about his travel plans for a man who believed his wife was seriously injured.

If they thought Gil hadn't fallen for their ruse—say, if they believed Fay contacted him before their second call . . . what would they do?

Surely the police know Gil would move heaven and earth to bring his family home.

That's it: the simplest way to capture us would be to know what Gil had arranged ahead of time. I don't know if the Moroccans have the ability to monitor his phone calls, but that strikes me as the absolutely most efficient thing to do. I'll warn Fay about the possibility.

I stroke the ostrich shell, so smooth under my fingers. Because it's fossilized, it isn't delicate, although one corner has broken off in the last hectic days.

The ostrich relies on cunning and surprise, not strength, in dealing with his adversaries. My talisman has gotten us this far. Could it get us across the ocean? Could it get us home?

Cunning and surprise.

And misdirection. Kicking sand into the lion's face. I close my eyes and shift the pieces in my mind. My nebulous plan begins to take shape.

Time passes.

The next thing I know, Fay is standing there handing out brightly colored packages like Christmas morning.

"Hi, Julie, you looked so peaceful lying there." She drops a neon green plastic bag on my lap. "Sorry to wake you, but—here—these are for you. I don't know if you heard me say I got one outfit for everybody. Sandals instead of shoes; they're easier to fit. Pants and shirts all around."

Fay also bought a couple of Moroccan-style chicken *shwarmas* and a long crispy baguette filled with tuna, boiled potatoes, and olives. Although we're famished, everyone—except Hamid—changes into clean clothes before gobbling the sandwiches.

My new clothes consist of loose brown cotton drawstring pants and a cream-and-gold-patterned shirt. Not my idea of gorgeous, but unobtrusive.

Nadia is the most changed in her smart Western clothes. Even with her unkempt hair, she's instantly more radiant.

"Where's the hairbrush?" I ask Fay when only crumbs remain of our sandwiches. "I'll help Nadia and Yasmin complete their makeover."

"Shit. I knew I'd forget something."

Their hair is going to be a problem now that it's not concealed. I can finger-comb my wispy curls into some semblance of tousled chic, but even Fay's well-cut hair is a matted disaster. Yasmin and Nadia both sport long, straggly locks. Clean now, but a tangled mess.

"Let me go," I say. "I haven't contributed much here. Give me some money. I'll get a brush and scissors at the outdoor market. D'you have any idea how much we need to save for gas to get to Marrakech tomorrow?"

That stumps the Moroccan women who've never filled a car before, but Fay and I work out the distances and come up with a generous ballpark figure.

"Is the car here yet?" I ask. "It's been an hour."

"I was going to look on my way in, but my hands were full of flimsy plastic bags threatening to disintegrate and spill everything. I thought I'd make a second trip to check. It's supposed to be a maroon Peugeot 407 and should be parked around back in the 'guest' area of the hotel lot. Unlocked, with the key under the driver's-side visor."

"I'll look." I hoist myself up, feeling more a sense of obligation to contribute than any eagerness to be exposed out on the street.

But before I leave . . . "Fay, walk me to the door."

Because it's so obviously a let's-speak-privately maneuver, she jumps up with a smile.

First, I explain my concerns about people tapping Gil's phone for information about us. Then I say, "I have an idea about getting us out of here."

Fay's eyes open wide. "What is it?"

And so I tell her.

"I didn't know that!" Fay claps her hands. "I'll call Gil right away."

* * *

I walk to the market the long way around, through the car park. A maroon Peugeot, a slightly larger model than our original rental, is there. I open the door. Yes, keys concealed in the visor. I pocket them, lock the car, and continue on my errand.

Across the street from the hotel, an outdoor market stretches back into a maze of side streets. Once you leave the oceanfront boulevards, you leave Europe and return to Morocco. Agadir's *souq* is an astonishing jumble, a place to buy everything from pottery to used sneakers, dried beans to zippers.

At the first boutique displaying drugstore-type personal wares, I buy a bright green plastic hairbrush with a design of a belly dancer on the back. The shopkeeper has colorful plastic clips, too, and a pair of scissors with long skinny blades good for trimming hair.

I'm distressingly out of breath walking back to the hotel; sweat beads on my cheeks and neck. Even the small bag weighs me down. My pace becomes slower and slower. I try to psych myself into progress with words of encouragement that have gotten me over other hurdles: *One step at a time; you can do this.* The clinic will have reopened by the time I get to the room. And now we have a car. Haircuts can wait; I'll get Fay to drive me there the second I return. Coming out was a stupid idea. *Hang in there; keep moving.* The hotel is maybe fifty or sixty feet ahead, close enough to see the front entrance with its portico surrounded by flaming scarlet bougainvillea, the sweeping circular drive, the gold-jacketed doorman—the three police cars, lights flashing, pulling up to the entrance.

CHAPTER FORTY-ONE

make a connection immediately to my repressed tingle of concern when Hachim, returning to the patio after getting dressed, ceased being argumentative and offered, instead, a prepaid hotel room. He made it sound like a compromise to get rid of us fast, but Hachim knew where we were going. After all, the cash he pulled from his wallet could've paid for several lesser rooms.

It would have taken Hachim only a single phone call.

All that goes through my mind in a split second. The red-and-blue-uniformed police—the paramilitary—are still milling around at the entrance. I have to move now. I sprint, panting and stumbling, to the back entrance we first used and make my way up the stairs. Colors fade to black, then glow painfully too bright.

I reach the door. Bang on it. Nadia opens it a crack. I push my way in. "Everybody out! Get out! Police. Downstairs. Let's go!"

Nadia scoops up Hamid and flees. Yasmin runs after her.

"Car in back. Go."

Fay's on the phone. She says something fast, hangs up, and streaks out the door. I have an awful time keeping up with her. Fay's trying to ask me something, but my ears are ringing. I bump into the wall when we turn a corner, banging my nose so hard tears come to my eyes. Then

Fay links her arm through mine one more time. Matching me step for step, she guides me gently down that last steep staircase.

Out the back door and around to the car park on the side. Yasmin and Nadia are hesitantly wandering around. "Maroon Peugeot" didn't register with them at all. Fay steers me toward the car; the other women converge.

"Key in pocket," I manage.

Fay digs in my pocket for the key. "I'll drive. Yasmin, in front with me. Nadia, get Julie comfortable in the back seat. Lying down helps. Could Hamid come up front?" Fay hugs me before she helps me into the back seat, her face tight with stress and worry. "Hang in there, Julie. We'll get clear of these guys and get you some help."

I try to tell her about the private clinic; words form, dissolve. Then I see, far away, like I'm looking through the wrong end of binoculars, the paper with the clinic's name and phone number on the table by the phone. Once the police enter our room, they'll find it. The clinic is no longer an option. We'll have to take a chance on a hospital after all.

Fay reverses out of the parking space and turns onto the boulevard. Resisting the urge to drive as fast and as far away as possible, she cruises sedately northward. Yasmin is useless with the map when Fay asks her to find a hospital on it. Nadia offers to look. Fay snaps at her. I try to speak again; the effort of trying to open my mouth exhausts me. Glare reflecting on the car windows turns the world into a kaleidoscope of confusing brilliance. Vertigo. I'm falling through space, my body spinning in circles.

My breathing becomes more labored. Then, beneath the flurry of pitter-pattering tremors my heart is producing, a deep strong ache grows, like a fist squeezing my chest. My vision fades. The chaotic contractions spike into an all-encompassing misery that surpasses in intensity anything I've ever known. My body is molten on the inside, a frozen shell outside. It takes more strength than I possess to maintain a flow of air into and out of my lungs. Nadia touches my forehead. I hear her say from a long distance away, "She's going—"

I'm in too much pain. I give up. Darkness falls.

CHAPTER FORTY-TWO

The light is too bright and the blurry shapes around me so bleached-out and ghostly that I have a fleeting died-and-gone-to-heaven scare. Just a passing fear, however, because the steady rhythm of my heartbeat rocks me gently.

I blink a few times. My vision clears. I'm in the back seat of the car with the door open. One of the blurry shapes is Fay, who's stuck her head inside.

"Ah, you're awake," she says. "That didn't take long."

"What didn't?" I can only whisper.

Fay lifts my legs and scoots in to sit with me. "You won't believe what Nadia did."

"Nadia?" I can't quite focus my mind—or my eyes.

"Yeah, good old damn-the-torpedoes Nadia. Turns out that Friday night when Yasmin gave her your pills to put in the sauce, Nadia chopped them into smaller bits so they'd dissolve quickly. One must've skittered off the counter, and she didn't find it until the sauce was ready. She said she started to drop it in." Fay extends her arm, thumb and middle finger touching. "But something stilled her hand. She stuck it in her pocket instead."

"So Nadia saved my life."

Fay laughs. "Of course, she totally spoiled what could've been the lifesaving gesture of the century by saying the old commandant had already come in to complain that dinner wasn't ready, and she worried the white disk wouldn't dissolve in time and they'd notice it. She said she figured she'd give it back to you later."

Nadia might be turning into a sensible and competent young woman, but she's not there yet. My head lolls from side to side. I don't know whether to laugh or cry.

"When you lost consciousness, she retrieved it and stuck it under your tongue. It was only a matter of a few minutes before your breathing settled down, so I kept driving out of town."

After a while, Fay helps me up. I ease out of the car and sit on the warm sand. "We're at a beach north of Agadir." She holds a bottle of water to my mouth so I can sip from it. "We got here about ten minutes ago."

The car is parked at the edge of a wide expanse of pale brown sand that rings a shallow lagoon, a semicircle of bright water. The farther reaches of the bay are encircled by tall boulders where the sea crashes. Gulls scream overhead. Salty smell of seaweed in the air. Picnicking families in the shelter of sand dunes.

Hamid comes over to the car with a bouquet of pink flowers that he thrusts into my hand. Nadia shows me a variety of seashells.

Planning has progressed in my absence. "At least Gil knows not to call the hotel," Fay says.

I join the conversation. "So that was Gil on the phone, back at the hotel?"

Fay pats my arm gently. "Yep, that was Mr. Fix-It himself. I told him about your coup in getting the car back—with my passport. And I asked him to check on what you heard in Ouarzazate. But you warned us about the police coming before we got into the details."

"Did you get him to use a different phone?"

"Yes." Fay nods. "To frustrate anyone who might be trying to listen in, I pretended the connection was too faint for me to hear clearly. I suggested Gil use the Rogers' phone—they're the people next door. I waited a few minutes and called him there. Gil doesn't know if the Moroccans can tap a cell phone in the States any more than you or I do, but he agrees that it's a small hassle that might pay big dividends if we can catch them off-balance."

"So we'll use his real phone for the fake stuff?"

"Should work," Fay says. "Before I had to drop the phone and run, we'd already agreed that I'd call him around six this evening, at the Rogers again, to find out what he was able to arrange."

"Do we need to go now?" The very *thought* of moving makes me shivery with fatigue.

"Not yet. It's only four thirty. You take it easy for a while. This is as good a place as any to complete the makeovers."

Take it easy—like I could do anything else. I rest my head against the side of the car. "Okay."

"We'll drive back into town when we're through here," Fay says.

No, please, we can't go back there. My post-pill calm instantly vaporizes.

At my look of alarm, Fay clarifies. "Not Agadir. There's a funky little place a few miles back. Full of surfers—if you can believe it. Very European. Shops with polyester sarongs imported from Taiwan. Galleries full of bad art. Seafood restaurants with menus in English. Buying a cell phone will take too much of Hachim's cash, but there are lots of *téléboutiques*. So let's finish the haircuts, phone Gil, and grab a bite to eat."

Nadia brandishes her new passport. "It's time for me to begin my life as Halima Mansour."

"Cool," I say. "Let me see."

Nadia opens it to the photo and kneels down in front of me, so her face is next to the picture. Fay bought her loose drawstring pants in the same style as mine, but Nadia's are dark blue with swirls of crimson. Her shirt, in the same crimson, has three-quarter sleeves and a square neck. The vivid colors of her outfit—possibly aided by a few days walking in the sunshine—bring out a glow that accentuates Nadia's high cheekbones. Seeing her smile is like watching a butterfly emerge from a cocoon.

"Wow, good job. It looks like all we'll have to do is cut bangs and twist your hair back in a knot."

Nadia closes the passport and lowers her head. "First . . . I believe it's important to make a clean and honorable start." She hunches down so low that her hand cradles her forehead. "I hated Fay," she says quietly. "I hated *you*, hated your nice clothes and your freedom. I hated your husbands and your vacations and your children. I even hated your lipstick and your earrings." Nadia raises her head, but her eyes remain downcast and one hand covers her mouth so it's even harder to hear her muffled words. "I'm thirty-five years old, and I've never had any of the things that seem so natural for you."

"Except Hamid." Nadia smiles shyly. "It wasn't really you, of course. You were simply a reminder of what I lost. But then you suffered along with us and didn't give up. You're smart and courageous. And you got us free. I'm sorry. It—" Tears well in her eyes, but after a couple of sniffs, she regains her composure. "It might take me a while to figure out . . . who I am."

My right hand touches my heart as though I've been making this simple gesture of sincerity all my life. "It's okay." Nadia's hesitation tells me she's gone as far as her jumble of emotions can take her. Her mood swings make so much more sense now that I know her better: A teenager who'd been a university student one day and a non-person the next. A girl callously uprooted and cast aside just as she sent out the first tendrils that would one day mature into a flourishing adult life. So that day never arrived. Until now.

I find myself thinking about my older daughter, Erin, who's maturing so fast these days. Soon she'll be a full-blown teenager; soon after that, a woman. Perhaps a mother, too, at some point. Her maturing is already bringing changes to our relationship, changes I expect—even if, as a former teenage menace, I'm not exactly looking forward to her full-blown-teen years.

But children grow into adults. They find love, partners. Spouses grow together—and apart. Parents age; they die, leaving bits of themselves as indelible memories. Sisters . . . well, sisters *do* change, and there can be stresses and tension, but it's a pretty durable relationship.

Fay has been sitting next to me, scissors in hand. "So let's finish turning you into Halima, a modern young French-Moroccan, and your son into Marc-André, the wily bug-catcher. Time for haircuts."

Curls shorn, wearing blue shorts and a white T-shirt, Hamid is indistinguishable from the other boys running around the beach. He even has grubby hands and a skinned knee. Nadia's dark brown wavy hair is now freed of its tangles and cut shoulder-length. Fay finishes by using one of the clips I bought to clinch her hair into a loose topknot. The silver threads sprinkled through it sparkle in the sunlight.

Lalla Yasmin refuses an extensive beauty treatment. "I'm not going to learn new tricks at my age," she says. "I'll probably always be more comfortable veiled."

So Fay crops her hair short to resemble the passport photo and brushes the curls behind her ears.

CHAPTER FORTY-THREE

While Fay brushes and snips, I swirl my fingers absently through the sand. Late Sunday afternoon at the beach. All around us, family groups sit on blankets, talking and drinking tea they brewed on tiny propane burners. A little girl with pigtails runs across the sand chasing a runaway bag.

Molly. Running across the sand to catch seagulls.

Only the adrenaline-blocking atenolol prevents me from drowning in a wave of anguish. Instead, my mind wanders to next Sunday... *next Sunday* I'd like to drive out to the shore with Steve and the kids. I don't care if it's freezing in Virginia. We can bring blankets and hot cocoa and sit in the sand together on the other side of the ocean.

That's a promise. *Next Sunday*. I just have to get home first.

When we drive into the picturesque, pretentious seaside town of Tamraght, I remain in the car with Hamid while the other women phone Gil. During dinner, which we eat in a bustling outdoor seafood restaurant, I nibble a salad and listen while plans for the next day are firmed up. In the incessant bustle of the restaurant, we're just one more group of sunset-seeking tourists in a sea of sunburned faces. Hidden in plain sight. Fay spreads out a map on the table and plots a promising route of secondary roads leading from here to Marrakech.

I become aware of the sharp tang of cumin sprinkled on the toma-
toes, the juicy crunch of the peppers, the succulence of the meaty olives.
I tear off a hunk of bread. I eat a piece of fish, some zucchini. Gradually,
I rejoin the living and am drawn into the discussion.

Fay replays the highlights of her last conversation with Gil for me.
"When I called him at six after our stop at the beach, Gil told me that
the second I dropped the phone in the Agadir hotel, he called the consulate in Casablanca to alert them to the potential arrest of US citizens.

"A man from the consulate phoned him back an hour later to con-
firm a police action in room 314 of the Hotel Kamal—although he said
the police categorically denied any Americans were involved. Instead,
the police reported that, acting on a tip, they'd planned to round up a
group of escapees from a maximum-security prison. The fugitives fled
in advance of the raid, however, and were presumed on the loose in
Agadir. At least one prisoner was thought to be injured."

The clinic name and contact number I'd left beside the phone.

"So they're canvassing hospitals and clinics. And within thirty minutes of the raid, they set up checkpoints around the city. All transportation out of Agadir—car, truck, bus, plane—is being monitored."
Fay squeezes my hand. "You saved our lives by getting us out of there
so fast."

I massage my cheeks and forehead hard. Perhaps greater blood flow
will translate to clearer thinking. "Fay, if they're watching *all* the traffic
leaving Agadir, it sounds like they didn't know Gil rented a car for us."

"Yep." Fay smiles. "Gil emailed his secretary to arrange for the car
and airline tickets, and she sent the info in a reply."

"That's good." The fog is slowly receding. "But it means we still don't
know if they have his phone tapped."

"I don't think we can be positive either way." Fay holds up first one
index finger, then the other. "Maybe it takes time to arrange—you
know, in another country and all. Maybe it's impossible. Or maybe they

won't even think of it. But whatever they do, we've flown under their radar this far. Your plan will help keep it that way."

Stealth.

I root under my new shirt for my pouch and pull out my ostrich shell talisman. "When are you going to talk to Gil again?"

"I'm supposed to call him after dinner. We both thought he should keep switching phones, so tonight, I'll reach him at the office on his secretary's line—we were careful not to use names, just in case."

Cunning.

"Good." I caress the smooth surface of the shell. "You know, there's *one more thing* I need him to check."

Misdirection.

I explain what I want Gil to do and pocket my talisman so I can easily reach it.

*   *   *

Fay's call after dinner takes a while. She comes back to the car flushed with excitement. "Gil had to put me on hold a couple of times while he checked, but you're right, Julie. The police believe they've got us trapped in Agadir."

"And the flights tomorrow?"

"He'll come up with a list. Which one we use will depend on what happens in Agadir."

"So we go with Plan A."

"Yep. Since we got away undetected in the car, we'll keep driving toward Marrakech. Meet Izri. Get my passport and your pills. Put Yasmin, Nadia, and Hamid on the plane to Paris. Call Gil when they're away safely. He'll let us know then if your plan is working on his end. If so, we're good to go."

"But we won't know definitely until then?"

Fay's face scrunches in uncertainty. "Gil *promised* he'd do everything he could to make it come together. He's going to work on it all night."

"Keep everyone focused on Agadir. That's the main thing."

I hardly dare believe the pieces of the puzzle we've put together will all work out, but it's a good plan, a plan that relies on who we are—each one of us. That was Ahmed's lesson to me: You do what you can with what you have.

And that's what we're doing. Nadia was right on target with her sweet words of gratitude—and if we didn't give up *before*, we certainly won't *now*.

"We'll use their knowledge against them," Fay says. "The tip to the Agadir police that led to us must've come from Hachim, don't you think? We'll give them something to find, all right."

Monday, January 24, 2005

Someone shakes me. After eons of fidgeting, I'd finally managed to relax in a position where my neck didn't instantly cramp and my legs didn't break out in pins and needles. I jerk awake and hit my knee on the window crank.

"It's starting to get light," Fay says. "We should get going."

With less than three hundred dirhams remaining after dinner, we resigned ourselves to one last night sleeping rough—but with full bellies, a ride to the airport, and cautious optimism. So we washed up in the restaurant bathroom, and then Fay drove a couple of hours inland. She pulled in behind a large vacant building of dissolving mud brick where the car would be screened from view. The Moroccans took the back seat; Fay and I made ourselves as comfortable as possible in the confined space of the front seat. No one noticed us except for the occasional pack of prowling dogs.

Fay straightens up in the driver's seat and starts the car—*on our way to Marrakech to meet Izri*. The early morning is cool, the summits of the arid hills are awash with golden light, the valleys filled with rising mist that glimmers momentarily as it meets the sun's rays and then dissolves.

Fay drives carefully and stays on sleepy back roads to avoid patrolling traffic cops—we've passed speed traps, legitimate ones, on the main roads in Morocco. The last thing in the world we need right now is a moving violation: license and registration, *madame*?

While Fay drives, I consider the next problem facing us. If Izri called me back at the hotel to change the time or to say his brother couldn't drive the car to Marrakech, he might simply have gotten no answer in our room. That's scary. Without my spare bottle of atenolol—and soon—I'll have to chance a clinic or hospital in Marrakech, a priority that conflicts with getting Gil's family to the airport on time. I just don't know how much time I have before I black out again.

Worse, however, would be if the police answered the phone. I don't know if the police would be convincing enough to get Izri to blurt out his message to them.

With that in mind, I tell my companions, "Since I'm the only person who can recognize Izri, I'll go into the café first. Alone. That will protect you. If he's not there or if I sense a trap, I want to be able to skedaddle. If he *is* there and looks scared or worried, ditto. He has such a guileless face; I think I could tell."

Scattered villages turn into frequent small towns; traffic increases. People on bicycles, men in trucks, groups of children in matching school uniforms holding hands, whole families on scooters, boys in donkey carts, all jostling for position on their way to work or school.

* * *

Disaster strikes on the outskirts of Marrakech, disaster in the form of an outbound *grand taxi* aggressively passing an overloaded truck that's slowing its progress. The truck driver, distracted by a heated fist-pounding, paper-waving conversation with the man in the passenger seat, fails to notice the overtaking taxi.

We see the taxi pull out, so the taxi driver ought to see *us*. Fay slows to let the speeding taxi slide into the gap in front of the truck before our approach closes it. But the truck driver doesn't slow. And instead of retreating behind the truck, the taxi driver honks repeatedly, to no avail.

At the last second, the taxi driver tries to scoot back in behind the truck to avert a collision with us. There isn't enough time; he's gotten too far out of position. In desperation, he cuts diagonally across the road in front of us.

Fay brakes with all her might, but the taxi's trajectory forces her to swerve farther and farther to the right. The gravel at the edge of the road spins our tires. The car skids sideways, broadsiding the taxi, momentum carrying both cars off the road. We come to rest with the noses of the cars in a shallow ditch, narrowly missing countless startled commuters and a spindly bush in a pot gracing the front of a pharmacy.

The truck keeps going.

Our engine dies; the taxi's is still racing. With a horrified look into the back seat, Fay orders us all out, and she crawls out on the passenger side after me. The front passenger door of the taxi, where our car struck, has buckled. The man seated next to it is bleeding profusely from a head wound. Hamid is screaming. Yasmin's arm is bleeding. I feel like I'm going to throw up. But we're all up and walking.

The taxi driver storms over, an angry bull bellowing about the preoccupied trucker. He got the truck's license plate, he says, and has called the police. Also, because *our* vehicle has hit *his*, we have to fill out forms. Besides, we saw everything, and he wants us to attest that our collision was entirely the truck driver's fault, not his. A crowd gathers. Someone says an ambulance is on the way.

From the worried looks on my companions' faces, everyone understands our predicament. The impatient taxi driver, whose aggressiveness was mainly responsible for the fiasco, is working the crowd: *Did you see that? What an asshole! We're lucky to be alive. Wait until they catch him.*

Unfortunately, his harangue—in which we're sometimes fellow victims, sometimes the ones responsible for the damage to his taxi—ropes us in too frequently for us to vanish. We absolutely *cannot* stick around for the police, though. None of us has a driver's license to show. There'll be questions, questions we can't answer. And even if we manage a legitimate excuse to get away, our car isn't drivable.

Fay sidles over to me. "Ideas? We've got to disappear before the cops show up."

The neighborhood is a mixed-use area: the pharmacy we almost crashed into, a shoemaker, a tire repair shop, and a small grocery store, apartments with people hanging out the windows. It's a long street, a long unbroken wall of attached cinderblock dwellings. No place to hide. "Alternate transportation?" I suggest.

Fay raises an eyebrow. "What? Ask where the bus stop is? Hail a cab?"
A cab.

Fay's still talking. "I can't see that man letting us wander off—"

"No, wait. Can you borrow someone's phone, Fay, like someone in the crowd here? Make an excuse, you know, 'I have to tell my husband what happened.' Whatever."

"Ye-e-es, I guess so. But who am I going to call?"

Fay and I have backed away from the blustering taxi driver. We're standing at the periphery of the crush. I turn my back to the crowd and lift the security pouch from under my shirt. Pills, lipstick, money—gone. But the paper clip that once secured my emergency cash still holds a few business cards. One is for the chatty cab driver who took us into town the day we arrived in Marrakech. "Just a minute," I tell Fay and enter the pharmacy.

When I come out, I hand her the card. "Call Abdulazziz. Remind him that he drove us into the city from the airport last week and gave us his card so we could go sightseeing. Tell him we need him to pick us up. Promise him anything, but get him here right away." I flip over the card. "I had the clerk write down the address of the pharmacy. How far away do you think we can drift without calling attention to ourselves—like to the little grocery store over there?"

"O-h-h-h . . ." Fay's catching on. "That would work. If someone notices us leaving, I'll say we need a bottle of water."

"Right. I can't see the grocery's name from here, so tell Abdulazziz that it's eight or ten doors farther from town than this address. Find out how long he'll be."

While Fay goes back into the crowd, I round up Yasmin and Nadia. "We're taking a short walk."

CHAPTER FORTY-FOUR

The taxi jounces to a stop in front of the little grocery store, and the driver waves to us with the enthusiasm of a game show contestant.

"You ladies again. I remember. Very happy to see you. We go to Koutoubia Mosque. Then I take you to palace. King not here today. In different palace today." Abdulazziz's tragic countenance would be more suitable on a sad clown. "But we can—oh, what's this? Is accident. *Aiee.*" He sucks air in between picket-fence teeth. "Too many crazy drivers in this country. Not safe."

He swivels to look at us. We're all squashed together in the sagging back seat, strained well past capacity by our combined weight. With widened eyes, he extends the hand that isn't on the steering wheel toward Lalla Yasmin's arm. A kind onlooker supplied a few napkins, which she used to stanch the blood. "You ladies in accident? In taxi?"

In light of Yasmin's injury, I have to agree that we were traveling in the taxi; otherwise, it would mean admitting we were in the other car. A car we were abandoning at the scene of an accident. The area isn't exactly Tourist Central, so those are the only two choices: innocent-bystanders-struck-by-shattering-glass isn't going to fly. It would be remarkably odd for us to be hanging around in the nondescript suburb.

Fay whispers in my ear. "Uh-oh. Hard to pretend that, on our way out of town, we were suddenly eager for a day of sightseeing."

"The taxi was turned sideways. I'm sure he couldn't tell it was outbound," I whisper back. "But now we have to duck out of his sightseeing trip."

"I can make it work," mouths Fay. "Do you remember the names of any of those fancy hotels on the same street as the café where we're meeting Izri?"

I nod. "The big one with the palm trees and beautiful garden is *Le Méridien.*"

Fay drops her head to Lalla Yasmin's shoulder. "You need to start feeling bad," Fay whispers. "Make it dramatic."

Yasmin goes right to work. I bend my head down like Fay, ostensibly consoling Lalla Yasmin who's moaning loudly.

An ambulance screams past, followed by a police car, blue lights flashing.

"Abdulazziz," Fay says, "my friend is in a lot of pain, and we ought to swing by her hotel to attend to her. Can you take us there first? It's *Le Méridien.*"

"Oh, okay." With another lugubrious grimace, he rotates to face the steering wheel. "After that, we visit mosque."

An eternity later—ten minutes by the clock on the dashboard, which already reads 9:32—the grand buildings that announce the city center come into sight. Abdulazziz parks in front of the hotel. "Okay, ladies. *Le Méridien.* I wait."

"How about if we settle up now?" Fay says. "We have to bandage her arm, and it may be a while before she regains her composure. We'll call you later."

His smile disappears. The poor guy thought he'd snagged a day-long guide-gig, not a single mediocre fare, for which he'd driven far into Moroccan-style suburbia. I feel terrible for misleading him. "I wait,"

Abdulazziz tries. "Have tea at Café Excelsior. Is convenient, next door only. Take you to mosque."

With an unexpected depth of acting ability, Lalla Yasmin groans again.

To get rid of Abdulazziz, Fay forks over a generous tip and, making up a room number and name on the spot, asks him to call for us at the hotel at noon. He drives away, mollified.

"Thank God we hadn't put gas into the rental car yet," Fay mutters. "That taxi fare ate up a lot of our remaining money."

*   *   *

I leave my friends sitting on cushioned wicker divans beside a fountain in the hotel garden and walk next door to the Café Excelsior. Tables spill outdoors, with green Perrier umbrellas shading the patrons. Izri isn't sitting outside.

The interior, accessed by a row of open arches, is deep and shadowy. I wander inside. Fewer than a dozen tables are occupied. No Izri, but also no other presence that sets off an alert. Only older men in business-suit versions of the djellaba—soft off-white wool robes, worn over slacks and polished Italian footwear. Most men hold a cell phone to their ear with one hand and a cigarette in the other. Espresso cups litter the tables. No one pays me any attention. I return to the fountain and report my lack of progress.

"Wait five or ten minutes," suggests Fay, "then try again."

So I do. And then I do it again. I'm more out of breath each time I make it back to the fountain. A half hour ticks by. It's after ten o'clock. We'll need to leave for the airport soon. The city is uncomfortably warm. Even the spray off the fountain, which occasionally blows over us, feels clammy, only increasing the humidity. My palms are sweating, and the polyester shirt sticks to my back. My face is flushed with the heat, but also with increased blood flow. If Izri doesn't show up, I'm going to need a hospital. There will be no Nadia-to-the-rescue this time.

My stomach growls. If only we all could sit under one of those umbrellas with sandwiches and cold drinks, but prudence suggests we save the last of our stash for an emergency cab to the airport.

Time for me to do another walk-through.

"Stay here." Nadia presses down on my shoulder when I begin to stand. "If you can tell me what this boy looks like, I'll check. You shouldn't be walking around in this heat."

"Thanks, Nadia. He's very much in the typical mold of a Moroccan teenager—you know, jeans and T-shirts." I stop. Nadia is just beginning to learn what the "typical" Moroccan teenager looks like these days. "I can't tell you exactly, but ten minutes ago the café was filled with old men. All you have to do is look for two young Moroccans—one a teenager and the other, well, his older brother. You want to try it?"

She's off before I finish the question. Back in a short time. Her glum expression says it all. We sit by the fountain, listening to the plink of water, heads down.

Fay is gnawing on the inside of her cheek. "I'd better leave you here to wait for Izri and the car. We'll have to take a taxi to the airport; otherwise, they'll be too late."

Please don't leave me alone. But I only shake my head and say, "You won't have enough money for a cab back here. And what if Izri never comes? How will we ever find one another again? Let's check once more."

"Once, but that's it." Fay stares off into space, lips pinched and making anxious cats' cradles with her fingers.

Nadia goes to the Excelsior again. This time, she sprints back. "There are two boys in the café now, and they're looking around like they want to find someone. Come see!"

I can tell it's Izri from a distance and run up to him. "Oh, Izri, you made it. I'm so glad to see you."

He tries to stand, but I bend over his chair, my face in his hair and my arms wrapped tight around him. "I have never been so happy to see anyone in my whole life!"

His face gleams with pride and satisfaction. When I finally release him, he stands politely. I introduce Nadia, explaining that she's one of the people Fay was helping, and Izri introduces his brother, Mennad, a taller, more solid version of Izri.

"I'm sorry we were late, Julie," Izri says. "Traffic was very bad coming into town."

"I'm just glad you're here." I hug him again.

"Are you sick? You look so tired and pale."

"I've had an awful week, and one of the reasons we need the car is for some medicine I left in it. Can we go get it now?"

"Let me take care of the bill." Mennad summons a waiter who scribbles numbers on a piece of paper and then drops it, along with a couple of decorative matchbooks, onto a saucer. Mennad digs in his pocket for change, which he throws in the saucer, reflexively picking up the colorful matchbooks.

They'd parked around the corner. When we reach the car, Mennad unlocks the trunk. I open my suitcase in a flash, take out my reserve pill bottle tucked into the side pocket, and swallow an atenolol. I don't have time to wait for it to take effect today; there's too much to do. I reach into the other side pocket and take out an envelope. Fay kids me about my security-conscious travel precautions, but this time they're going to save our skins. Inside the envelope are photocopies of my passport, our itinerary . . . and a spare credit card I stuck in. Just in case my purse was stolen.

"Okay, Izri," I say, "we're back in business now. I'd give anything to have time for a relaxed conversation so I could tell you everything that's happened since I last saw you. The thing is, we don't have much time before we have to be at the airport. Do you think we can all squeeze into the Peugeot and run an errand before we take you to the taxi? You can tell me all about your holiday."

It isn't really a question. Fay, Yasmin, and Hamid come running around the corner. I give quick introductions, and we cram into the little car. First stop is an ATM. I max out. Giving Mennad a big chunk of the cash, I thank him profusely.

He tries to hand most of it back. "This will take care of our expenses. Izri and I were happy to help."

We play the polite *please take it . . . no, I can't . . . I insist . . .* I finally prevail by telling him the truth. "Without you and Izri, my friends and I would be stranded indefinitely in Morocco at a far greater cost than what I'm proposing to give you. I want you two to share it with our gratitude."

I let Mennad assume the greater cost I'm talking about is money.

Not to be outdone, Mennad tells me, "If we accept all this, it's with the understanding that you will be our guest the next time you visit my country."

Since my chances of returning to Morocco are approximately zero, I agree instantly. "We should keep in touch."

"Let me write down my contact information." Patting his pockets produces a pencil stub but no paper other than the little matchbooks he just picked up. Mennad scribbles on the inside. "Until we see you again, please send us news of your life and your family."

I looked down at what he wrote. "Email?" *Geez, if only the rest of this trip had been accompanied by 21st-century technology.*

"Yes, I manage inventory for a chain of clothing stores. We use it at work." I write my email address on the inside of the other matchbook and hand it back to Mennad.

We drop the brothers at the *grand taxi* rank next to the Bab Doukkala market. They squash into the last two spaces in the back seat. Since their arrival fills the car, the taxi driver cranks the engine. No time for extended goodbyes. We each promise, "I'll write."

Remembering the harrowing ride over the mountains at the hands of a possibly lunatic taxi driver, I yell "Be safe" as they pull away.

"*Bon voyage*," Izri calls back, waving until he's out of sight.

On the drive to the airport, Fay squeals into a department store parking lot. "Wait here." She dashes into the store with a wad of cash and returns a few minutes later with a small suitcase in each hand and fat plastic bags squashed under her arms. "Traveling without luggage raises too many red flags these days," she tells Yasmin and Nadia. "Fill the bags with these bulky sweaters and robes I bought."

She's behind the wheel before the words are out of her mouth. We speed up the wide boulevards to the airport entrance and drop the car at Europcar, almost empty of gas and at the wrong office. They efficiently add the extra charges, and I hand over my little piece of plastic—I *so* don't want to see the bill at the end of the month. Access to money makes such a difference. Pay now and worry about the fallout later.

We pick up our suitcases and walk away from the car rental office. Now will come the serious hurdles, the kind money *could* buy immunity from, but in our case probably would not.

CHAPTER FORTY-FIVE

The wind rustles the fronds of the decorative palm trees by the airport, creating a constant susurration like surf on a stony beach, and brings with it the faint fragrance of flowers. The Atlas Mountains circle the horizon and they're still stunning, but I've seen the spine under their snowy exterior. I've driven through rocky fields to the summit on corkscrew roads and down the other side to the dry valleys at the edge of the desert. And beyond, into the Sahara.

Our pace flags as we approach the terminal. I can see reflected in the expressions of my friends my own dread of the obstacles in our path. Nadia, of course, has put on her brusque face, the tense and irritable one she first showed us. Yasmin puts one foot in front of the other with barely enough energy to make forward progress. My sister, looking almost as grim and worn out as her mother-in-law, holds Yasmin's arm and encourages her.

Streams of passengers from other walkways converge in a bottleneck at the entrance. Everyone struggles to keep their suitcases and children in hand. Inside, echoing chaos. Fay leads the way, and we walk single file in her slipstream toward the Air France check-in.

"It's already after eleven," Fay says. "You need to get in line."

We stand in a tight circle, for once at a loss for words, but in that respect, we don't look different from other family groups on the brink of tearful goodbyes.

"You know what to do." Fay wraps her arms around both women and pulls them close. "Stay calm. If you have any questions at the airport in Paris, call that number for Gil I gave you. He'll fix things, and he'll meet your plane in New York. And I'll see you there." Fay's voice breaks. "Soon."

Of course, that's when Yasmin breaks down crying, which seems a perfectly natural reaction to airport leave-taking. Nadia gravely kisses our cheeks and wishes us a simple *bonne chance*. Then she takes Hamid's hand and purposefully heads for the Air France counter. Yasmin peppers us with kisses until, reluctant to be alone in such a strange place, she bolts after Nadia.

Fay and I stake out seats in an alcove that offers a view of the head of the line. Every few minutes, one of us stands and stretches in order to look around the corner. The women move glacially toward the front. Every group ahead of them seems to have some time-consuming issue that involves rummaging for misplaced documents or shifting the contents of an overweight bag or gesturing wildly over an aspect of their trip that requires a supervisor's calming presence to resolve.

Finally, Nadia comes into view. Sweat breaks out on the back of my neck. The next agent waves her over; she approaches, Yasmin and Hamid trailing. They proffer their passports; the man at the desk swipes one through a machine. He lifts his head and asks a question. I hold my breath. Nadia says something to him. He types some more. He frowns and asks another question. Nadia points down to the hastily put-together suitcases. *He's only asking about luggage.* I let out a shaky breath. Nadia lifts one bag onto the scale, Hamid—rather, Marc-André—doing a cute-tyke job of assisting. Laughs all around.

Fay exhales. "They're going to make it, aren't they?"

I cross the fingers of both hands but don't speak, afraid to jinx them. The second suitcase receives its coded tag and is whisked away. The airline representative hands over papers and points to the left.

They catch sight of us when they walk away. Yasmin waves sur-
reptitiously, an excited smile alternating with a nervous compress-
ing of her lips. The security line lies ahead. Luggage and jackets
on the conveyor; electronics out; passports and boarding passes
in hand. Thank God we remembered to coach them in the car. As
French-Moroccans on a holiday visit, they should know the ropes
of post-9/11 air travel.

We reposition ourselves and again stand watch. The women look a
little nervous, but many other travelers do, too. When they near the
front of the line, Fay's hand finds mine. We hold on to each other, too
nervous to speak. Anticlimax. Without more than a cursory look, each
walks through the metal detector. And they're gone.

"Time to call Gil," I say.

"No." Fay pulls me across the room to the large monitor displaying
arrivals and departures. "We have to make sure they're in the air first."

We mark time—an eternity of scrolling departures rolling up the
monitor—while Air France changes the flight's status from "on time"
to "25 min delay" to "boarding" to "departed." Immediately, Fay rushes
to a pay phone and dials Gil—by prearrangement at yet another phone
number.

"They're off," she says. "No, no problems. Right." She listens for several minutes, punctuated by the occasional "okay."

While tension shows clearly in Fay's furrowed brow and hunched
shoulders, she keeps nodding, keeps agreeing with whatever Gil is telling her. He must've been busy since we last spoke.

"We will. Love you, too." Fay hangs up. "So now for the bluff—Plan
A for the time being."

"So Gil found someone to coordinate things in Agadir?" I ask,
relieved. Like Fay, I'm convinced the police believe us contained in their
dragnet in Agadir, and Plan A was designed to give substance to their
suspicions, thus giving us breathing room to maneuver in Marrakech.

"He got in touch with a human-rights lawyer from Casablanca," Fay says, "a man he met at a conference a few years ago."

"But—Casablanca?"

"Yeah." Fay flaps her hand in a don't-worry flutter. "It's only a five-hour drive from Agadir. Once Gil explained our situation, the lawyer put Gil in touch with a private detective, someone he said was discreet and resourceful. *And* one hundred percent on board with thwarting the monarchy's extrajudicial schemes. The detective hired decoys last night—a tall woman with long blond hair and one with short dark hair. They drove down to Agadir early this morning and are now waiting."

Waiting to be captured by the police.

Our getting out alive isn't okay if it means others' imprisonment. "Those other women—how much trouble are they going to get into?"

"It will only be tense for them until we've left the country. They'll come to the airport in a taxi, with bags like they plan to travel. Dressed in traditional clothes, but without passports, tickets, or any other ID. The women called Gil's cell phone from a *téléboutique* in Agadir this morning, just like we planned. They went through the script we drafted—Gil said he'd booked them on the 4:50 Ryanair flight to London and that when they got to the airport a man in a blue suit would hand over the tickets and documents they need to leave the country. Gil had them describe what they'd be wearing so he could tell the man how to find them."

I heave a sigh of relief. "So if the Moroccans *have* tapped Gil's phone, they'll have everything necessary to zero in on them . . ."

"Right." Fay's hands transform into thumbs-up fists. "And if not, they'll simply see two women with a good likeness to us. And body-cloaking clothes that will make it seem like we're trying to disguise ourselves as Moroccan women."

I hug my arms around myself. "I'm still worried about them."

"We've got it timed really well." Fay gives me a reassuring pat. "Here in Marrakech, there are a slew of international flights around four p.m., so they'll arrive at the Agadir airport at two thirty. The women need to get noticed *there* in the narrow window that includes the time when the flights *here* are ticketing and boarding. We'll buy our tickets, go through security, and get on our plane while the police are preoccupied *there.*"

"But what if we can't get on an international flight?"

Fay flaps her hand again. "Don't worry about that part. The flight choices may narrow by the time we buy our tickets, but right now most flights have available seats. Anyhow, we can't risk giving our names out until the last possible minute."

"All right." We've talked everything over and over; we both know what we have to do. I simply can't quiet the incessant worry-loop cycling through my head.

"Worst comes to worst, it's Plan B," Fay says.

"Right," I say again. Plan B: we walk out of here and make tracks for the consulate in Casablanca. Probably in a *grand taxi*. A taxi driver wouldn't check ID, but we'd be vulnerable to random or targeted roadblocks. It would be more dangerous and a lot more trouble. And we wouldn't get home today. But back to my previous worry: "Those women—"

"If they don't attract police attention in the first five minutes, the detective is going to call in a tip that he's a taxi driver who noticed something odd about two women he'd just driven to the airport—they were traditionally dressed but speaking English. He'll give a complete and accurate description."

"What'll happen to the women then?"

"They'll be questioned, of course, but they'll claim to be who they really are—Moroccan women on their way home to Casablanca, and they'll insist they're waiting for the male relative they're traveling with to arrive with their passports and tickets. When the detective hears that our flight has departed, he'll show up with the passports that verify their identities and tickets to Casablanca—*home to Casablanca*, see, not overseas on Ryanair to London like in the decoy message. They may have an intense few minutes, but they know what they signed up for—and we're paying them a small fortune."

"And if they aren't noticed after the phoned-in tip?"

"The detective will start an argument with them. Make a stink. Call the police over."

Fay's talking too fast. She's had just about enough. I touch the front of my shirt to reassure myself my atenolol is still in the pouch, still within reach. I'll definitely need more today. Not yet, but soon.

I set this in motion, but those abstract people-pretending-to-be-us are now two women walking into danger. I only hope we can leave Moroccan airspace while the police are still merely checking their story and treating them decently.

I shake my head to dislodge my misgivings. As Fay said, those women—unlike me—knew what they were getting into.

CHAPTER FORTY-SIX

"We need to lie low for a while." The big digital clock above the arrival and departures monitor reads 1:52. "I'll check in with Gil at two fifteen and then again every fifteen minutes," Fay says. "For now, let's wander around separately so we don't call attention to ourselves. Meet me here, by this monitor, after each call, okay?"

"Good plan. I'm going to grab a sandwich now. Want one?"

"Eat-like-a-bird Julie." Fay's faint smile ends with a tight compression of her lips. "You go ahead. I'm way too stressed out to be hungry."

The closest thing to edible food is a dryish roll with a slab of—I think—turkey, a single pickle, a slice of pale pink tomato, and a limp leaf of lettuce. After a few bites, I toss it into the trash.

I'm still sipping the lukewarm cranberry juice, though, when Fay sidles up to me after her two fifteen call. "The detective watching at the Agadir airport told Gil the police set up a gauntlet through which everyone entering the airport has to pass," she says quietly. "That's different from screening for flights. They'll be looking at everyone coming in, not just those ticketed."

"So they'll catch them trying to enter the airport?" I cross my fingers again. That's the best possible news.

"Seems likely." Fay is squinting again, like she has a bad headache. "Just a little longer."

I don't know how she's coping. Now that it's almost time, I'm light-headed with fear, right on the edge of full-blown panic. When we separate to wait for the next call, I take an extra piece of atenolol and resume my amble around the terminal.

Fay is even more keyed up when we meet at the departures monitor after her two thirty call to Gil. Her eyes are shiny bright, and she keeps licking her lips. "The police picked them up. Since they got nabbed so quickly, the women are going to stall, make it confusing so it sounds like there are holes in their story."

I send up a silent prayer for their safety. And for ours. "Now—what about us?"

"Our best bet is a Swissair flight to Zurich. There are more than a dozen seats available and it leaves at 4:09."

As one, we raise our heads to the big overhead clock: 2:37.

"I bought a wallet at the gift shop," Fay says, "so I won't be pulling a wad of your cash out of my pants pocket."

"Did you take enough for the flight?"

"Yep." Fay's quick, shallow breathing scares me. She's operating on too much nervous energy and too little sleep. "Time for me to go. But remember, I go first from now on. Stay away from me when I'm in the ticket line. And if *anything* weird happens—if the agent picks up the phone or calls another one over—get the hell out of here. Don't wait until the police come running. Walk away. Call Gil from someplace safe—you have the phone number he'll be using, right?"

I nod yes.

"Then head for the consulate. As fast as you can." Fay smooths her hair, gives me a wobbly nanosecond grin and, without a backward look, marches briskly to the Swissair counter. Even in the black desert, I never felt so alone.

This is the critical point.

We are betting our lives on my casual conversation with Fatima, the restaurateur's wife in Ouarzazate, about her son's journey home from France. Fay asked Gil to check Fatima's information. Pretending he was trying to locate a friend who'd missed a connecting flight in Marrakech, Gil got the same answer from several international airlines—*exactly* the same thing Fatima told me: Passenger manifests for all flights originating in Morocco remain solely on the local area network within the airport, so they're shareable by ticketing and gate agents. *But* because the infrastructure hasn't yet caught up to the demands of constantly updating traffic, a flight manifest is only uploaded to the main airline servers after it's complete—with the flight boarded and door closed. If that is accurate, we'll be on our way to Switzerland before our names show up.

That won't matter, of course, if the police have put out a nationwide alert for us. Since her purse is gone, Fay's paying for her ticket with some of the cash I got at the ATM, but she still has to provide her passport. We both do.

I've gone over it a million times, though, and every time I end up at the same place: the authorities would have to notify every airline, every airport, and every desk agent in the country. And why? They think we're trapped by their dragnet in Agadir.

To distract myself from the looming unknowns, I concentrate on the other folks waiting to travel. In any other circumstance, this would be delightful people-watching. Businessmen in suits, businessmen in djellabas, European hippies in torn jeans and T-shirts, Moroccan women in kaftans and veils—I check out their feet and legs, of course. Lots of pant legs and sneakers show under voluminous kaftans, just waiting to be revealed after that first visit to the airplane bathroom. People speaking Spanish and French, English and Arabic, and other languages I don't recognize.

Like all airports in this security-conscious era, armed soldiers are out patrolling two-by-two. They're strolling casually, though, just keeping an eye on things. They aren't scrutinizing faces or checking identification.

The atenolol is working. My breathing has calmed and quiet observation is replacing panic, just as it did when I took one after injuring my ankle that horrible day alone in the desert.

Then it's Fay's turn. Despite my chemically induced anxiety reprieve, I bring a clenched fist to my mouth, sucking my knuckles to keep from humming with fear. Fay speaks briefly, opens her new wallet. To look at her you'd never know she spent the last three days and nights on the run from the police. The agent scratches her cheek with long red fingernails. She types on her keyboard. Looks up, says something. Fay slides her passport across the counter.

The woman swipes it.

Now. I bite down on my knuckles.

But there's no alarm. No buzzer. No bells. No armed men rushing over. Not the slightest twitch of alert from the agent. Fay receives her boarding pass and walks toward the security line, disguising a fist pump in my direction as a struggle to get her carry-on bag onto her shoulder.

I join the ticket line after Fay snakes through the first looping turn at security. With Fay's success, the pressure has abated, but when an agent down at the far end of the counter waves me over, it's as though all motion in the airport has ceased and a spotlight shines on me alone. I trip over my suitcase when I try to lift it. The clasp pops and my pile of dirty clothes spills onto the floor. Two soldiers in tan uniforms, long black guns swinging at their sides, rush toward me from a hundred feet away. My heart must've stopped beating for several long seconds. They screech to a stop by my side and stand, glowering.

No, not glowering. Merely puffing from their brief exertion. But still they stand there without speaking, without smiling. Shuffling their feet.

After catching the hesitant looks passing between the men, I realize they're reluctant to barge in and manhandle my female belongings. I scoop the clothes from the floor into the open bag. One of the soldiers bends to redo the clasps. Then he lifts it onto the scale and tips his cap. I hope I said thank you; I meant to, but all I recall is being speechless with terror.

Somehow, I make my voice work at the ticket counter. "I'd like a ticket on the four o'clock flight to Zurich." I hand over my gold card and passport and, before I know it, I, too, have my boarding pass in hand. I breeze through security, this time without committing any attention-getting faux pas.

Fay is sitting in the boarding area of the gate just beyond security. She runs toward me. "Thank God."

Fay's hands on my shoulders are icy. *She's running on fumes* is my first thought when I see her up close. To the casual observer, she still *looks* chic, but there's wildness in her eyes, like a cornered animal that doesn't know which way to run.

"Come on." This time, I link *my* arm around *hers* and tuck her freezing fingers into the crook of my arm.

Our flight to Zurich is leaving from Gate 25. Because of lousy airport karma, it's a foregone conclusion that every gate for every flight I will ever take in my entire life is at the far end of the longest concourse. Gate 25 is indeed the last one, in a curved cul-de-sac. We pass signs for flights to Nantes, Malaga, Toulouse, Brussels, Bologna, Seville, Amsterdam, Bonn, Milan . . .

A stream of pent-up arriving travelers zigzag across our path, desperate for the bathroom or a smoke or overeager to be pacing at the baggage carousel before their luggage has even been released from the bowels of the airplane. Running children crisscross the concourse, their squeals adding to the cacophony of distorted, over-amplified announcements.

Almost there. Fay's footsteps slow. She gulps. "Oh no."

I look up. Standing next to the counter at Gate 25 is a uniformed soldier.

CHAPTER FORTY-SEVEN

Fay drops into a chair at Gate 22 and puts her head in her hands.

"It's okay, Fay," I say quietly. "If they'd picked up on us when we got our tickets and had our passports scanned, they'd *know* we were in the terminal. They wouldn't have let us get this far—and if they did, they would've sent a bunch of men to lock this place down and arrest us. Really." I sit next to her and bend my face toward hers. "Only Gil knows what flight we'll be on."

"What if they heard my first call and caught on to what we were doing and stayed one step ahead of us? So they were able to listen in on that last call to him?" Fay's pale skin is blotchy, her face a mask of pain and misery.

"But they wouldn't send *one* soldier to arrest us here. Didn't you see all those soldiers walking around the terminal in pairs?"

"What if he's only a lookout and the others are hiding? What if they wait until we're boarding? What if the airport people told the police not to make a scene and scare the other travelers?"

"They could've pulled us out of the security line, Fay. You know, pretended there was an issue when our luggage scanned."

"But what if there were too many people bunched together and they couldn't get close enough without calling attention to us and they were afraid they'd lose us if we ran?"

And here we are at the end of the line. No place to run but out.

Although I've marshaled all the logical arguments and Fay's *what-if* house of cards is unlikely, her terror is catching. *What if...* "It's a coincidence." *It has to be.*

"No, I can't walk past him. I won't." Panicky though it is, there's unexpected resolve in Fay's voice. "I can't bear any more. I'm so tired. I want to go home now."

I want to go home, too.

If Fay weren't half-dead with fear and exhaustion, she would do something unexpected now, like she did all those years ago at Mardi Gras when she saved us from being arrested at that crazy drunken party. Like she did a few days ago in the most desperate time of her life. When they locked us in the back of that van, Fay turned our thoughts from passive despair and channeled our energy into positive avenues. She led us to believe we could prevail.

I want to go home. So, if I'm going to see my family again, it's up to me this time. I picture us at the beach: we're huddled in blankets, drinking cocoa. Steve's arm is around my shoulder. The children are laughing. Or maybe they're arguing. It doesn't matter. We're together.

It's up to me to get us home.

So how can I get rid of the soldier? The cul-de-sac at the end of the concourse where we're sitting has five gates, and it's congested. Children play between the chairs. Teenagers pulse to the inaudible rhythm of their iPods. Old women sit heavily, occupying two chairs at a time, smelling of expensive French perfume, their faces obscured behind layers of fabric.

Although every gate has a crowd, every chair an occupant, and every destination a departure time, the only military presence stands directly in front of the door we need to pass through.

"He's the only soldier around," I say. "If we can get him away from the gate ..."

Fay looks up dully, but I spot a tiny spark. "He's young," she muses. "Yes, and he doesn't look very serious or alert."

Fay gives him a long reflective stare. "Do you think he's just a bored and lonely boy eyeing a pretty girl?"

"Maybe." I think about it. "Or maybe it's simply a convenient location for spotting trouble at any of the gates in this area."

Fay rubs the back of her neck.

"Fay, you said yourself there's heavy security at the Agadir airport. That must mean *no one* knew we were going to be on this flight—at least until you bought your ticket. Which wouldn't have left much time for him to get into position. And don't you think we would've noticed if he rushed down the concourse ahead of us?"

We're quiet while my unvoiced what-ifs reverberate like rolling, late-summer thunder: What if the soldier was already in the concourse on a normal patrol? When alerted, he wouldn't have to run to get here ahead of us; he could simply get in position. What if Fay was right that the police decided there were too many people in the way in the main part of the terminal or too many places for us to evade them? Too messy and not enough control. Or—my breath catches—what if they wanted *both* of us and Fay had already passed through security before they identified me?

I'm sure Fay's rolling the same dice I am—do we dare walk past him, identification out for inspection?

There's this, though: the total nonchalance of the ticketing agent. *Both* ticket agents. And those two women assisted us randomly—one customer done, call the next in line. They *both* couldn't have been such talented actresses.

Still ...

"Like you, I'd feel a lot better if we don't take a chance," I say. "We have to get him out of the way. Look, we're fifty feet from the jetway. Our passports scanned without incident; we got through security ..."

"We need a diversion."

I thrust my hands into my pants pockets, fingering the ostrich shell on one side—remembering *cunning over strength*, remembering how Ahmed said *you do what you can with what you have*. My other hand touches the pack of matches in the other pocket—the one on which Mennad wrote his email address.

I was just thinking about our disastrous New Orleans trip, how Fay created enough confusion for us to slip away by pulling the fire alarm—I put it all together. "And a diversion is precisely what we're going to create." I hold up the matches. "We don't want an actual fire—that might cause undesirable complications, like clearing the boarding area."

I don't need to say another word. Fay's mouth curves into a dazzling smile. "Right." Her gaze swivels side to side . . . assessing. "Smoke maybe?"

"What would you say to a failure in the fire *sprinklers*?"

"But how—"

"Remember the time Greg and I got in trouble for smoking pot at Grampa's office?"

"Oooooh, a flood." Fay's face lights up.

"In the ladies' room?" Keeping my hand in my lap, I point with a discreet index finger to the universal symbol marking a women's restroom. It's less than twenty yards from where we sit at Gate 22—and only slightly farther from the lone soldier at Gate 25.

"That'll give me some privacy." Then, thinking about the circumspect soldiers who hesitated to help with my suitcase, I say, "And it'll provide an extra layer of confusion."

Her face scrunches up in thought. "When?"

"We wait as long as possible. We want him busy—out of sight, out of hearing range—while we board. And without enough time to call for backup."

"Want me to start the flood?"

"Nah, you've done enough for one day. I've got this." I'm not going to tell Fay she looks so wiped out I can't imagine she has enough energy to strike a match. "What row are you in?"

Fay checks her boarding pass. "Eleven."

"Good. Almost everyone will be on the plane by then. I'm in fifteen, so I'll start when they call the group that includes my row."

We don't have long to wait. The gate agent chats with the young soldier. Periodically, the agent's phone rings and she excuses herself to answer it. Each time, I hold my breath. Each time, she speaks briefly, matter-of-factly, and hangs up. And returns to her conversation with the soldier. A second agent arrives. Then a third hurries to the counter and opens a folder.

The loudspeaker crackles. *"Mesdames, messieurs, l'embarquement pour le vol Swissair numéro 670 peut maintenant commencer à la porte vingt-cinq. Nous invitons actuellement les passagers de première classe à se diriger vers la porte d'embarquement."*

The first-class passengers make their way to the gate. The agent who was chatting with the soldier moves to the side of the counter to process boarding passes, putting the soldier directly behind her. He might've been checking names—or he could simply be ogling her décolletage.

After first class, she calls rows 38 and higher ... rows 26 to 38 ... rows 14 to 26.

"Showtime," I whisper.

CHAPTER FORTY-EIGHT

stand. "When I come out of the bathroom, I'll stick around to make sure the water leak gets noticed promptly. *You* start walking slowly across to our gate. The second the guard leaves, step on the gas. Get in line and get on board."

Fay gives me a quick hug, and I stroll across to the ladies' room. One stall is occupied, and one woman is at a sink touching up her hair and makeup. A glance at the trash bin nearest the door confirms that it's three-quarters full of used towels, soiled diapers, and greasy food wrappers. Perfect.

My idea behind triggering the sprinkler was another blast from my teenage past. Our whole family had flown to Chicago for a two-week-long Christmas visit with Mom's parents. Christmas was over; our friends were a thousand miles away; the weather sucked. Our grandfather was the manager of an insurance agency. He insisted Greg and I come to work with him one day—Fay being excused in order to show Gramma all the doll clothes she'd made—and we were both bored out of our minds. Greg must've been nuts to suggest smoking pot with all those grown-ups around. And I definitely was for agreeing.

We went down to the basement—file storage and a little-used bathroom. Knowing we had to get rid of the telltale smell, Greg opened the only bathroom window, a long, narrow one high on the wall next to the toilet. We took turns standing on the toilet and aiming our exhales out the window.

It didn't quite work out the way we planned. The wind blew briskly, directly *into* the open window, and created a smoky haze in the bathroom. I was stoned. I panicked and jumped onto the toilet next to Greg, intending to rip the joint away from him and throw it out the window.

One, Greg was not ready to give up the joint.

Two, atop a toilet seat is a lousy place for a tussle.

Three, neither of us remembered the screen on the window.

When I grabbed for the joint, Greg flung his arm out of my way. Our momentum carried us toward the window, and I saw my chance—or thought I did. I leaned harder on Greg, hoping our combined weight would get me in a better position to hurl the joint outside. Instead, my foot slipped. Greg pulled away from me when I fell. His hand hit the screen. When he ricocheted wildly to keep his balance, the lit joint raked the industrial smoke detector—and the sprinkler erupted.

Smoke is *not* what activates a fire sprinkler system, I learned that day—from the stern captain of the fire truck that arrived, siren screaming, before we escaped. "If it was smoke," he said, "burnt toast would cause daily kitchen floods. It's the heat rising from a fire."

We were grounded for months.

Now I'm proposing to re-create that fiasco.

I spend a few minutes dragging the belly-dancer brush through my short curls and preening at the mirror. The second the woman at the sink walks out, I take a wad of paper towels and use them to dig out a diaper that's merely damp, not gross. I'll use it to protect my hand from the heat. Then I grab another fistful of towels and lock myself into a cubicle. At the same moment, a toilet flushes and the other woman comes out to wash up.

While I wait for her to leave, I make a nest of dry paper towels inside the diaper and stand on the toilet. The ceiling is awfully high, but I've chosen a cubicle with a sprinkler unit directly above it. I test my range by briefly raising my hand. I can reach to within a foot of the sprinkler.

I need to light the papers on fire when I'm alone in the bathroom—without witnesses and so I can get out of there *fast*, before I get drenched. Just as the second woman finishes washing up at the sink, however, a group of Moroccan women with several young children in tow come in. I flush the toilet but stay in the cubicle.

The women pee; the children pee. They change a diaper, retie sneakers, wash hands, readjust their voluminous outer layers. The clock is ticking, and I am jiggling with butterflies. The second they leave, I light a match. The paper towels blaze. Ashes fly, then drift down like gray snowflakes and disintegrate.

The paper towels burned too fast; I need something denser. I spy an unopened roll of toilet paper on the back of the toilet—a solid cylinder of highly flammable paper.

I rip off the outer covering and strike a match inside the cardboard roll. It catches. The reddish glow spreads from the cardboard to the surrounding paper. A flame rises, spiraling like a birthday candle. I hold it up and count: one, two, three, four, five . . . Before I get to six, spray erupts from the pipe.

I jump off the toilet, dropping the diaper and burning toilet paper into it, and run out of the stall. Finger-combing my damp curls, I exit the bathroom.

Fay's standing at Gate 22. I give her a quick thumbs-up, then bend my head to the water fountain.

There was a constant stream of women when I wanted the restroom to empty. Now, it seems that everyone in our area is lining up to board the plane. *Come on. Someone* must need a pee-break before an international flight.

A thin stream of water trickles from under the bathroom door. *Come on, come on. Notice.*

Fay is halfway to the gate. The soldier hasn't moved. Although I don't want to raise my profile, perhaps I'll have to be the one to "discover" the deluge.

A man pushing a wheelchair moves to the far side of the concourse, where the bathrooms are, to keep clear of the clump of travelers waiting to board. The wheels glide over the water. The man is talking on a cell phone, and he walks through the puddle without appearing to notice.

The old man in the wheelchair, though, tugs on the man's arm and points. The man looks down. A stream slithers like a snake from under the door. He scoots away from the spreading water. "Hey, hey. There's a problem here."

No one hears him over the chatter in the echoing waiting area.

A man. In this conservative society, he won't dare open the door to a women's bathroom. "Hey," he calls again, louder.

This time his cry gets the attention of a large woman dressed head-to-toe in black. He points; she elbows her way toward the bathroom door. I imagine her saying, "For heaven's sake, get out of my way. I'll do it."

The woman opens the door—and a torrent sluices out. She tries to jump out of the way; her feet slide; she topples, landing on her *derrière* with her headscarf skewed to the side and the lower half of her dress sodden. And her shrieks rise over the noise in the concourse.

Other women rush over to help her. The bathroom door drifts shut once the built-up wall of water escapes, but from inside comes a continuous hiss of spraying water. A crowd forms and writhes aimlessly, like a snake without a head. Water continues to run under the door.

Our flight to Zurich is almost entirely boarded. *Notice the damn commotion.*

One of the gate agents—not the attractive one checking boarding passes—touches the soldier's arm and points to the disturbance. His eyes and mouth open to twin Os, but he stays put.

I've been trying to walk a thin line between causing such a dramatic problem that security would clear the airport and creating a mini-tempest in a teapot that would too easily resolve itself. Either I guessed wrong about what would get the soldier's attention or he has orders to remain by the gate. There's only one way to find out which one it is.

It's up to me to create more urgency.

I move closer to the milling crowd. "Did you hear that?" I ask the first person I come close to. "There's someone inside. I think someone is hurt in there." I repeat it to everyone I pass. Murmurs grow louder.

Within a minute—music to my ears—a woman yells that someone's inside the restroom, someone's injured. "Listen, she's calling for help." Others take up the cry.

In truth, you can't hear much, but *finally* the soldier trots over to take charge. Fay picks up her pace and presents her boarding pass before he reaches the door. The gate attendant doesn't give her a second look. She, too, is absorbed in the drama at the ladies' room.

First, the soldier calls into the bathroom. The ambient noise has reached such a crescendo that, of course, he can't hear any reply. So he pushes open the door and steps into the restroom.

He's still inside when I get to Gate 25. A family of four cuts in front of me, oblivious to my presence and puffing like they've run the entire length of the concourse. They board. I hold out my papers.

"*Merci, madame.*" The young woman's attention remains on the disturbance.

Fay has lingered in the jetway, and I catch up to her. We link arms.
"You okay?" We speak at the same time.

Fay nods, the wild look in her eyes subsiding.

Instead of answering directly, I propel her forward. The line that normally clogs the jetway has already dwindled. "We did it." There's a catch in my voice. "Time to go home."

All of us—me, Fay, Yasmin, Nadia, and Hamid. Home to our families. Home without souvenirs to hand out or photos to share. Only Molly has a present, the magenta slippers I bought in Ouarzazate. With my camera gone, no nature snapshots for Alex. No pictures to remind me of Izri or Ahmed, the men who saved my life. None to document my days wandering in the desert or the glade where we bathed in the stream. The glitzy hotel room in Agadir or the serene lagoon where I sat in the sand. Or the dead soldier.

I don't need the pictures really. I will carry them in my soul for the rest of my life. I've often said I like to travel for the serendipity of not knowing what I'm going to find. This time, to survive, I found myself.

We've reached the cabin door when an announcement comes over the loudspeaker: *"Embarquement immédiat pour le vol 670 à destination de Zurich. Ceci est le dernier appel."* Last call.

"That was," Fay says, "way too close for comfort. Next time, let's do something ordinary." Fay nibbles her lower lip while she sneaks a look at me. She's worried her part in this adventure has driven a lasting wedge between us.

We're standing next to row eleven, where Fay is sitting. The flight attendants have begun walking up the aisle to get passengers settled. I need to move on to my seat in row fifteen, but I can't leave my sister wondering. Sometimes there's no simple way, no perfect way forward—whether we're talking about family or anything else in life. Like Ahmed told me in the black desert, you have to do the best you can with what you have. And, I add to myself, *who* you have at your side. "Next time," I tell Fay, "I want a nice relaxing vacation."

Fay's tremulous smile is sunshine breaking through clouds. "With museums and five-star restaurants."

"Or beaches and tall iced drinks." I pause. "Next time, no secrets. No games. And I get to pick."

"Deal."

AUTHOR'S NOTE

I first arrived in Morocco on the ferry from Tarifa to Tangier.

That sentence is true.

We all make stories from our life experiences and, because this note follows a work of fiction, it's a good place to share the story of Bonnar Spring, unreliable narrator. For years, I described how I came to Morocco this way: On vacation in Spain with my dear friend Jan, the weather had turned so dismal that we didn't even get out of the car to see the monkeys at Gibraltar. Instead, we drove west along Spain's southern coast. When we approached Tarifa, a sign directed traffic to the Tangier ferry. And we said *what the heck* and took it.

Anyone looking at my sequence of photos from that trip would know I couldn't possibly be telling the truth—we visited Gibraltar *after* our return from Morocco. But it does make a good story.

The truth is more prosaic. At the end of my Peace Corps service, I'd passed up a jaunt to Morocco in favor of heading back to an old boyfriend in the States. Big mistake—and a missed opportunity that gnawed at me. Jan, who's a wonderful painter, was also interested in seeing Morocco. We'd both heard stories about Tangier's elegant old Hotel Continental, which is perched above the port in the town's old medina. And in southern Spain, we'd be so close . . .

After the clouds and rain in Spain, arriving in sunlit Tangier was a Wizard-of-Oz moment, a glimpse into a remarkably vibrant Technicolor world that was different from any I'd ever known. Jan and I stayed at the Continental and explored the medina's twisting alleyways and chaotic, teeming markets. We ate and ate and ate—Moroccan delicacies that were new to us and classic French cuisine.

Over many years of visits, though, it's the *people* I remember most about Morocco. From that first trip:

Jimmy (his sign reads "Patronised by Film Stars and the International Jet Set") who sold me my first rug and gave me a silver bracelet, probably because I paid too much for the rug.

The vendor who wrapped my pottery bowl in a piece of newspaper with a sudoku puzzle on it and asked me if I knew how to work them. So we did one together, with me explaining it in a mix of French, Spanish, and English.

And then there was Ali.

I began this note by talking about the stories we tell. Even true stories take on a patina with the passage of time. Here's how I remember leaving Morocco that first trip—and I believe it's mainly true:

The Strait of Gibraltar was too rough for the small ferry that brought us to North Africa. While we waited—outdoors—for a larger vessel to be brought around, we started talking to Ali, a Moroccan man who worked as a circus performer in Spain. The wind was whipping, so I tied a scarf I'd bought around my head to cover my hair.

After a while, Ali asked, "Do you hear the men salaaming you?"

I listened. Each man who passed nodded politely and said, "*Assalamu alaikum.*" Greeted me, Bonnar, veiled and sitting on a suitcase on the ferry dock. In just a few days, Morocco had gone from being the strangest place I'd visited to one where I felt at home.

Here's the thing, though—a proper thriller must include Bad Guys.

Yes, we *were* stopped by the police and we *did* pretend we couldn't speak French—twice that I remember—but the policemen gave up with good grace and without giving us a speeding ticket, which was the whole point of our charade.

Yes, we picked up hitchhikers and stayed in some really out-of-the-way places.

And, yes, we traveled into the aptly named Black Desert as well as into the Sahara. We picked up seashells on the desert floor, saw Neolithic animal drawings, rode camels, and wandered around Roman ruins.

We discussed politics, cultural differences, and the pace of change over many cups of tea—and once with the most amazing avocado smoothie (made by the wife of a man we'd picked up hitchhiking in the mountains).

The beauty of Morocco and the generosity of its people are real. The villains are all products of my overactive imagination.

PUBLISHER'S NOTE

We hope that you have enjoyed Bonnar Spring's *Disappeared*.

This is Bonnar's second international thriller. We trust that you, the reader, felt as if you were in the deserts and the cities of Morocco with Julie and Fay. And that you were able to breathe a sigh of relief when they both boarded that airplane.

Bonnar's debut novel, *Toward the Light*, is also a nail-biter. Here you will meet Luz Concepcion as she returns to Guatemala to murder the man who destroyed her family. Luz is a strong female "everywoman" protagonist confronted with an overwhelming moral dilemma and physical danger far beyond her limited abilities to counter. Bonnar immerses her readers in the Guatemalan setting and culture as Luz encounters a mission more complicated and personal than she could ever have imagined.

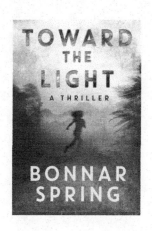

"*Toward the Light* is a high-stakes thriller set in the mean streets of Guatemala. Family secrets drive this impressive debut novel, a tale of revenge and redemption, to an exciting finish."

—Hallie Ephron, *New York Times* best-selling author

For more information, please visit Bonnar Spring's website: www. bonnarspring.com.